Hard to SCORE

NEW YORK TIMES BESTSELLING AUTHOR

K. BROMBERG

PRAISE FOR K. BROMBERG

ALSO BY K. BROMBERG

Published by JKB Publishing, LLC

ISBN: 978-1-942832-33-1

Cover design by Helen Williams
Cover Image by Rafa G Catala
Cover Model: Jorge Del Rio Romero
Editing by Marion Making Manuscripts
Formatting by Champagne Book Design
Printed in the United States of America

Hard to SCORE

Prologue

Drew

I PULL MY HELMET OFF, LEAN MY FACE UP TO THE SKY, AND WELCOME the cool air against the sweat plastering my hair to my head.

And really, I'm just buying time. Giving myself a minute to still my nerves that have been humming beneath the surface for the past few hours. Allowing myself a moment for this to sink in.

That I'm here at the NFL Scouting Combine, and I just gave the performance I needed to give.

"That was one incredible show."

I turn to face the man with the slightly southern accent who's bearing down on me. He's tall with broad shoulders and a double chin, but his eyes are the same as the younger version of him I saw in picture after picture from my youth. And he's wearing a polo shirt with an emblem on the left breast that would make any football player salivate.

The Tennessee Tigers.

Super Bowl champions four out of the last eight years. One of the most loved, and therefore often hated, teams in the NFL.

Of all the coaches in this damn Combine. Of course, he's the first to seek me out.

Goddamn fate.

"Thank you." I nod. "I got lucky today."

The man—Roger Molleman—barks out a laugh. "Seems to me someone might be lying through his teeth, because that's a talent that's hard to hide."

"Thank you," I repeat as he stops a few feet from me and angles his head to the side as our eyes meet—hold.

"Your name again?" he asks, despite knowing damn well it's written on the sheets pinned to the clipboard he has sandwiched between his arm and torso.

And everything I've worked for over my short lifetime comes down to this one moment. To selling this one lie.

"Drew Hemmings." The name still feels foreign on my tongue all these years later. "Or Bowie. I answer to just about anything."

"Where'd you go to school?" he asks. "It says something on the stat sheet but—"

"Butler University."

"Can't say that I've ever heard of anyone going pro who played at that college. Hell, I don't even have the slightest idea of where it is. But by golly, son, why haven't we heard about you? Why haven't you been playing at a PAC-12? How do I know the numbers you gave today weren't flukes?"

"You don't." I shrug.

"For a man trying to get drafted by the NFL, I don't see you trying to sell yourself."

"I'm confident in my abilities. Someone will pick me up."

He laughs again and looks around at the five other coaches standing about ten feet away, arms crossed over their chests, and apparently waiting to talk to me.

My pulse races at the sight, but all Roger sees is cool, calm, and unaffected.

"You're cocky. I like cocky."

"Quarterbacks have to be."

He angles his head to the side and studies me with a quiet scrutiny. "The way you play . . . you remind me of someone, and I can't seem to put my finger on it."

Do you know you held me when I was a baby?

Do you remember the man you used to call a best friend was my father?

But none of that matters.

The only thing that does is that I'm here now and I'm going to capitalize on any opportunity I'm given.

That's my father's past.

This is my future.

"Doesn't every player remind someone of somebody?" I ask to divert his attention.

"True." He glances over his shoulder again to the other coaches waiting. "Do you have some kind of pitch you want to make to me? Something for me to take away so on draft night I say your name instead of one of the other quarterbacks out there?"

My dad's advice runs through my head. *Roger doesn't like kiss-asses. He likes aloof confidence. He likes to answer the questions himself. He has to be the one in control.*

"Nope. Nothing to say. Your team and its record speak for itself just as my stats and performance today does." I set my helmet down on the bench. "Thank you for your time."

I reach a hand out to shake his and he stares at it for a beat before reaching out and shaking it. "That's it?"

"That's it."

"You've got nothing else to say?"

My smile is slow and steady as I meet his eyes again. "Like I said, I like to leave it all on the field. That should be proof enough."

He stares at me with an incredulity I love. That means I'll be memorable. That means I did my job.

"We'll be in touch," he says, hands in his pockets as he rocks back on his heels.

"I look forward to it."

And those five words are the only inkling I give him that I'm interested in playing for the Tigers.

The only inkling at all.

And when all is said and done—when I've spoken to coaches and chatted with other players I've previously admired from afar—I take a seat in the stands of Lucas Oil Stadium and look around.

I take in the rise of the seats around me, the rows going up one after another until they become huge walls that form an oval around us. I can imagine what a packed crowd sounds like. I picture being on the middle of the field with cameras flashing and fans cheering so loud that I have to shout the cadence before the snap—and even then, I doubt my offensive line would hear me.

There would be adrenaline. A rush that edges on what I'd assume getting high would feel like . . . and even then, it couldn't rival the feeling of sixty thousand people cheering *or booing* you and your team.

How could he have walked away from this without a fight?

But as I sit down on the bench and breathe it all in, I know my secret must keep. I fear if all is found out, the one thing I want the most, might all come tumbling down.

When it comes to athletes, fans and history remember two types: the undeniable stars and the ones who caused scandals.

I could be the first one.

But my fear is that the second one will rob me of that possibility.

They say the sins of the fathers are to be laid upon the children.

For my sake, let's hope that's not true.

Chapter ONE

Brexton

"So I'm the reason you've been hanging around," Justin Hobbs says with a half-cocked smirk before readjusting the towel that covers his freshly showered lower half.

"I have lots of reasons for hanging around, one of which was to watch the scrimmage this afternoon," I say of the last preseason game the Raptors had before the season goes into full swing.

I take him in. Typical quarterback's body. Lean and tone with not too much excess, say like an offensive lineman, who has to throw his weight around. Handsome in a dime a dozen way. He looks like any Midwest boy raised on beef and beer, complete with the farmer's tan evident because of his shirtless torso.

The difference is he's from California, has a cannon for an arm, and an ego to match.

I'd been warned ahead of time.

"And?" he asks.

"And, the team played well. It was preseason but if it's any indication of what the upcoming season's going to look like, I'd say you're in great shape."

"I know I am. Thanks."

This is the part where I want to turn around and walk out. This is the part where my job becomes so predictable and, just once, I want it not to be.

"I meant the team in general."

"And I'm the heart of it, so . . ."

There is no shame there. Not an ounce. But I smile anyway.

"Then that does mean it includes you," I acquiesce begrudgingly.

"Of course it does. What would a team be without its quarterback?" He glances around and flashes an arrogant smile at one of his teammates before focusing back on me. "But I'll be the first to admit, my precision was off. I plan on putting more time in to fix that."

An ounce of humility. I grab it and hold it tight, because that's something I can definitely work with.

"That's good to hear." I nod.

"So what can I do for you, since you're standing before me and definitely wanting something?" He licks his lips and takes his time glancing up and down the length of my body. He likes what he sees no doubt, but then again, as rumor has it, he's not exactly indiscriminate when it comes to the company he keeps. When he's done giving me the once-over, his eyes meet mine again. "Should we go out and have a drink or two to discuss whatever it is you want from me?"

"I hear you're unhappy with your agent." I take a glance around. Only a few players are left in the locker room, which is why I chose to enter now. Fewer ears overhearing mean fewer rumors being spread.

But they will be spread.

I'm counting on it.

"Isn't everyone unhappy with their agent?" he asks.

"Not my clients." I flash a smile and extend a hand to him. "Brexton Kincade. Kincade Sports Management."

He takes his time shaking my hand in that way that screams of a man who thinks I'm charmed by him. My only response is to withdraw my hand when he releases it while holding his stare the entire time. "Well, *Brexton Kincade*, I do think that you owe me dinner and a conversation to discuss how exactly you can be of service to me." He takes a step closer to me. "And make no mistake, I demand a lot of service."

Gag.

He seriously just said that?

My smile doesn't waver as my *gross-o-meter* hits its maximum capacity. "Good to know. Maybe we can schedule something later in the week? I've been given access to the conference rooms for meetings this week, so that would be a great time and place to discuss things."

Where most guys' expressions would fall after their innuendos were ignored, Justin's towel "accidentally" falls instead. And in true asshole fashion, his amused eyes hold mine to see if I look.

I don't. I refuse to give him the satisfaction.

Instead, I hold a business card out to him, completely unfazed by his average-sized dick simply hanging there in my periphery. "Here's how you can get in touch with me."

"I know how *you* can touch me."

I lift a lone eyebrow. "I'm flattered. Truly, I am."

"Come on." He chuckles as he tries to figure another angle to entice me.

"I look forward to hearing from you." I take a step back. "Oh, and you seem to have mistaken me for someone who actually cares if you drop your towel."

I turn on my heel, catch a couple of coughed-out laughs from his teammates who overheard our conversation, and lift a hand in silent greeting. As the door closes behind me, I overhear one of the guys giving Justin shit for being a dick.

At least someone's calling him out on it.

Normally it would be me. I'm the Kincade sister with the loud mouth who's known for voicing my opinions, but not this time. Not when my dad has given me the task of recruiting Justin Hobbs away from his agent, none other than the prick extraordinaire, Finn Sanderson—otherwise known as FuckFace in my phone contacts.

Justin will be a pain in my ass. A player an agent tolerates simply because he's a great commission despite being a cringeworthy human. But if he's going to help Kincade Sports Management get some of its shine back after Finn tried to lessen it, then I'm game.

Anything for my family.

Or at least that's what I said before meeting him.

Now as I make my way through the maze of corridors in the underbelly of the stadium toward my next meeting of the evening, I cringe at the prospect of possibly working with him.

But that cringe pales in comparison to the yawns of boredom I endure for the next few hours, as I negotiate and cajole and persuade the general manager of the New York Raptors that my free agent linebacker would be a great fit with the organization.

I love my job, I truly do, but as of late, I'm getting a little sick of inflated egos with ridiculous demands. *Especially* while I try to save their asses from whatever they did that was caught on a phone and is now viral.

I'm not burned out, but rather just totally sick of the bullshit.

Where did all the nice guys go?

It's the question on repeat as I make my way from the confines of the now almost empty stadium, toward the far end of the parking lot.

I grumble at how far I have to walk across the lot in my heels, but it's my fault. There might come a time in my life when I'm actually not running ten minutes late.

Maybe.

But I'm not holding my breath.

I startle at a noise to my left. It sounds like heavy breathing mixed with grunting combined with who knows what. It's a sound most normal women would scurry away from. I head toward it and find myself on the outskirts of the parking lot, looking through a chain-link fence, down at the team's pseudo practice field.

Or at least it used to be until the team built a fancy one outside of the city a few years back.

Nonetheless, in the moonlight, I see a figure down on the turf. He has what appears to be a headlamp attached to his helmet that bobs with each and every move he makes. He has about twenty footballs set up on kicking tees all around the scaled-down version of the field. I watch as he randomly picks a football up and then fires a throw into one of five target nets set up in various distances away from him.

With each grab of a football, he dances backwards a few steps, arm cocked back with the football in hand, and then fires a rifle straight into the target.

I take in his red T-shirt, gym shorts with a towel tucked in the waistband that he dries his hands on after every couple of throws, and the white of his helmet.

"Well color me impressed," I murmur to myself, surprised to see him out here, but so very pleased that he is. "Justin Hobbs is the real deal."

I can't tell you the last time I saw a professional athlete finish a game, be unhappy with his performance, and then head straight to the field to improve it.

Now this? This is a man I can represent and sell.

One after another he hits his target with both natural talent and finesse that's astounding. This is what Justin was missing in the game tonight. Sure he's skilled, but there's an instinctual confidence about him right now that he needs to translate to the field or else I fear it's going to be a rocky year for him.

That is what I didn't tell him to his face.

Those are things you reserve to tell people when they're your contracted client, not when you're trying to win them over.

But there is a massive glimmer of hope in what I'm watching and that, in and of itself, is worth me standing out here in the summer night air instead of driving myself home.

I don't know how long I observe from the fringes of the parking lot, awed by Justin's talent and contemplating why he's not making use of the lights that tower above the practice turf, but it's long enough for him to run through the cycle of throws three times.

It's only when he jogs to the side of the field, takes a seat on the bench with his back to me, and takes his helmet off that I walk through the open gateway in the fence.

He turns when he hears the click of my heels at the same time that I speak. "I'm impressed. Practicing after a game? Not many players do that these days."

"What . . ." The word falls from his mouth at the same time his eyes meet mine, but the man with a rifle of an arm isn't Justin Hobbs.

Not in the least.

No, the eyes that meet mine are a mixture of blue and green and are the same ones that stopped my heart many times in my teenage years.

Recognition flickers in his just as quickly as his expression falls before a slow, reminiscent smile spreads on his lips. "Well, if it isn't Bratty Brex."

My heart jumps in my throat at his voice and a thousand teenage dreams about my first crush come flooding back. My heart feels like it just turned over in my chest in a way I haven't felt in forever.

But my own smile remains steady even if the ground beneath my feet feels like it just trembled.

"If it isn't Dreadful Drew," I repeat the childish nickname of our youth while remembering the secret ones my girlfriends had for him later in our teens. *Sexy Drew. Dreamy Drew. *Sigh* Drew.*

"God, I haven't heard that in forever." The second string quarterback for the New York Raptors chuckles softly and angles his head to the side to take me in.

I study him in turn. His dark, short hair is wet with sweat and going every which way from him running his hand through it. His skin is tanned from being out in the sun, and those eyes of his are unrelenting as they meet mine again.

"What? I mean—*why*—or rather how come..." I shake my head as nerves I shouldn't feel tinge the edge of my voice.

How have we avoided each other this long?

How are you?

How have we been in the same industry for so long and our paths never crossed until now?

"Probably because of the same reasons as you," he says when I don't complete my scattered thoughts.

"What do you mean?" I ask.

"You always struggled to complete your thoughts when you were flustered. I always thought it was cute."

"I'm not flustered. *Or cute.*"

"You're right. I was wrong. You're not cute at all." Drew's tongue darts out to wet his bottom lip. "You're gorgeous."

There's a brief beat where I simply stare at him, eyes blinking to make sure I heard him properly, before I burst out laughing. This is not something Dreamy Drew would say to me.

This is something I might have dreamed and wrote in my diary that I wish he would say, but it's not something I know how to process ... so I laugh clumsily.

And luckily he does too, because there's a sudden awkwardness between the two of us—two kids whose parents were best friends, who vacationed together ... and then acted like the other didn't exist after scandal hit.

"Thanks. I mean . . . yeah, thank you." I shift on my feet and try to look anywhere but at him. "Why are you out here? Why don't you have the lights on? Why—"

"You still ask a million questions, don't you?"

I pretend I'm not melting inside at his shy smile and playful tone. *But I totally am.*

"And you still get annoyed by it," I say, waving a hand at the field in front of us. "What are you doing out here in the dark?"

"Doing the same thing I do after every game."

"Which is?"

"Putting in a full game's worth of passes by myself since I didn't get to touch the field today." He nods. "I've got to keep my skills sharp in case I'm called to play."

I'm impressed with his response.

Even more so with his dedication.

"Are the Raptors too cheap to turn the lights on for you?"

He laughs. "No, I don't want them on. Lights mean people look and I don't want people to look."

"Why not?" It's a legitimate question, but perhaps I'm a little over-zealous in the way I say it, because Drew's head jostles at the words. "From what I just saw you're every bit as good as Justin is. In fact, I'd put my money on your accuracy percentage being higher. I don't know your other stats but I'm not exactly sure why you're complacent with sitting second string here when you could be starting with so many other teams."

"Humph." It's all Drew says as he rises from his seat and gives a sharp shake of his head. "That's the same question I've asked myself for years. Wonder why that could be?" Sarcasm laces his tone and every part of me stills at the words.

"Do you really think it's because . . ."

"I've been contracted in the NFL for seven years, four of which have been with the Raptors. I find it interesting that numerous people have said the same thing you just did—that I'm good enough to be a starting quarterback—and yet backup is all I've ever been."

"I don't understand—"

"Don't try to. The mental gymnastics is exhausting, and you never reach a definitive answer." He looks over to the person helping him. "You good, Steve?"

"Yeah. We should be set to go again in a few minutes," Steve says.

"'Kay." Drew turns back to face me. "It was good to see you again, Brex, but I've got to get back to work."

"Yes. Sure. I . . . it's great to see you too." We stand a few feet apart, eyes locked, with a sudden unease taking hold. "I didn't mean to interrupt. I thought you were Just—"

"Justin Hobbs. Yeah, I figured that's who you thought I was." There's a trace of annoyance in his voice as he pulls his helmet back on. "For the record, Justin never puts extra time in. If you're here to recruit him then you should know that."

"Who said I'm recruiting him?" I ask, suddenly wondering why I haven't set my sights on Drew.

"Everyone." His smile doesn't reach his eyes.

"Thanks for the tip," I say and take a few steps back, hesitant, almost as if I don't want this conversation to end—despite its sudden awkwardness. I feel like there are so many things I want to say, and yet, I haven't seen this man for almost ten years. In fact, the last time I did, he was wearing board shorts with floppy surfer-style hair and I was watching him from afar, wishing he'd notice me as someone other than a family friend's daughter.

"I'm sure I'll see you around," he says and then jogs back onto the darkened field without another word.

I stand and stare after him for a moment, stuck in the weirdest feeling of indecision. Wondering how a conversation that started out so playful and fun ended up giving me a sour taste in my mouth.

"Well . . . okay then," I mutter to myself as I kick an imaginary rock with the toe of my shoe and head off the field the way I entered.

As an agent, I know better than to annoy a player when he is practicing. *I do.* Then why is it so damn hard to make my feet move one in front of another and walk away from him?

I slide into the driver's seat of my car, turn my key in the ignition, sit there, and stare at the darkened lights towering over the practice field where Drew is.

Maybe I lost track of him on purpose. Surely we've crossed paths before at some point considering we work in the same industry. Of course, there are thousands of athletes and agents, but perhaps us missing each other wasn't just a coincidence.

Maybe just like his life had been turned upside down when the shitstorm surrounding his dad happened, mine did too when my mom died two weeks later. Did he feel the same way? Like a part of his life—his innocence—was over, and everything he'd known as normal had changed? Was it easier for him to walk away and never look back?

Then again, maybe he'd already broken my heart way back when without ever knowing it, and therefore I avoided thinking about him, my first unrequited love.

One thing is for sure . . . the teenage boy I used to have a massive crush on ended up growing into an incredibly handsome man.

A man who seemingly doesn't care about time lost.

And yet, there's me, the woman who can't stop thinking about him as I drive street after street on my way home.

Chapter TWO

Drew

You're gorgeous?

I pick up the football from the kicking tee and shuffle back a few feet on my heels, arm cocked back, eyes on the farthest target.

You're gorgeous?

I release the ball and it sails two feet wide.

"Fuck!" I bark at no one. Steve stops midstride and looks my way before being cut down by my glare. He throws his head back and laughs at my miss, and I grit my teeth.

I'm never distracted. *Never.* And one fucking chat with Brexton goddamn Kincade and now I'm missing my mark?

What the hell, Bowman?

I run a cadence through my head before grabbing another football and going through my paces again. I hit the top of the target and the ball falls to the side of the catch net instead of inside of it. Fucking missed again.

Why would you say something like that to Bratty Brexton? Why would you tell her that she's gorgeous after everything that happened? After everything . . .

"Christ."

I lift my face to the night sky and take a deep breath to clear my head. But all I see are her mile-long legs, knockout body, and stunning face.

It's true. She *is* gorgeous. It took me a second to process she really was Brexton Kincade because my memories of her are gangly limbs, a gap-toothed smile, a flat chest, and unruly hair.

It's almost as if my mind has purposely skipped over that last summer we spent together. Like it never happened.

But that was a fluke.

That was two teenagers caught in a peer-pressure moment.

That was something I'd convinced myself never happened.

Until now.

Now she's *that*. All woman, all desirable, all . . . *Jesus Christ*. This is Brex, we're talking about here. I can't be thinking about her like that.

I can't be wondering how to hit on her when we used to run around like lunatic kids chasing fireflies in Allegheny on family summer vacations.

And I sure as shit can't act on it.

Not after what happened.

Not after my life was turned upside down at the hands of her father.

And as another pass sails wide, I grunt in frustration.

Get any ideas out of your head, Drew.

You need to stay as far away from her as possible.

Her last name alone should tell you that.

Chapter
THREE

Brexton

I FEEL LIKE A STALKER.

Or rather, I *am* a stalker. How can I not be as I sit across the street from Drew Bowman's house with the determination I had more than an hour ago now waning as reality sets in. As I wonder what exactly he's going to think when he opens the door to find me on his doorstep.

But I can't let this go.

Not the incredible talent I saw two nights ago or the notion that he's sitting second string, when I know so many teams who would kill to have his arm behind their offensive line.

And while that's all true, it's also a huge lie. *Major.* Maybe I'm sitting here like a crazed fangirl because . . . I really want to see him again.

He was the boy's face I pretended my pillow was when I "practice-kissed" it every night before I went to bed.

My first real *kiss.*

The boy I had wild fantasies about—holding hands, Homecoming dance date, college sweethearts.

All those things died a quick death when our lives irrevocably changed.

Maybe I never laid them properly to rest and right now I feel like if I see him again, I'll know if I'm just manifesting something that doesn't exist.

Besides, he called me gorgeous.

The hopeless romantic in me sighs at the words, at the soft smile on his lips when he said it, and ridiculously wonders if this chance meeting was meant to be.

But when it comes to matters of the heart, nothing good has ever come from my romanticism. Just a whole lot of heartbreak that had me swearing off love the last time it happened—a whole four months ago.

Good thing when I looked him up I found out he wasn't married. Even better when I asked his teammate, my client, about Drew, he let it slip that Drew didn't have a girlfriend.

Let's hope that's true or this might be super awkward.

Nonetheless, I shake my head and force myself to get out of my car. I'm here, I might as well follow through. The spiel I practiced in my head over and over—the one about how I'd be interested in representing him if he wasn't happy with his current agent—Ari Longmire—is on repeat in my head as I put one foot in front of the other and cross the street.

His house sits in a quiet upper-class suburb across the Hudson. Mature trees line the street in front of perfectly manicured lawns. Drew's house is large but not flashy with a ledgestone front and a massive wooden door. It sits back from the street on a large lot with perfect landscaping and stonework.

I'm not sure why this picture of suburbia surprises me. Maybe I expected a sleek condo overlooking Central Park for him, but I welcome the surprise.

Regardless, I'm standing here staring and shouldn't be surprised if any of the neighbors in this high-end neighborhood have called the cops on the woman loitering on the curb.

That puts my ass in gear and has me walking up the long pathway to the front door where I ring the doorbell.

A dog barks somewhere down the street as my resolve waivers with each passing second.

A muffled, "Just a second," can be heard from inside. My heart jumps in my throat and the stupidity of what I'm doing kicks in.

The lock turns.

The door rattles.

And when the door swings open, Drew Bowman is standing before me in a pair of Raptor sweatpants and nothing else.

I struggle to speak. I mean, no sane woman would blame me for my complete loss of intelligible thoughts if she were looking at the eight-pack of abs on display in front of me. I try not to look, I really do, but how can I not glance down when he's there looking like that?

"Brex? What—how did you—what are you doing here?" Drew asks as he leans against the door frame, casual as can be, and crosses his arms over his chest. And crosses them in the way that their sculpted firmness is innocently displayed.

"I don't know. It's a long story," I finally spit out before I sigh and point at him. "You. You said the other day, 'probably for the same reasons as you.' What did you mean by that?"

So not what I had planned on saying . . . but it's out there nonetheless, and now I'm stuck standing behind something that he might not have remembered but that rooted itself firmly in my brain.

"You mean why our paths never crossed until the other night?"

I shrug as he angles his head and studies me for the longest of beats. "I guess."

He chuckles. "*You guess?* And yet you thought it was an important enough question that somehow you found out where I live and are now standing on my doorstep?"

"You do have a point." I bite my bottom lip, in that state of awkward limbo. I didn't chicken out but of course, now I don't know what to do. A sigh falls from my lips and I throw my hands up. "Honestly? I don't know why I'm here. I know that I saw you the other day and since then I haven't stopped thinking about when we were growing up and I don't know . . . thought maybe we could catch up for old time's sake."

His stare is unrelenting and then a slow smile ghosts over his lips. "I was just about to throw a steak on the barbeque."

"I couldn't impose."

"Good. I wasn't going to share my steak with you anyway. I just thought you'd prefer to sit and watch me eat it." My head startles as his words hit my ears and then he belts out a laugh. "You're still easy as hell to rile up, Brex. Time sure as hell changed a lot of things about you, but it didn't change that, now did it?" He takes a step back into his house and opens the door wider. "I was joking. I have plenty. Stay?"

"I wasn't looking for you to invite me in."

"No? If you'd prefer to keep stalking me, that window right there has a clear shot to the kitchen if you press your face up to it. But then again, that might call attention to the neighbors, and I'd think coming in through the front door would be a better time for you than being led off in handcuffs as a peeping Tom."

"Very funny." I snort.

"Then come in."

Every part of my teenage heart flutters when he flashes me a grin as I walk past him and into his house. I don't know what to think other than the house fits him. Or at least, what I think would fit him despite not really knowing him. It's an open floor plan flooded with a ton of natural light against neutral walls with accent colors of grays and blues. While it looks like someone with a keen eye decorated it, each and every room I pass as I follow him to the kitchen looks comfortable and lived in.

I study the muscles in his back as he moves in front of me. His broad shoulders. His trim waist. I admire a well-trained physique like the next woman, but just like when I was a teenager, there is something about Drew that makes me want to sit and stare.

That makes me want to follow when I am definitely not a follower.

We move into the kitchen area. While it's large in size, there's an understated elegance to it that masks the ridiculously expensive appliances and cabinets. One that doesn't make you feel weird pulling up a barstool for fear you might ding or scratch something.

"I was just about to have another beer," Drew says as he rounds the island. "Would you like one or maybe a glass of wine? I have some red and some white. Don't ask me what kind though or if it's good because it's simply on hand in case someone else wants some." *So he entertains enough to have wine he doesn't drink on hand. Who though? The team? Women?*

"At least you're honest."

"Always."

"I'll have a beer. Whatever you're drinking."

He lifts an eyebrow. "Women who wear heels as high as the ones you were wearing the other night usually don't opt for a bottle of beer."

He noticed the heels I was wearing. Let's hope he also took note of the long, shapely legs they were attached to.

"I'm far from typical, Drew."

He stops mid motion and meets my eyes. There's a quick flash of surprise in his eyes that stutters his smile, and I can't say that I mind it. "Good to know," he murmurs as he opens the refrigerator door and pulls out two bottles of a particularly good IPA, opens a bottle, and then slides it across the counter to me.

"Thank you," I say as I turn to track him when he walks over to a huge, gray leather couch, grabs the T-shirt hanging off the back of it, and slips it over his head.

I want to groan in protest and tell him it doesn't bother me that he's shirtless, but that would sound quite weird.

So I force myself to appreciate the way the plain black shirt stretches over his body and smile when he turns to face me. Our eyes meet as he leans his butt against the back of the couch.

"So you want to catch up, talk about old times . . . yet you're not talking."

"It's only been a few minutes."

"So you need to get warmed up?" He nods. "Okay. You pretend you know what you're going to say, and in the meantime, I'm going to throw the meat on. Sound like a plan?" His chuckle should irritate me but it does quite the opposite.

My sigh fills the space. "I didn't mean for this to be awkward."

"It's not. But it's kind of like a first date in a sense. We don't know much about each other and what we do know isn't exactly who we are now . . . so we'll talk, we'll drink, we'll eat . . . and we'll get to know each other."

A first date?

In that case . . . and then I shake my head at my own stupidity for taking him so literally.

There's an easy charm about Drew I didn't expect and simultaneously appreciate as I follow him out a pair of French doors into his backyard. Like his house, the backyard is grand but welcoming. A covered patio sits apart from the house with what looks like a whole second kitchen, complete with a barbeque, television, sink, and refrigerator. There is a large patch of grass with some elaborate stonework that matches the front of the house, which leads to what appears to be a spa.

"It's a little slice of heaven out here," I murmur.

The steaks sizzle as he puts them on the grill. "A lot of the guys laugh at me for not living in the city, but"—he motions to the backyard—"it's nice to just be away from it all. To feel normal. Even if I feel like I'm never home."

"Whereas I live in the city and there are so many nights I'd love to be able to walk out my back door and have all of this to relax and enjoy. Rooftops are great for views of the city but there is no peace and quiet like there is here."

"You never left?" he asks and I turn to find him studying me.

"For college, yes. But my family is here. My job. I travel a lot because of it, but there's nothing quite like Manhattan."

He purses his lips. "We moved . . ." He doesn't finish the sentence as he averts his eyes and turns to check on the meat he just put on. "I was first drafted to Tennessee and was contracted there for the first two years. Did one year down in Florida. Now I've been back here for the last four and hopefully will continue to be."

"So you do like it here then? In New York?"

He eyes me almost warily before he nods. "I do, yes."

I hold my face up to the late afternoon sun and close my eyes. "Every time I say I'm sick of it, I travel for work and realize how much I can't wait to get back home to it."

"Hmm," he says, and then he falls silent. I watch him for a few moments as he sprays water on the grill to calm the flame and then moves them to the other side of the grill.

I'm not sure exactly how I expected this to go so I have no stick to measure it against, but a part of me feels like it's failing. The other part of me thinks the fact that we can do comfortable silence well is a good thing.

"Remember that time when—"

"The stingrays!" he says.

"Yes!" I shout as we both laugh. I certainly notice that he completed my thought for me.

"There was that crazy lady screaming every time one came near her even though we were there in—where were we?"

"Grand Cayman."

"Yes. That's right. It was Grand Cayman and we took that boat out to that shoal in the ocean where there are tons of them."

"But that lady," I say with a quick shake of my head. "Man, she screamed as if a great white shark was eating her any time a ray came within ten feet of her."

"That was a great trip. So many fun memories. Before everything changed."

I finish the sip of my beer, trying to figure out what to say, how to say it, but not wanting to ruin the mood. But just when I start to speak, he changes the subject.

"Remember when we rented that place down in the Florida Keys?" he asks.

How could I not?

I was fifteen and when the Bowmans showed up at the house we'd all rented, something had shifted. I hadn't seen Drew in almost a year but this time when he walked into the house with board shorts hung low on his hips, his skin tanned and chest bared, I realized he wasn't a little kid anymore.

And I sure as hell wasn't a clumsy little girl.

I'd spent those whole two weeks hoping he'd notice me. Every time he told his parents he was going to go off and explore, I prayed he'd ask me to come along. And the one time I caught him kissing the local girl he'd met on the beach, I was crushed it wasn't me.

So those last few nights I maneuvered myself any way I could to be in his path, even if it meant stepping out of my comfort zone and into a situation that left me in tears.

Something had shifted between us that summer—hormones, puberty, life—but it was only one-sided.

Our families parted ways at the end of that trip. I was in love and he didn't have a clue.

"I do. I seem to remember you having a different girl following you back to the house every night. You'd sit on the porch and do who knows what with them until your mom would make you come inside."

"Oh, to be a teenager and carefree again."

I stare at him, almost daring him to meet my eyes to see if he remembered *that* night or not.

Probably not.

"What was it called? *Forced family fun?*" I ask and smile.

"FFF." He chuckles. "I'd forgotten that term."

"Your sister made it up, didn't she?" I ask, remembering the aloof roll of her eyes when we had to all play UNO together one night. But I'm so caught up in the memory that I almost miss the shadow that drifts through his expression.

"Maggie did. And for the record," he says as he checks the meat, "forced or not, I have a hell of a lot of awesome memories from when our families vacationed together."

Chapter
FOUR

Brexton

DREW'S LAUGHTER RINGS OUT, DROWNING OUT THE SOUND OF crickets and a motorcycle revving somewhere down the street. Evening has taken hold as we sit across from each other, empty plates now pushed to the side with several empty beer bottles beside them, and a whole host of laughter and memories shared between us.

He's obviously more than easy on the eyes. I knew that when I knocked on his door. What I didn't expect was to be charmed by his personality as well. What I never considered was that spending time with him would spark something more than that teenage crush.

Not in a million years.

But it has.

Sitting across from him, his easy smile, and his incredible sense of humor, has only made him more attractive to me.

But I've sworn off men. Too much heartbreak and not enough heart filling.

Keep telling yourself that, Brex.

"So after the Olympic trials, what happened?" he asks.

I shrug with a frustration I still feel all these years later. "I blew out my knee the first day at the Olympic Village. The turf had a tear in it that snagged my cleat, and down I went."

"You must have been heartbroken."

"To put it mildly. But I'm lucky. So many athletes spend their lives competing and don't have anything to fall back on. I had my degree, and when doctors told me that if I played field hockey again, I had a chance of ruining my knee forever, I made the decision to have a real life."

"Do you miss it?" he asks.

I angle my head and stare at him as I think it over. "I miss the competition and that anticipation in the air before a game. I miss the smell of a real grass field just after it's been mowed, and knowing I was part of a team . . . but I have no complaints when it comes to my life now."

He twists his lips and stares at me, eyes growing darker as they narrow in thought.

"What is it, Drew?"

"So you're after Justin, then?" he asks.

"That's who I've been tasked to acquire, yes."

"Do you mind if I ask why?"

"Because it's the name of the game in this business." My answer is lame, but it's a difficult thing to answer. Not to mention, I don't want to have to explain anything about rival agent Finn Sanderson and our family pact to take back some of the clients he's stolen from us over the past few years.

"Big-ticket players also come with big-ticket headaches."

"I won't argue with you there." I take another sip of my beer.

"Just be careful with him."

"What's that supposed to mean?"

"Just be careful." He shrugs with his hands and meets my eyes. "Obviously you're working with Kincade," he continues, speaking of Kincade Sports Management.

It's the first time either of us has delved into this realm. We've spoken about past family vacations, about college years, about the mundane, but we've avoided—perhaps purposely—what happened and the current day.

But now he went there and I have no choice but to respond.

"Yes. We all work there." I lean back in my chair.

He falls silent and takes a sip of his beer, but his eyes stay fixed on mine, almost as if he's trying to figure something out. "Is that why you're here, Brex? To recruit me? Because if it is, you can save your breath. I'm not going to switch agencies." He leans forward and rests his forearms on the table. "And if that is the reason, it's pretty shitty to come here under the guise of catching up only to know you want something from me."

"Drew. That's not . . ." I bark out an uncomfortable laugh. "I should be offended by your question but I understand where you're coming from. Yes, I'm an agent, but I'm not so conniving that I'd come to your house, get you buzzed, and then try to sell you why your agent is doing you no favors whatsoever."

"I think you just kind of tried to." He laughs and holds up his thumb and forefinger a little bit apart. "Just a little bit."

I roll my eyes. "Agent or not, anyone can see you have a shitload of talent just sitting there not being used. Has Ari tried to—"

"Brexton." My name is a resigned sigh.

"No, I'm serious. Your arm is remarkable. I was looking at your stats. There's no way what happened with your dad—"

"And you just made my point. Thanks for a walk down memory lane, but it's probably best if you get going now." He pushes up from the table and starts collecting the plates.

I sit there with the taste of rejection in my mouth and a weird panic flickering in my veins. I can't remember the last time I had this much fun or relaxed so easily.

There's still something about him that makes my heart flutter all these years later.

"Drew. Wait." I scurry after him and have my hand on his arm the minute he sets the plates down. "I'm sorry. I'm not here to push or prod or anything, I'm just at a total loss why your talent has gone unnoticed and why you seem completely fine with it."

"Because." He throws me a lopsided smirk over his shoulder that I don't quite buy.

"Because why?"

"First, I don't care if you understand why. And second, I love my life. It's steady and stable for reasons that are no one's business but mine. I get to stay in one place, I get to play a game I love, and—"

"But you're a competitor and competitors like to compete. It doesn't make sense. I don't understand."

"Stop trying to. I'm not the kid you once knew and you're not the little girl I used to know either." His eyes roam up and down the length of my body. "A lot has changed."

"It has but the other night you implied it's because of your dad and that—"

He turns abruptly and faces me, hand grabbing my arm in return, and the look on his face stops me cold. We're in each other's personal space and, where there was awkwardness, there's now a strange tension that I'd swear was sexual if his expression wasn't one of irritation.

"I've had fun tonight, Brex. More than I thought I would when you showed up on my porch a few hours ago. I'd like the evening to continue because it's been a long time since I've had someone who I can talk this easily to. You're witty and intelligent, and God knows how hard that is to find in a conversation these days. The little girl I knew is all grown up and frankly, I'd love to get to know her better . . . but only on one condition."

"What's that?" I ask as I swallow over the sudden lump in my throat. He smells like soap and sandalwood, and I feel ridiculous focusing on the little things about him—the shadow of his stubble, the ring of dark blue around his irises, the very subtle scar through his eyebrow that I remember was the result of a skateboarding accident gone wrong.

"The past is the past. What happened is what happened. We don't talk about it, we don't pick it apart. It's history for a reason. We don't try to solve it . . . and we'll be good. Got it?"

Chapter FIVE

Drew

THERE'S DEFIANCE IN HER EYES THAT IS EQUAL PARTS INFURIATING and fascinating. Both war through her expression. Both give and take and struggle to subside.

I hate that my next thought is how I want to taste her lips.

And then my next after is *how can that even cross my mind?*

How can I look at her and want her, knowing part of my fate is because of that last name she has?

"Brex?" I ask.

Her breath is shaky. Hesitant. *Affected.* That last part is such a turn-on even when I swear to fucking God I don't want it to be.

"Deal," she murmurs, but I don't let go of her arm, and she doesn't step back out of my space.

Indecision lingers where normally I would dive right in. That history I told her to forget clouds my mind and sidetracks the thoughts I'd love to act on.

"Brexton." Her name is a whisper laden with intention.

Seconds feel like minutes and each breath is like another push of momentum to kiss her. The woman I shouldn't want.

The woman I am already thinking about having.

We jolt apart at the sound of the doorbell followed a second later by pounding on the door. It's rapid and insistent, and my heart drops into my stomach because I know that knock.

I know that fervor.

Not now.

Not fucking now.

"I need to get that."

"Is everything okay?"

"Yes. It's . . . why don't you go out back and grab another beer."

Confused eyes meet mine but a soft smile warms them. "Sure."

I wait for her to go out the back door before I head toward the intermittent yet demanding knocking. With a deep breath, I prepare myself for what I'll find when I open the door this time.

But it doesn't matter how much I prepare, I'm still knocked on my ass when I swing the door open and find my sister standing there, the visual reminder of the rippled effects of the betrayal. What Brex's father did to my family. The toll. *How Brex's dad hurt us all.*

Like my younger sister, Maggie, standing here. Her eyes are hollow, her collarbone is poking through whatever you call what she's wearing, and her body twitches in a way that says she's coming down from whatever withdrawal she seems to be riding today.

But it won't last long.

It never does.

She'll find someone to give it to her or sell *something* to get it.

The sight of her rips every shred of emotion from me—anger, disgust, sorrow, resignation—just like it does every time we're back in this space.

And it's been too many to count.

"Maggs," I say, disappointment flooding through me. "Long time no see. Apparently, it's been long enough though for you to start using again."

"I am. I was. Things got tough," my sister explains as she remains in a perpetual motion of twitches and feet shifts and neck jerks.

"I see." My sigh is heavy enough for the both of us. "And by tough, you mean what? The last check I sent you ran out? The one that was supposed to help you with living expenses but, from the sight of you, went to other things?"

"Don't you stand there and cast judgment on me, Drew. Not you in your fancy house, perfect life, and all your money. You don't get to judge me or look down upon me or—"

"You had a good run. I'm proud of you," I murmur as I try to remember what her sponsor from her last rehab stint instructed me was best to say to lessen her agitation. As I try to bite back the anger that eats at me with each and every passing minute. "Is everything okay? What do you need?" We've played this delicate game more times than I care to count.

Maggie stares at me as she zones out for a second. I'm used to this from her, but the seconds give me time to study my sister and despise her even more for everything she didn't become.

My once gorgeous sibling is now a shell of herself. Her hair that used to be glossy and the envy of her friends is now brittle and dull. Her model-worthy cheekbones now look like harsh angles. Her full lips are cracked and hiding stained teeth.

"If I ask, you'll get mad."

"Try me."

I shut the door at my back and lean my shoulder against it. The last thing I need is Brexton coming out to this shitshow and having to explain yet another Bowman family embarrassment.

"What is it you need?"

She dances on her toes and then rocks on her heels, all the while her hands are continuously touching her face, her hair, her arms. It's a dizzying constant that has to be exhausting. "Do you think you could spare some money? Please, Drew? Could you help me out?"

"What are you using this time? Meth? Crack? Or have we moved on to heroin?" My voice is as cold and flat as my expression.

"Does it matter? I just need a hit. Just something to take the edge off and then I'll be able to think clearly."

"When's the last time you used?" I ask, trying to get as much information as possible to give to her sponsor.

"It was just today. Just yesterday. I swear." Panic flutters in her voice and desperation owns her eyes. "I had some bad news. My job. I lost it. I was down and needed the pick-me-up."

I nod as if I care, nonchalant despite the fury coursing through my veins.

"I'm sorry. I'm so sorry. I wish I were stronger. I wish I could beat this but I swear to God, Drew," she says as tears well in her eyes and defeat mirrors her posture. "It has its claws in me and no matter how hard I try, it keeps dragging me back down. I promise I'll go back to rehab. I promise I'll get better. If you'll just help me tonight."

Do I give her the cash and enable her? Do I push her away knowing she's going to find her fix somewhere else—somewhere most likely more dangerous?

The same questions I ask myself each time.

The same difficult answers each and every time.

"*Please.*" She gives me a smile. She doesn't realize she looks like a broken clown with makeup smeared beneath her eyes. "It'll be the last time I ask."

"Until the next time.""

"No."

"You haven't asked about *her* once, Maggs. Not once."

"I know she's okay."

"You do? Is the high so important you've lost sight of what matters? Like, your three-year-old daughter? You know. . . Charley?"

"I love her. Don't you dare accuse me of not loving her."

What a waste. The thought runs on repeat as I look at her, and then think of the angel of a little girl who deserves so much better.

How is it that one thing, one event in time, started the slow demise of a family? It's like a ball slowly gaining speed and power, trying to take out everything that it comes in contact with.

I think of Charley and the life she deserves, of the mother she deserves, and I take a step

toward my sister, hating myself before I even speak. "Here's what's going to happen. You're going do whatever it is you're going to do tonight . . . and then tomorrow afternoon, your sponsor is going to meet you at your house. From there you will check yourself back into rehab."

The first tear spills over. "I don't know if I can go back there. I don't think—"

I step toward her and put my hands on her shoulders, holding her body still. "You can and you will. I'm not giving up on you, Maggs." My heart aches in my chest at the empty words even I don't believe anymore. "And we're going to get you better, okay?"

She nods enthusiastically. "But can I have some cash for tonight? Please. I won't ask again."

"I'm sorry. I love you, but I can't. Just like I didn't last time. And the time before that. It's clear the money I used to pay your rent only allowed you to use whatever cash you made to buy drugs . . . so obviously we need to make some changes when you get out of the program this time."

"Drew. *Please.*"

I enter the house but she doesn't move. She used to fight me, try to push the door in, but there's resigned sadness to her this time that tells me she knows better.

"Good night. Tomorrow, I'll have your sponsor call you to set up a time. And if you don't show, then I'll make sure you never see Charley again."

"You wouldn't dare!" she screams.

"Try me."

Without another word, I shut the door in her face and rest my own forehead against it. The bleak, downtrodden, and desperate image of her is ingrained in my mind and, just like every other time my sister walks away, I wonder if it'll be the last time I see her alive.

Fuck.

I thought this last time was going to be *the time.*

I thought this last facility would be the *final one.*

However, just like my sister, I don't understand the claws that own her either.

Chapter SIX

Brexton

"Everything okay?" I ask as Drew comes onto the patio but the sight of him—a strained smile and taut shoulders—tells me whatever the raised voices were about isn't okay.

"Yes. No." He chuckles. "As okay as it's ever going to get."

"I'm assuming that's cryptic and that's all you're going to give?"

He takes a long swallow of his beer and gives a quick shake of his head. "Pretty much."

The mood has shifted. The sexual tension that was vibrating between us no less than fifteen minutes ago has all but dissipated.

I wish I hadn't picked everything up and cleaned the dishes while he was outside, because it's awkward and I have nothing to do.

"Well then," I say as I rock on my heels and chuckle nervously when he falls silent with a pensive expression. "I guess I'll be going. I've already hijacked enough of your evening. I don't want to take any more of it."

He stares at me for a beat, as if it's taking a second to register what I've just said. Then he takes a few steps toward me. "I'm sorry. I don't even know—that was Maggie."

"Your sister?" My voice escalates in pitch as I think of all the fun the two of us used to have. Not to mention all the trouble we got into as well. "How is she? How is . . ." But his expression stops the words on my lips. "*Drew?* What is it?"

He shakes his head and takes another long swallow of his beer. "Remember when I said the past is the past and we don't talk about it?" he asks in a definitive tone, and I nod. "That's exactly what that was."

I stare at him, blinking, wondering what he means. Obviously, even though I knew her in the past, she's still here now. "Sure. Okay. I don't . . . okay."

And then it dawns on me. While I'm here and he's fine with it, maybe he doesn't want his family to know I'm here. Maybe that would tear open a wound to the past he's not ready to confront with them yet.

Especially when, who the hell am I? Just a woman who stopped at his house and invited herself in for dinner?

It's not like we're dating or anything.

Why would he tell Maggie that I'm here and cause a rift?

"I'm going to grab my purse then," I say and throw my thumb over my shoulder before heading inside to find it.

Drew follows.

A part of me hopes he'll tell me to stay. That we can sit back down at that table in the backyard, fall back into that easy camaraderie we had, but I know the moment has passed.

And even worse or weirder or whatever you want to call it, I'm confused on why I want to so badly.

He watches me silently as I grab my purse and slide the strap over my shoulder. "I'll walk you out," he says.

"No need. I can manage on my own." I offer him a smile that I don't think reaches my eyes and head for the door.

"Brex. Wait," he says just as my hand reaches the handle. When I turn to face him, I'm surprised to see him so close to me. "Thank you for stopping by. I had a good time catching up. I apologize for this." He waves his hand in the space between us. "Maggs is Maggs. I need to stop hoping she'll somehow be different so that I stop being disappointed when she isn't."

I don't understand what he's talking about, but I smile and nod. "The only person you can control in life is yourself, Drew. You know that."

"I do, but it doesn't make it any easier."

"I know, and I'm sorry." I reach out and squeeze his hand. "Thank you again."

"Maybe we could do this again sometime. Finding friends who *knew me when* are far and few between most days."

I nod, trying to not be miffed by the friend comment, and smile softly. "I'd like that."

And I would. There's something about him that makes me remember how easy life used to be before adulthood happened.

"'Night, Bratty Brex."

"Good night, Dreadful Drew."

This time when I walk away, he lets me.

But after I climb in my car and glance back at his house, he's still standing there in his doorway watching me.

I wave and drive away with a crush that has been rekindled. And that's all it can remain. My heart has been hurt so many times before that I wish it were more jaded, because there *is* comfort in spending time with a friend who *knew you when*.

Chapter
SEVEN

Drew

"YOU REALLY SHOULD KEEP YOUR FRONT DOOR LOCKED," I WARN AS I stride into my parent's house irritated at how my evening has turned.

"Drew. Oh." My mom claps her hands in front of her where she stands in the kitchen when she catches sight of me. "You paid us a visit."

"Anyone can walk right in here." I walk toward her and press a kiss to her cheek, noticing and grateful my father is nowhere in sight. "We live in a good neighbor—" But when her eyes meet mine her words fade. "Drew?"

"She's using again."

Her sigh is as audible as the shake of her head is resigned. But it's her eyes widening that tells me she gets my gist. That she understands that Maggie might come by only to steal something to feed her habit.

Some things are like clockwork in this family and that's one of those things.

"How do you know?" Ever the mother, she shakes her head as if she rejects what I'm saying. Maggie could never do wrong in her eyes and even all these years later, it's still hard for her to see otherwise.

But I looked like him. I played the same sport. It was much easier for her to shift blame on me.

"She came to my house asking for money."

"I see," she says quietly. "And you did what?"

"I told her no. I told her—"

"But, Drew, what is she going to do to get money?" Desperation and fear are woven into every thread of her voice.

I bite back my sharp rebuke, knowing it won't do any good. "I don't know, Mom. The same thing she does every other time she needs it. I pay for her home and her utilities. It's not my job to feed her habit, and I'd hope if she showed up here, you'd feel the same way."

"Of course," my mom says with a wave of her hand as if my suggestion is nonsense. At the same time though, I know how hard I struggle with the decision to keep Maggs at arm's length, so I imagine it's even harder in Mom's shoes. "You came all the way over here to tell me that? You could have just called."

"That would mean you'd actually have to carry your phone with you and answer it," I say, referring to a long-running gripe I have. They got rid of their landline, but they forget to answer their cell phones.

She gives me *the look* that every kid knows from their mother. The one that says drop it. "Did you tell Wayne?" she asks, referring to Maggie's ex and Charley's father.

"He was the first person I called," I say, thinking how I stood at my front door watching Brexton's taillights until they disappeared down the street. How I wished I could have my evening back with her instead of dealing with this bullshit. "He said not to worry. Charley is and will be fine."

"It still makes me nervous." She moves around the counter and points to the couch for me to make myself at home. "Please don't tell your father. When he gets agitated, everything flares up, and we've been on a roll of good days lately."

I nod. "Yeah, I forgot. I need to start tiptoeing around here to forgo the inevitable fight."

"That's not what I said."

"You didn't have to."

She moves closer and lowers her voice. "Maybe you should try talking to him again."

My laugh is caustic. Memories slam into me. His sharp words and cold shoulder. The man I love more than anything feels like he gets further and further away from me when all I want to do is understand.

Why he walked away.

Why he can't come to my games.

Why he resents my career because he didn't fight for his.

"Surely you don't mean that. Last time was a disaster." And last time was before his diagnosis.

When I dared to ask him for all the details . . . and we didn't speak for over a year.

She stares at me, a woman who I think knows way too much and is stuck between her husband's secrecy and her son's need to know.

I don't envy her.

Not one bit.

And that's why I'm about to leave well enough alone when I hear his voice.

"Drew. What a surprise," Dad says as he makes his way to his chair and takes a seat. I watch each movement for signs of progression, but my mom is right, despite the tremors in his hands, he seems to be doing okay.

The untouchable man I've always hoped someday to be close to again.

"Dad," I say with a nod as I meet his eyes.

The strain is still there, even after all this time.

The sense of betrayal still between us.

The distance can't be resolved.

I'm the kid who went against his parents' wishes. The son who played a game his father left behind and a father who has resented it ever since. I'm the child who has lived a great, upstanding life while Maggie has screwed up everything she touches—everything but Charley, of course—and yet I'm the one who's still on the opposite end of the awkward silences.

I'm still the one who feels like I don't belong.

"I watched the game the other night," he says. "Hobbs needs work. He looks rusty. You need to tell Bellinger that you deserve a chance."

"Hobbs scored four touchdowns."

"But his mechanics are off. His elbow was too low and he was missing the obvious pass most plays."

I nod as he continues through his analysis of the man who starts in front of me. An analysis that can be so critical and cutting it can be debilitating.

I happen to know from experience.

But when such critiques come from one of the best in the game of his time, you shut your mouth and listen.

The upside? That man is my father.

The downside? The same.

"Should I type up notes and send them to him?" I ask as my mom takes a seat beside Dad. "Or better yet, I'll give them to his agent so he can shop for a better team for him."

His eyes flash up to mine and he points a tremoring finger at me. "The last thing you need to be doing is talking to any agent."

His tempered words are an ever-constant reminder of what happened.

Of why Brexton Kincade is another element of my life that needs to stay firmly in the past.

Chapter
EIGHT

Drew

9 years earlier

"But I don't understand." I sit on the couch in the middle of the living room staring at my father. He's a hulking figure in the space, all six foot five inches of him, as he stares at Maggs and then me with a look I know I'll never forget. Sadness, fear, confusion, and the one I'll never understand, resignation. "What does it mean you're no longer playing football? That's who you are. What you do."

"It's not for you to understand, Drew. It's for you to simply accept." He glances over and meets my mom's eyes, and she swallows nervously.

What the fuck is going on?

I mean, I know what's going on—he's explained it to me no less than twenty times and we've been living with its fallout since—but this makes *no* sense.

He didn't do it.

He told me he didn't.

"Mom?" I ask for clarification from her but she just looks at my dad and waits for him to continue.

"Earlier today I tendered my resignation to the Patriots and the NFL Players Association," he says somberly.

"Dad?" Maggie's voice vibrates with the same uncertainty I feel.

Our life has been turned upside down for the past few weeks—press on our lawn, rumors going crazy, my dad suspended—and now he's telling us that's it?

Just like that?

"You're just going to walk away?" I shove up out of my seat, fury suddenly in my veins, and disbelief owning me. "You said you didn't do anything wrong. If you didn't do anything wrong, then why aren't you fighting it? Why aren't you—" I run a hand through my hair and pace from one side of the room to the other.

Not only is football his identity, but it's also been mine for as long as I can remember. He's Gary Bowman, the star quarterback, and I'm Gary Bowman's son. The one who's going to follow in his footsteps.

It's all I've ever wanted to be.

It's all I've ever planned for despite my parents telling me I have to go to college first.

"This can't be real," I mutter, but when I turn back around and look at the people in the room—my mom, my dad, my sister—I feel like I'm at a funeral. Everyone looks so glum.

He meets my eyes and nods like a scolded puppy and there's something about the sight that eats at me. "Sometimes in life, Drew, what's best and what's right aren't always the same thing."

I stare at him, then my mom sitting idly by, and I shake my head, hands fisted. "But you told us to always fight for what's right. And you didn't do this!" I shout, confused when the past few weeks have been confusing enough. "Why are you walking away? You're breaking records and will be in the Hall of Fame and I don't understand . . . Why aren't you fighting?" My voice breaks as I step toward him, needing to look into his eyes, wanting to understand.

Needing to understand.

"Drew." He reaches out to touch my arm. I yank it from his reach as the anger bubbles over and the disbelief keeps rising. "I know it will be an adjustment for all of us, but it's for the best."

"You said they were wrong!" I scream, his lack of a reaction only adding fuel to my fire. "You told me it was a lie and you didn't do it, and yet you're just walking away? What are people going to think—"

"That's enough!" His voice thunders through the room and sucks all of the oxygen from it.

My head spins. My heart races. Everything in my orbit tilts off its axis, and I can't find my balance.

"I wanted you to hear it from me before you catch wind of it from the press. And after we leave this room, we'll never speak of it again."

"But—"

"Goddammit, Drew!"

His words startle me. Almost as much as his fist pounding on the TV cabinet beside him. They knock me back into the moment, into a reality I can't comprehend nor do I want to.

"Did you throw the game, Dad? *Did you?*" I scream, not caring about respect or that he's my dad. How is this happening? *How is this possible?*

"Son."

"No." I back away at the word, head shaking, mind not wanting to believe. My dad isn't someone who would risk everything, risk our safety. He's strong, he's loyal to his team, his friends—*He's loyal to his friends. He'd do anything for them* . . . No. Surely not. But what else could it be? *Fuck.* "It was Kenyon, wasn't it?" I grasp at straws. "I heard—in the Keys. You guys were drinking and you were talking about betting on games. I thought . . . Oh my God." I pull down on the back of my neck as my feet move, eating up space to abate my anger. "He did it, didn't he? He did it and you're taking the fall for it. That's why you refuse to talk to the press about it. That's why you're slipping away quietly. Claire Kincade died and you're going to take the fall for him, aren't you?"

There's a worried glance that my mom gives my dad. The look every kid knows that means you've caught them in something and she's warning him to not speak.

Their eyes hold for a beat as Maggs looks over to me, tears welling in her eyes. She saw the look too. She knows something bad happened too.

"Dad, don't bullshit me."

"Drew!" My mother shouts—definitely at my cursing and defiance—but I don't care.

"It was Kenyon, wasn't it?"

"Drew! Do not mention his name in this house ever again," my mom says sternly, her eyes meeting my dad's briefly but I'm too amped up, too confused, and only feel like it reinforces what I've just said.

I'm in his face again, my chest bumping his, wanting a reaction out of him—*needing* a reaction from him. Needing to know that I'm right. "You would never do this. It's not possible."

But instead of him responding like I need him to, he turns his back to me and walks toward the windows. The ones that have their blinds closed to prevent the prying eyes of the press, who have been camped out in the front yard for the past few weeks.

They're as hungry for an answer from my dad as I am.

"There will be some changes going forward," he says when he finally speaks. "A new life for our family. Adjustments will have to be made." And he continues on and on, but I stop listening, because he's not saying the things I need him to say. The things I need him to explain.

And when he walks from the room, leaving us there with absolutely no answers, both my sister and my mom remain while I jog after him.

"Dad." Desperation is in every thread of my voice and when he turns to face me, where he's standing in the hallway, he's framed in a way so there is no mistaking how beaten down he is.

Tears fill his eyes as our gazes meet. He offers me a somber nod, an apology without giving one, before turning his back and walking down the hall.

And it hasn't been discussed since.

Chapter
NINE

Brexton

"So things were fine and then they all of a sudden weren't?" Dekker asks from where she stands in the doorway. The sun reflects off her engagement ring and sends prisms all over my office, as I silently chastise myself for saying anything at all.

Of course, she was going to grab hold of that tiny morsel of information and demand a whole feast.

So much for me and my mouth. When am I ever going to learn?

"Brex? Don't you dare be close-lipped on me now. You know you offered the info up because you're dying to tell someone about him. I'm that someone, so give me the deets, woman."

"It was nothing. Never mind."

"Ha." She crosses her arms over her chest and levels a stare at me. "So either tell me what happened or I'll go tell Dad and then you can tell him the juicy details."

"There are no juicy details. And Dad? Really? Can't you be more original than that?"

"You know as well as I do that keeping a secret from Dad is next to impossible." She shrugs. "So it's me or him."

I hold her gaze and know she's right. I'm dying to tell someone and telling our dad right now isn't really an option. When it comes to him, questions lead to more questions and I'm nowhere near ready to go into full confession mode.

My sigh is my answer and her smirk tells me she knows she's got me.

"So things were fine and then they weren't?" she asks, picking back up to where we left off.

"So to speak. We were standing in his kitchen in that suspended moment when you're holding your breath because you think you're going to be kissed—"

"You're the only person I know who'd ever say those words out loud." She laughs and lifts her eyebrows. "You sound like a romance novel."

"And there's something wrong with that? It seems you found your happily ever after with Hunter so how can you tell me they don't exist?"

"Touché," she murmurs with a gloating grin. She's so damn cheerful since finding and falling in love with Hunter, it's nauseating. But in that good, I'm jealous but happy for you, kind of way. She plays with the rock weighing down her ring finger and even though I roll my eyes, it's all for show. I'm more than thrilled for her. "So? You thought he was going to kiss you and then what?"

"The doorbell rang. He disappeared and dealt with it, and when he came back the mood was gone."

"Who was at the door?"

I have to stop myself from saying her name. "His sister."

"Buzz kill."

"Yeah, but it was more than that. They were arguing about something and . . . I don't know, the mood was gone."

"I'm sure it wasn't gone, gone."

I snort. "He made sure to drop the *friend* term as he saw me out."

She hisses in response. "Ugh. That sucks." She plops down in the seat in front of me. "What was his name again?"

"I'd prefer to not say," I say nonchalantly and shrug before leaning back in my chair to stare at the city streets below. Kincade Sports Management is fifteen stories up, dead center in Manhattan. There's always plenty to look at outside of its walls, especially when you want to use it to avoid answering your older sister.

"Ooooh," she says, her ears perking up with a sudden interest. I mentally chastise myself because once again, I'm just drawing her in further. "That means I know him," she says in a sing-song voice with a clap of her hands.

"I never said that."

"You didn't have to. I know you better than you do. So . . . how'd you meet him?"

"Work," I deadpan without batting an eye. She was the oldest kid between our two families and, was more times than not, the ring leader with Drew when it came to planning all our shenanigans. Hell, she probably played with Maggs more than I did now that I think of it. She'd probably remember even more about the sequence of events leading up to Gary Bowman's scandal. The last thing she needs to know is who it is or that I camped out on his doorstep.

"Amusing. Dare I ask if he's a client or not?"

"Why?"

"It's just a question," she says coyly.

"Please spare me any lecture you're conjuring up about not dating clients. Talk about the pot calling the kettle black." I snort considering Hunter was her client and clients technically should be off limits.

"So it *is* a client."

"Does it matter?"

"Simply trying to narrow down the field so I can figure out who the mystery man is."

"He's not a client. That's all I'm going to give you."

"Why the secrecy, then?" Her brows narrow and I can see the cogs of her mind turning as she tries to figure it out.

"Because you guys are assholes," I say. I'm more than used to their ribbing about the revolving door of my love life. The sad thing? I wouldn't want it any other way.

Not that I'm ever going to admit that to her.

"And your point is?" She grins.

"I stopped telling you about love interests years ago. The teasing got old."

"Oh, come on. It was all in good fun. I mean, can you blame us? Your love life is like a soap opera."

"Like you've ever watched one."

"You know what I mean." She waves a hand my way. "You love to be in love."

"Who doesn't?"

"Me. Lennox. Chase," she says, naming my sisters.

"Don't be a hypocrite, Miss-Madly-In-Love." Sarcasm owns my tone.

"It's different."

"Of course, it's different. Is this when you pull the first-born card?" I tease, hating how rules always seem different for her than they do for me since I'm the younger.

"I'm not pulling any card. I'm simply saying you're just built differently from us so we don't understand it."

"No need to try to understand seeing as I've sworn off men."

"Doesn't seem like it by the topic of this conversation and the supposed Mystery Man."

"Well, I have. I'm sick of getting hurt." I give a resolute nod as if that's going to convince both my sister and my heart of the oath.

Dekker's expression softens and she leans forward in her chair. "You and Micah ended things over five months ago. Are you still upset over—"

"Yeah, well . . .unlike the rest of you cold-hearted bitches, I ended up with the soft one."

"Cold-hearted?" She laughs the words out. "I'll remind you of that the next time you're looking for a sympathetic ear." But as soon as the words are out her smile softens, her voice even more so, as she kicks into big-sister and chief-consoler mode. "Are you going to see *him* again?"

My sigh fills the room as I meet her eyes. "That's the real question, isn't it?"

"This is the part where I remind you that you swore off men."

"I did. I have. *Completely*," I admit, knowing she's right. I did swear off them. I now need to forget that silly crush I once had on a man I don't really know anymore. "So obviously the answer to that question is a moot point."

"I bet it is." She shrugs and offers a coy smile. "Maybe you should invite him to the McMasters' wedding. You replied with a plus-one for Micah and now there is no plus-one."

"Not even remotely funny."

"Why not? There'll be fancy suits and alcohol and a romantic atmosphere. I mean—"

"First off, the best way to scare off a man is to take him to a wedding, and second, I'm perfectly fine attending it on my own. I may love being in love, but I do not *need* a man to go with me. I'm perfectly comfortable with flying solo."

"I think you should bring him. Find out what his true character is."

"I'm serious, Dekk. The last thing I need right now is a man."

"You do need one. You—"

"Oh my God, you're infuriating. I don't need one—"

"Justin Hobbs," she says, bringing the conversation full circle to what she came into my office for in the first place. "He's the man you need." She smiles and bats her lashes. "Correction, he's the man we at KSM need you to need."

"He's an arrogant ass." I snort but welcome the change of topic.

"You knew that going in to recruit him." She chuckles. "Besides, isn't that the norm these days? If you're a hell of a player then you have to be a dick? Arrogant or not, keep the eye on him as the prize."

"Jesus. Now you're starting to sound like you love Justin as much as Justin loves Justin." I roll my eyes.

"That bad?"

"He pulled the old, *oops, I dropped my towel* trick."

"Of course, he did," she says with a shake of her head.

Being women in a male-dominated industry, all four of us have been subjected to the towel drop. To an athlete's need to put us in our place or sexualize our interaction in one way or another.

While we may be used to it, it's in no way acceptable.

"Was he at least worth the towel drop?" she asks.

"Dekker." I spit her name out.

"C'mon, you know you noticed." She laughs.

I laugh. She's right. I did notice. "Pretty average."

"Maybe he's a grower and not a shower." She rises from her seat. "Let me know if you need any help with him. He may be average and arrogant, but I hear he's a difficult one."

"Thanks. It's nothing I can't handle."

Chapter TEN

Drew

"Great practice today, Bowman." I glance over to Coach and nod.

"Thanks," I say the word, but know it doesn't matter how great my practice is because I won't touch the field in the game this weekend.

I'll get suited up. I'll warm up. And I'll sit and watch the game from beneath a set of football pads on the sidelines without ever getting to step in between them.

But there's been something about Brexton's words from the other night that have gotten stuck in my craw. Honest comments about the amount of talent I have that's being wasted.

Comments I'd like to take at face value and not read into . . . but struggle doing.

I know I'm good.

I know I have the work ethic and the drive.

I know I'm damn talented.

And yet other than my one shot with the Tigers in my early years with the NFL, I've been relegated as the backup quarterback in this league ever since without ever really being given a chance to prove myself.

Sure, I've gotten some time in when the starting QB is hurt or we're winning by a ridiculous margin, but it's typically in a game where whatever I do doesn't really affect its outcome. It's almost as if there's a clause in my contract that says "second string only."

And sadly, until Brexton said those words to me, I didn't realize how much I had grown to simply accept that fate. I'd bought the line I kept telling myself. The one that told me I was still an asset to the team, still vital in preparing my teammates for game day.

I'd talked myself into accepting this norm because between Maggs' disfunction and my father's disease, while I might not be taking center stage on Sundays, at least the position allows me to be near my family. And if I were starting QB, it would most likely be elsewhere—another city, another state—since Hobbs is here. With my current family situation, that would make things more difficult.

So is that why I haven't fought harder? Haven't been more vocal? Haven't demanded my agent help fight for me?

Or is it all of that along with the fact that after what happened with the Tigers, I decided maybe less is more. Maybe I convinced myself that if I'm in the spotlight for too long, another accusation will be made and tarnish everything I've worked for.

The admission, even if just to myself, is hard to hear. Hard to acknowledge.

When did I become the coward? The guy who didn't fight for what he wanted because he was afraid? I bulldozed my way into the NFL and then one situation, one incident, and I allowed myself to disappear into the shadows much like my father did.

The facts don't sit well with me.

It weighs heavily in my gut, much like my thoughts weigh on my mind during my shower, and well into the time I'm about to head home.

I have a zoo date with Charley. One of those perks I get to have by living here in New York. My normal in the crazy family of mine.

As I heft my bag onto my shoulder about to head out to pick her up, I stop when I hear Justin on the phone as he walks into the locker room.

"Did I wait the appropriate amount of socially accepted time before I called you back after you gave me your digits?" Justin asks and then barks out a laugh that is pure ego and cheese.

The man is on the prowl.

Then again, that should come as no surprise considering he always is.

"So you *do* want me. I knew you couldn't resist me." He emits a louder than normal chuckle to make sure we're all watching him. And by the glance I give some of the linemen on the other side of the locker room, they're annoyed by him too.

The problem is, you can only stay annoyed with Justin for so long. There's something about the guy that makes you like him, even when you want to hate him.

"C'mon, you know me better than that by now. I'm expecting grand gestures. Signs in the sky professing your love for me. Hoops for you to jump—or dance—through. Is that too much to ask?" he jokes and then pauses with a shit-eating grin on his face as he listens. "Okay. I guess that will have to do, but I'm telling you, I'm not a man who likes to settle."

I half listen to the rest of the conversation, curious who it is because Justin's really turning on the bullshit.

"Who was that?" I ask, with a lift of my chin when he ends the call.

"This chick who wants on my jock." He winks.

"According to you that would be every chick."

"Can't fault me for being good and desired." He shrugs with his hands up as I shake my head. "I'm a two-for-one special."

How does a cocky asshole with an arm like he has and a fucked-up attitude get to be a starting quarterback?

I'm better.

I know I am.

"C'mon, Drewski," Justin says as he takes a seat and starts to lace up his sneaker. "One day, *you too*, can be like me."

A player? An asshole? Egotistical? Hated as much as he's loved?

Oh, the many sides of Justin Hobbs.

He lifts his eyebrows as if I owe him an answer, but the one I want to give isn't deserved. Mine stems from frustration. A frustration that I've been complacent for so long. Discontent.

He sighs when I don't bite. "Brexton. It was Brexton Kincade."

And with that name, he has my complete attention. The damn woman has owned my thoughts. Because of her insistent praise of my skills? Because she opened my eyes to my discontentment?

No. It's more than that.

If I'm honest with myself, it's because she's gotten to me.

I miss the smell of a real grass field just after it's been mowed, and knowing I was part of a team.

She's right. Fuck is she right.

Of course, I get to smell the real grass, but only from the sidelines. Only with a clean uniform. I've forgotten what it feels like when an offensive line is charging at you, competing to take you down and dirty so their team has a better chance at winning.

But you're a competitor and competitors like to compete.

Her opinions, her comments, they just keep circling in the background, just keep taunting me in the best of ways. In the worst of ways.

Brex and I have history, we connect even now, but I can do nothing about it, *about her*, other than defend her out of professional courtesy from a douchebag like Hobbs.

"She's a sport's agent trying to win you over. I doubt she wants your jock, Hobbs. I hate to break it to you, but I assure you all females aren't dying to be with you. She's simply trying to do her job."

He emits a suggestive chuckle. "Yeah, her job is to *do me*."

I grit my teeth. Fucking prick needs to be taught some manners about how women weren't put on earth to bow down to him.

That and the fact that I might feel slightly jealous when it comes to how much attention he's been paying her.

Ridiculous but still true nonetheless.

"Real classy."

"Can you blame me? Who would pass up a chance at having that banging body and burying your face between those thighs?"

"Cut the shit, Justin," I say and take a step forward. He always takes it too far. "We can all agree that she's hot, but don't be a dick. She's doing her job and doesn't deserve to be subjected to assholes like you."

He nods, and I wait for him to come back at me but he doesn't. Rather he hangs his head back and blows out a long breath. "Fucking Finn."

"Sanderson?" I ask referring to his agent.

"Yep." He meets my eyes and lowers his voice. "No offense to *the NYC*."

The NYC? Only douchebags say shit like that.

"But Finn would love for me to stay here forever, man, but it's not my vibe. I could use some Cali sun and those gorgeous women. Big tits. Tiny waists."

"Good personality. Good morals. Intelligence," I throw out there to highlight how shallow he is.

He shrugs unapologetically. "Hey man, it doesn't matter if they understand quantum physics. All that matters is how they look on my arm and how their ass looks when I'm fucking them from behind."

I run a hand through my hair as I come to the realization. He really just said that out in the open without checking to see if there were any reporters nearby to quote him.

Thank fuck, there aren't.

"If you plan on moving there, the last thing you should do is call it Cali. Big faux pas."

"Faux what?" he asks.

"Never mind. Just don't call it Cali. That'll get your ass kicked right out."

"Noted." He tosses his towel at the dirty towel bin across the room. "Any advice on Finn?"

"Advice on Finn? I thought you were just talking to Kincade?" I ask, fighting the moral dilemma. If he stays with his current agent, it sounds like Finn will keep him in New York. If he were to switch agencies over to say Kincade, then maybe he'd be traded to California and I'd get a chance at starting.

The problem? That pushes him into Brexton's realm, and history or no history, I hate the idea of him being anywhere near her for an extended period of time.

"Nah, man. Why would I do that? Finn's the one I want to fight for me. Brexton's the one I want to fuck."

"Cut the shit, Justin."

"Christ, man. Relax. I'm just teasing. She's hot. I'm hard to resist. We'd be good together."

"Too bad she has a long-term boyfriend," I lie through my fucking teeth. *What the fuck, Bowman?* Brex is a big girl. She works in this industry, so I know for a fact she can handle herself.

She's not a princess. She doesn't need saving.

And yet when Justin lifts a lone eyebrow at my comment, I don't flinch.

"That's right. I forgot you know her. Steve said you were talking to her after the game the other night." I nod. "So she really has a man?"

"From what I gather."

"And you think that scares me?" He throws his head back and laughs. "No one can resist me."

"You need serious mental help."

"No, man. What I need is advice. Care to give me some? You've had skin in this game a hell of a lot longer than I have."

Spoken like a true dick. *Thanks for pointing out you've been in the show two years while I've been sidelined for what feels like forever.*

"Tell your agent what you want and if he can't give it to you, then move on to one who will."

He nods with a dramatic flair. "Yep, but that motherfucker keeps telling me to stay here. That this is the team I need to be on. It's the right makeup, management, offensive coordinator."

And Finn is right. This team, this offense, is best suited to an arm like Justin's, just like it suits mine.

But I keep my mouth shut.

"Finn works for you. Not the other way around. You're his paycheck, and he doesn't get paid unless you do."

He stares at me with blank eyes as if I just spoke an epiphany. It's common sense. How in the hell does he remember our playbook during games?

"Huh. That was solid, man."

I nod and fight the shake of my head in disbelief. "You're the one whose contract is up at the end of the season. Tell your agent what you want, and if he doesn't comply, then get a new agent who will."

Chapter ELEVEN

Brexton

"IT'S BEEN AWESOME SEEING YOU AGAIN TOO," I SAY AND HUG AN OLD friend before she flits over to another couple she swore she hadn't seen in ages.

The wedding was lovely, *and boring* in that way most weddings are. Lots of words that no one really listens to until they lead to that one moment. The *I dos*. The *you may kiss the bride*. The first time the couple turns to face the audience as a Mr. and Mrs.

The cocktail reception, while my old college friend and her groom have their wedding photos taken is even better. The iconic Tavern on the Green lit up with fairy lights and lush greenery—a little piece of country in this concrete-laden city—isn't a bad place to be with a glass of wine in hand and a heart full of the romanticism of the moment.

The night is warm and the music is soft, as I move across cobblestone pavers toward the doors we've been summoned to for dinner service to start.

But when I look up and see Drew standing across the patio, my feet falter and my heart skips a beat.

Drew Bowman is hot in a football uniform. He is sexy at home, barefoot in his sweat pants. But in a dark suit and tie? He's absolutely devastating.

I look away for a split second as I try to process all the emotions swirling inside of me. Or maybe it's just sheer lust from the sight of him.

The problem?

When I look back up, he's staring straight at me and now I have nowhere to hide. Not that I want to.

He walks toward me, one hand holding a drink, the other buttoning up the buttons of his blazer/suit jacket. His expression reads confused but his smile lights up the night.

Too bad when he speaks, the irritation in his voice sounds nothing like his smile looks.

"What are you doing here?" he asks.

"Look at you all fancy and dressed up."

"What are you doing here?" he repeats, accusation in his tone.

"Jules is one of my good friends from college."

He nods and takes a sip of his drink as his eyes take an unabashed stroll up and down the length of my body. I know desire in a man's eyes when I see it, and it's there all right.

"Small world," he murmurs and starts to walk away, completely dumbfounding me.

"What? Wait!" I grab his arm and he turns around. "Why are you here?"

The muscle in his jaw tics. "Because Archer McMasters is my friend."

"Small world," I repeat as we start moving with the herd of guests inside the decked-out ballroom. Intricate arrangements of flowers line surface after surface in white and beige tones. Fabric drapes from the ceiling and crystal lines the tables. Somehow, it's elegant yet shabby chic all at the same time.

"It sure is," he says.

I was hoping to have heard from you.

"I hope whatever happened the other night . . . that you were able to resolve it."

"Yes. It's fine." His eyes hold mine, and I swear it's like he's struggling with something. Then he offers me a tight smile. "Good seeing you, but if you'll excuse me, I need to get to my table."

I watch Drew walk away, more than befuddled over how this is the same man I had dinner with the other night.

Did I do something wrong? Say something?

How did I misconstrue the vibe I got from him at his house? The almost kiss I'm certain was going to happen? His comment suggesting we do it again sometime?

Am I that off my rocker and desperate for love? That pathetic?

I know I'm not.

I know for a fact, and yet . . . maybe Dekker was right. Maybe I see things through hopeless romantic eyes, even when there isn't anything there to begin with.

With confusion owning my thoughts and dampening my mood, I head for my assigned table. The irony? When I approach it, I find Drew standing there, staring at the place cards—one his, one mine—seating us next to one another.

I should've guessed when I was assigned to table thirteen that it was a bad omen.

Now I know it is.

"Looks like we're sitting next to each other," I say and infuse cheer into my voice that I really don't feel. While he's not exactly being the most cordial, he at least has manners and pulls my chair out for me.

He sits down and grumbles under his breath as others are taking their seats, and the first round of food is being served.

Everyone at the table introduces themselves. There are two couples who know the bride and groom from work, two childhood friends and their spouses, an empty chair where my plus-one would have been, and then there's Mildred.

Sweet Mildred with her auburn-colored hair and raucous laugh, and who has declared herself to be ninety-five years old and states, "I'm too old for this shit," when a salad is slid in front of her.

She's my kindred spirit, and I think she knows it too by the way she keeps eyeing and smiling at me through the centerpiece on the table.

"Mildred? How do you know Archer and Jules?" I ask.

"I'm Archie's great-grandma." She waves a hand. "We go way back."

Everyone at the table stops chewing at her comment and then starts laughing when we all comprehend her joke.

"You don't want to sit with family?" the lady to the right asks.

Mildred snorts. "Family is boring. I already know their secrets. I asked to be put at a table with some hot young men so I at least have something good to look at."

There are several coughs mid-chew in response. Luckily, we're all saved by the main course being served, because Mildred is a lot to take in and you're not sure if you should encourage her or fall silent.

"You ready for Sunday?" I ask Drew quietly, cryptically asking about their upcoming game without outright asking so he won't get the million questions that normally follow when one learns you're an NFL player.

"Drew?" When he doesn't answer, I touch my hand to his arm to ask again, and he politely but deliberately moves his arm out of the way.

"We can't do this," he murmurs. "This can't happen."

I turn and look at him while he waves to someone across the room, and I swear it's just to avoid me. "What can't happen? Me sitting with you?" I emit a disbelieving chuckle. "I'm not sure you get a say in that since it was Archer and Jules's decision where we sit."

"Not that. *This.*"

"This?" I ask.

"Do you two know each other, dear?" Mildred asks from her prying perch across the table, drawing six sets of eyes our way.

"No," Drew says.

"Yes," I say at the same time.

I offer a tight smile in response, hoping the servers clearing dishes and asking if we'd like more to drink will be enough distraction so we don't have to answer.

I turn to face Drew and lean in. "I don't understand what your problem is. Is this about the other night?"

"Drop it, Brex."

"Why?" I demand in a hushed voice. "We had a good night. Then we didn't."

"It's complicated."

"How so? I wasn't asking for anything more than friendship," I say and know deep down I'm lying. Making a house call to a client who isn't yours is just a piss-poor excuse, even to my own ears, and yet, what else am I supposed to say?

"Are you two ex-lovers?" Mildred asks loudly.

"No," we both say in unison.

"Just friends," Drew corrects.

"It seems you two are in the middle of a juicy fight and frankly, my ninety-five-year-old self misses those kinds of fights where you claw at each other until it turns into you can't take your hands off each other." She wiggles her shoulders. "Is that what we're in for? Should I see if the staff here can procure a hate-fuck room for the two of you?"

"Oh my God," the guest to Drew's left laughs out as I stare at Mildred with a lax jaw and shock. She really did just say all of that.

And by the way I accidentally hit Drew's knee with mine and he yanks his away, I know for a fact she did just say that.

"Do you like mustard, son?" she asks Drew. "I bet you do. Loving mustard is a sign of being stubborn. And stubborn lovers are the best kind." She shivers as if she's reliving a memory before a grin slides onto her lips. "Am I right?"

"No. We're not. He's not." My words fail me.

"We're just *friends*," Drew says and I hate the way that word makes me feel. Almost like we're back playing spin the bottle in Deadman's Cove when we were teenagers. When he made sure that everyone knew we were *just friends*.

The rejection tastes just as bitter now as it did back then.

The difference? The difference is this time I have confidence and a backbone.

"You do have quite an active imagination, Mildred, but I hate to disappoint you. Drew is someone I knew way back when, when we were just kids."

"Even better." She rubs her hands together. "There's still time for some fireworks to happen yet."

We both chuckle politely as the awkwardness grows between us.

"It's been nice catching up with him, but if you'll all excuse me, I'm going to go mingle."

I stand and down the rest of my wine, setting the glass down without caring what I look like to those at the table.

There seems to be some fun happening on the dance floor outside and it's time to let loose and do the same.

Screw Drew Bowman.

He can be attractive and sexy all he wants. He can have a laugh that makes you smile and an intellect that makes you think.

But he doesn't get to be a dick to me.

I didn't need him before, and I sure as hell don't need him now.

Chapter
TWELVE

Drew

I WASN'T ASKING FOR ANYTHING MORE THAN FRIENDSHIP.

Her voice—those lips—saying that phrase repeats over and over in my head is stuck in my craw.

Especially when every time I look up, she's right there, front and center, shaking her ass on the dance floor.

Who the fuck am I kidding? I haven't looked down once. Hell, I haven't taken my eyes off her. I feel like the creepy asshole standing in the darkness of the patio, leaning against the rail with a drink in my hand, staring at her.

Friendship, my ass.

Is that what's bugging me? That friendship is the last thing on my mind when it comes to this woman and yet that's what she asserted? That's why I'm pissed?

Or is it just the plain question of *who is this woman?*

She's so very different from the teenage girl who feared being the center of attention. The one who shied away from groups and preferred her romance novels to interaction at times. The wallflower who is most definitely now shining.

She is in the middle of the dance floor with her arms in the air, her head thrown back, and her hips swaying to the beat in a way that should be illegal. Talk about breathtaking.

Confident.

Sexy.

Stunning.

I can't take my eyes off her when every part of me knows I need to.

She's like a Juliet whose family lead to the demise of mine.

Yet I'm still looking, still watching . . . still trying to rationalize how I could be with a woman like her when all is said and done.

And if my parents were to find out? The fight we had a few years back would pale in comparison to what this one would be. Am I willing to risk that?

But how can I say I'm not to blame for the sins of my father when I'm blaming her for hers?

"Fuck," I mutter with a shake of my head.

There are other stunning women here tonight. In fact, there are plenty of them. Some I've spoken to. Some whose eyes I've met across the room and politely smiled back at.

But not a single one has held my attention like Brexton has.

I grit my teeth as a man moves onto the dance floor and begins dancing with the group of women. But he has his sights on her. Anybody can see that.

Or maybe I'm the only one who's watching.

When he steps in front of her and they both laugh before moving to the beat, I tilt back the remainder of my old-fashioned.

It's time for me to go.

Or I'll do something I might regret.

Chapter
THIRTEEN

Brexton

I SWAY TO THE MUSIC STILL PLAYING IN THE OPEN COURTYARD BEHIND me as I make my way through the gardens, onto the patio, and toward the lobby.

My feet are sore, my buzz is still strong, and there's a smile plastered to my face because that was fun. I can't remember the last time I danced the night away without caring who I was dancing with or who was watching.

It was just what I needed.

A little release from a stressful few weeks. A lot of hope that true love really does exist. A lot of happiness seeing old friends again.

And yes, I'm just plain ignoring whatever the hell was going on with Drew. At the end of the day, he doesn't get to steal my sunshine because he chose to be a thunderstorm.

I have a bounce to my step as I head out the entrance, uncertain if I want to head home yet or just have a breather. Regardless, I startle when I see Drew there.

His ass is resting against a brick retaining wall that lines the path, the neck of a beer bottle is between his fingers, and his head is angled to the side as he takes me in where I've stopped a few feet in front of him.

It's funny how you spend years and years not seeing someone and then in a span of a week you see that person several times. Almost as if once your body is aware of *him*, it just gravitates toward him.

And believe me, mine is aware of him—even when I don't want it to be.

"You're still here," I say.

"Yep. That I am," he says with a laugh. "I've been standing here for way too long, trying to decide if I should stay or leave."

"Good for you." I nod.

"Seeing as we're *friends* and all." His eyes narrow as our eyes meet.

"Yep. Friends." I offer a tight smile and cringe at the word.

"We should make that a drinking game. Every time that word is said, we take a drink. Like this. *Friends.*" He lifts the bottle of beer to his lips and takes a long swig. "Friends." And another. "Being friends is *so* much fun," he shouts with his arms out to the side. It's then I realize that his smile is a little lopsided. He's just as buzzed as I am. "Do you like being *friends*, Bratty Brex?"

"So now you're going to make fun of me?" I take a step forward, uncertain if I want more attention from him or if I'm mad at him. None of this friend shit is making any sense. "We're not teenagers anymore, Drew. I have no problem standing up for myself now."

"I'm sure you don't."

"And what's that supposed to mean?" I ask on the defensive. I'm so done with his shit.

"That means you have a reputation for being a ball-busting bitch who doesn't take no for an answer."

"And the problem with that is what?" I snap.

"Not a goddamn thing," he says but the sarcastic chuckle he emits eats at me and eggs me on.

"Since we're into being honest," I say. "How about I let you in on a little tidbit?"

"Lay it on me, Brex," he says pushing himself off the wall and holding his arms out, not caring who walks by or if they see anything. "I'm all fucking ears."

"I look at you and see one of the most gifted and talented quarterbacks I've ever seen but the man beneath is too goddamn afraid to step into the limelight. It's hard to score if you never want to touch the fucking field, Bowman."

"This is where you stop talking," he says, anger in his voice, but oddly no belligerence. There's clarity in his eyes, a challenge, that frankly is the most honest thing he's shown me yet.

"You don't have the right to tell me what to do anymore," I shout. "Just like you didn't when we were teenagers in the Keys."

"Bullshit," he sneers. "I had every right to."

"Give me one reason why you think you can."

"Because . . ." His eyes roam the length of my body, but this time they don't do a very good job hiding what they're thinking like they did earlier. This time they telegraph every goddamn thought. Lust. Need. Greed. And I'm confused why we're fighting when he looks at me like that. "Because . . ."

And with no pretense or preamble, Drew Bowman steps into me while dropping his bottle to the grass. His hands frame my face, and he kisses me.

It's heat and need. It's demand and desire. It's a soft tongue but a greedy mouth.

He tastes of anger and longing, and every ounce of pent-up frustration I feel toward him I sense it back from him.

There are no thoughts of the people at our backs. No second given to where we are or how this happened. It's just Drew and me and a teenager's fantasy coming to fruition.

"This is wrong," he murmurs and then kisses me again. "So fucking wrong." He rests his forehead to mine, his hands still on the side of my face, my own pulse so loud in my ears I swear he can hear it.

"Drew." My breath is unsteady.

Much like my heart is.

"Just friends."

It's my turn to laugh, step back, and look at him like he's the lunatic he sounds like.

"Are we back to the drinking game again?" I ask.

A sheepish grin slides onto his lips and every single thing about him right now—disheveled hair, crooked tie, incredible eyes—owns me completely.

"If I keep saying we're friends it will remind me that we are. That I haven't thought about you way too many times in the past few days. That we don't have a tangled history neither of us want to address."

"I thought we weren't allowed to talk about our history."

He throws his head back and emits the craziest laugh that has me shaking my head, trying to figure out if he's losing it.

"Do you know how many years I've waited to do that? *To try that?* Ever since that stupid goddamn game of spin the bottle." He runs a hand through his hair as he hangs his head sheepishly, stumbles slightly, and chuckles. "*Now I know.*"

"Now you know," I repeat, more than shocked at his confession.

Wasn't he the one who hesitated to kiss me when the neck of the bottle landed on me? More importantly though, did our first kiss affect him as much as it did me?

But if he was interested, how come he never acted on it? How come … But I know why. It was the last night of our trip and teenage crushes fall to the wayside when your family life falls apart.

He takes another step back and looks at me with astonishment. "That ball-busting bitch thing? I'm sorry. I didn't mean that. I just needed something to get mad at you for so I wouldn't want to kiss you."

"Obviously," I say as Drew goes from angry to sweet in a matter of seconds.

"Because I like that about you. I like that you're not afraid to go after what you want. I like that you stand up for yourself."

"And how exactly would you know that?"

"Because I asked around." He shrugs like a little boy, odd given the person who just kissed me was all man. "I wanted to know more about you. In fact, I kind of needed to know."

"Okay." I fight my smile as he bites his lip, as if he's trying to make sure he just said what he needed to say.

But the two of us stand there in the early fall evening, staring at each other, and trying to figure out what just happened.

Or maybe not so much what happened, but more like, what to do about it.

"Fuck," he barks out and laughs crazily.

"What?"

"Why does it have to be *you?*"

"Excuse me?"

"Of all fucking people, Brexton Kincade, why is it you," he shouts, pointing both hands at me, "that I can't seem to get out of my head?"

"I—uh . . ." I'm at a loss of what to say, because he's shouting but he's not angry. He looks bemused and perplexed and astonished simultaneously, and there is something about it that makes him even more endearing to me.

Before I can answer him, he jogs a few steps away from me before turning back around and laughing.

"Where are you going?" I ask.

"I've been drinking."

"Clearly."

"And since I've been drinking"—he points a finger up as if he's just had the best idea ever—"I need to go home."

"Okay, then." I draw the words out. He's definitely cute when he's drunk.

"Oh, and I have a game too. On an airplane." He holds his arms out and mock flies in a circle like a little kid.

"You're playing on airplanes now?"

"I have to take one to get there, silly." He waves a hand at me and rolls his eyes, then his face suddenly turns serious. "So this can't happen yet."

"*This?* What exactly would *this* be?" I ask.

"Me wanting you."

He says it so matter-of-factly that I stumble for words.

"Brexton Kincade," he shouts.

"Yes?"

"The next time we kiss . . ."

"There's going to be a next time?" Did I really just say that out loud?

"God, I hope so," he says and closes the distance between us before planting another kiss on my lips. "Because next time? Next time I'm going to be sober so I don't miss a fucking thing about doing this thing we just did."

"You mean kissing?"

"Yes. *That.*" He starts to head away from me and stumbles. "Mildred's right, you know," he says, turning to face me, his arms out at his sides, the pathway light directly overhead, illuminating a circle around him.

"Right about what? *Mustard?*"

"No. About *hate fucks*. They're awesome. But not for the first time." He shakes his head.

"*Oh.*" Parts of my body ignite at the dark promise of his words. "That's good to know," I all but squeak.

"*You.*" He points to me. "Goddamn you, Brexton Kincade. You made me start to believe. You made me want. And now I have to figure out what the hell that means."

I'm sure that makes perfect sense to him, but now isn't the time to ask. Now is the time to stand here and watch him walk away with his laugh echoing around me and the warmth of his lips still on mine.

What just happened?

And more importantly, when can it happen again?

Chapter
FOURTEEN

Drew

10 years earlier

Spin it.

Spin it.

The twenty or so teenagers sitting around Deadman's Cove chant the taunt over and over.

It's late, but I have no worries. It's our last night here in the Keys, and our parents let us roam free. It's safe in this small paradise where we rented a house for two weeks with the Kincade family, and besides that, I'll be seventeen in a couple of months so I can take care of myself.

Add to that? Mom and Dad partied a little too hard with the Kincades today and are no doubt fast asleep.

Today? More like this whole trip.

But that's okay. That means they won't know how many beers I've had because they won't remember how many they drank.

A fucking win for me.

It also means I've made fast friends with the locals here. Anyone who can supply the beer is someone they like. Besides, they're starving for outsiders to save them from the boredom of this small-town, island life.

"Let's go, Bowman. It's your turn. Whoever you land on you get five minutes of heaven alone with them behind the Coconut Shack," the local ringleader Hank says, referring to the beachfront walk-up ice cream stand that's now currently closed.

I stare at the empty bottle sitting on top of a piece of cardboard and wonder who it's going to land on.

"Fine. I'm game," I say, willing to try anything once.

"So you know the rules?" he asks.

"Yeah. You draw four numbers and whoever has those numbers are the contestants. I spin and whoever I land on is who I get time with."

"Yep."

"Fine. Sure. Bring it on, man."

I've kissed plenty of girls. Ones I like. Ones who like me. Ones who just want to kiss Gary Bowman's son so they can say they are that much closer to the future Hall of Famer.

So I'm game. What guy is going to turn down a chance to sample the goods to see who he wants to hook up with again during the rest of his vacation?

Not this guy.

Not on your fucking life.

Hank stands atop a wood stump beside the bonfire raging at our backs. "Drumroll, please," he says as he digs his hand in a bucket to pull numbers from. "Number ten."

"Right here!" Sassy Sarah steps forward with her hand raised and her tits bouncing. She's known for that teeny-tiny bikini she loves to wear and for her dad giving us discounts when we buy snacks at the bait shop he owns down the pier.

No complaints there whatsoever.

"Number two," Hank continues.

"Woohoo!" comes from the darkness as Delilah from Kennebunkport jogs forward. Her grandparents own the house next to our rental and, so far, the chick has been down for anything. I'm not sure if that scares the shit out of me or excites me.

Maybe both.

"Number three," Hank shouts and cheers go up to the right of him.

"I was hoping I'd get picked," Glenda says. The local guys here refer to her as the Good Witch behind her back, because she's fast and easy and usually willing. "I need some variety."

I have her pegged as all talk, but I'm a horny sixteen-year-old guy who's sick of using his hand and the Internet for inspiration.

"And lastly," Hank says as the three ladies sit cross-legged in the sand around the board, "number twelve."

"She's right here," someone shouts in the back.

I strain to see through the darkness at the girl walking forward slowly. And when I see her, I open my mouth to protest but don't say a word.

It's Brexton.

Fucking Brexton.

With those huge hazel eyes and that shy smile. With . . . all *that* going on. That meaning every part of her that every guy here tonight is currently looking at as she makes her way to the circle. We parted ways on our Christmas ski trip with her looking like a baby giraffe—gangly and clumsy—but she showed up here for our summer trip with curves and that red polka-dot bikini that she's currently wearing.

It's fine.

This is fine.

"Spin the fucker already," Hank says as chants of *spin it* fill the air again.

"Yes. Sure." I look across the cardboard the bottle's on and smile at Sarah, Delilah, and Glenda. I can't bring myself to look at Brex. Not now. Not like this.

She's just a kid.

She's just . . .

Hoots and hollers carry against the crash of the waves on the beach as I spin. The brown glass bottle goes around and around until it slows down and lands pointing directly at Brexton.

I stare at its neck but don't meet her eyes, as everyone starts clapping and shouting.

I would have kissed any one of them by now. Sarah. Delilah. Glenda. I would have pressed my lips to theirs, and given myself something to remember for the spank bank later.

But Christ, this is Brexton, and . . .

"Let's go, Bowman. Don't be a pussy."

I lift a middle finger in the air, roll my eyes as the guys laugh, and hate that as I rise from my seat in the sand, I know what every guy here is thinking about and wanting to do with her.

But it's Bratty Brex, and I'm struggling to figure out why all of a sudden I'm nervous to kiss her, when I'm never nervous for shit like that.

"Hi," she whispers when I step up to her. "I'm sorry it's me."

"Don't be. It's just . . ." But there's something about the way she looks at me that stops the words on my lips. It's the flames from the fire reflected in her hair. The quick intake of her breath. The way her eyelashes flutter when she looks at me.

Jesus, when did she become so pretty?

"Just what?"

When did she go from being Bratty Brex to Beautiful Brex? How did I not notice?

"Let's go, man. Time's a-wasting. *Or*," he says with a dramatic pause, "are you two too chicken to follow through?"

"Yeah, yeah," I say and then step forward to stop my overthinking and press my lips to hers.

Holy shit.

I've kissed a lot of girls—pecks on the lips, tongue action, you name it—but there's something about when my lips meet hers, when our tongues touch, when her fingers tense against my chest, that makes every part of me feel like I just touched a livewire.

I jolt back, electrified with a desire I don't quite understand yet that's edged with anger, and stare at her.

"What?" she whispers as she worries her bottom lip between her teeth, confusion in her eyes.

I just stare at her. At the reflection of the fire on her lip gloss. At the doe-eyed look she's giving me. At how her mouth parts and her breath seems a little faster—kind of like how mine is—and I wonder why I feel so lightheaded all of a sudden, why my stomach suddenly feels like it's tied in knots.

"Holy crap, everyone," Hank shouts, stopping the hooting and hollering I didn't even hear. I snap my head his way, suddenly aware of everyone around us. "I do believe that Drew and Brexton here already have something going on. Do you two sneak into each other's beds at night when your mommies and daddies fall asleep? Do you—"

"Cut the crap, Hank." It has to be the beer I've drank. "I assure you, we are only friends," I say with as much conviction as possible.

Definitely the beer.

"Friends with benefits," he shouts and everyone starts laughing. I glance at Brexton, who steps back into the shadows away from the fire.

If I look at her, he'll think I'm lying, but that wounded expression on her face tells me she's upset.

"Not in the least, dude."

"So then why aren't you taking your five minutes behind the Coconut Shack with her?" he taunts.

"No thanks. We're *friends* with a capital F. Believe me."

"I'm just fucking with you," Hank says as he slaps me on the back and cracks another beer. "I'll give you a do-over. Who you kissing next, since obviously you need to wash that friend taste out of your mouth?"

I laugh and go along with the guys but when I look back over my shoulder, Brexton is gone, and I'm left wondering what the hell just happened.

Chapter
FIFTEEN

Brexton

Drew: So about last night . . .

I BREATHE A SIGH OF RELIEF AT THE SIGHT OF IT. THE SAD FACT IS IT'S been a day since Jules and Archer's wedding and I'm stuck in a state of limbo. The kind where you wonder how much time you should let pass before you call back the guy who just left you a message for the first time.

To know if he remembers what happened or regrets what happened or anywhere in between.

But he texted.

And at least that's a start.

The problem, now that he has? I'm stuck staring at it and trying to not overthink how exactly I should respond.

Do I just come out and scream from the rooftops that it's about damn time for him to communicate or do I play it low-key cool?

I take a deep breath and type.

Me: You mean the part where you pretended to be an airplane? That part?

Drew: Yes. That. Exactly.

Me: lol.

Drew: I'm sorry about everything.

Me: Everything?

Drew: The kissing you part.

My heart falls. I stare at the blinking cursor and hate how everything, when it comes to him, seems to be a mindfuck. Two steps forward and then ten steps back.

I bite my lip and wonder how I should respond. Because I *have* to respond.

What's the worst that can happen? I say what I really want to say and he either gets spooked by it or welcomes it? Either way, I've gone almost ten years without crossing his path, so I'm sure if this is a disaster, I can figure a way to avoid him for the next ten.

What is it you want though, Brexton? You've sworn off men and relationships. You've promised yourself that you're not going to fall for anyone anytime soon.

And now you're stuck between a rock and a hard place and wanting that hard place to be one Drew Bowman.

I reread our texts again, teeth worrying my bottom lip, and wonder if he's on the other end feeling the same way. Wondering how he's in this situation with an old family friend from his past.

Maybe I just need to get him out of my system. If I fulfill my unrequited teenage fantasies—but now on a more grown-up scale—perhaps the mystery would be gone and there'd be nothing between us.

I poise my fingers to type, the angel and devil on my shoulders having a field day in their spotlight.

I suck in a breath and hit send. You only live once, right?

Me: What if I'm not sorry, though?

I squeal and put my face in my hands like a teenager who can't believe she just said or did something in front of the most popular kid in high school . . . and I wait for him to respond.

The three dots blink slowly on the screen for some time as he types, while I'm silently freaking out on my end.

Drew: Is this coming from Bratty Brexton or Gorgeous Brexton?

Thump. My heart is ridiculously influenced, and I don't care that it is in this simple moment.

Me: Both.
Drew: It can only be from one or the other. Pick.
Me: The latter.
Drew: Say it. Own it. It's true. I'm waiting.
Me: Gorgeous Brexton.
Drew: So we officially have a dilemma.
Me: ??
Drew: Are you telling me you want to play spin the bottle again, Brex?
Me: Spin it. Spin it.

I can still remember the chant that night. The awareness of having everyone's eyes on us. The way his lips felt against mine as my heart fell to the ground at his bare feet.

My cheeks hurt from smiling as I hold my phone in my hands, the memory coming back to me. My first kiss. My first love.

"Not in the least, dude . . . We're friends with a capital F. Believe me."

"I'm just fucking with you," Hank says, slapping Drew on the back. He cracks another beer as I slink into the shadows. "I'll give you a do-over. Who you kissing next, since obviously you need to wash that friend taste out of your mouth?"

Drew laughs. Loudly.

My first heartbreak.
And now, this second chance.

Drew: When I get back, we just might have to see about that. 'Night, Bratty Brex.
Me: 'Night Dreadful Drew.

But hours later, the ridiculous smile is still on my lips and I'm ignoring every part of me that's saying I need to slow everything about my thought process down.

It's hard, though.

So very hard.

Chapter SIXTEEN

Drew

THE ROAR OF THE CROWD REVERBERATES IN MY CHEST. THEIR CHEERS come together and create a wall of white noise that makes it impossible for the offense to hear Hobbs's call.

My body vibrates with anticipation I haven't felt in forever.

One that's bone-deep, unmistakable, and that has been lost behind apathy I refused to acknowledge.

Until now.

I look at you and see one of the most gifted and talented quarterbacks I've ever seen but the man beneath is too goddamn afraid to step into the limelight.

Brexton's words are on repeat in my head as I watch Hobbs jog back with his arm cocked, and struggle to find someone open to throw it to. Even though he throws it away, I can see the play clearly in my mind. If he had scrambled right, it would have bought a second for Grinkleman to be where he needed to catch the pass and gain ten yards.

Easy to say from the sidelines. Even harder to do under pressure with huge linemen bearing down on you . . . and yet I *know* I could have made that play.

I grimace as Justin airmails another pass as they blitz him. Klaus, the offensive coordinator, glances back at me, just like he does every game Hobbs is struggling, and gives me the *you ready to go in* look.

But I no longer get excited like I used to. He can give me that look all he wants. I'm never going in.

At least that's what I've always thought, but fuck if Brexton's vote of confidence doesn't have me dreaming bigger again.

Have I been sitting on my ass—resting on my laurels—because I'd accepted a fate that wasn't mine to accept?

I have my reasons for not rocking the boat, I sure as fuck do, but when did I stop fighting to play the game I love on my terms—on the field?

Klaus throws his clipboard at the ground, and then his headset, as Hobbs's next throw is intercepted. The Lions run it all the way down the field for a touchdown.

And four minutes later as the clock ticks below the twenty-second mark and they're still in possession of the ball, they win the game.

⌇

"Tough game out there today," I say as I walk by Hobbs. His head is down, his forearms are braced on his thighs, and his shoulders are sagging in defeat.

"Fucking bullshit is what it is."

I nod and take a seat in front of my locker, waiting for the press to clear. "It happens. You can't be a hero every game."

"Says who? Says a guy who's played second string his whole career? Rumors are you'd throw a game just like your old man did, but since I don't see you touching the field any time soon, I'm not sure why people even talk about you anymore."

"I warned you to never say that to me again." Fury is ripe as I kick his feet farther apart. His head yanks up in shock, and I'm right there in his face. My dad may be too much of a pussy to set people straight but I sure as shit will. "This is coming from a snot-nosed rookie with less than eighteen months in this league." I see the rest of the guys in the locker room take a step forward as they wonder how far I'm going to take this.

It takes a lot for me to lose my cool—I've been on this team long enough for them to know this—but fuck if I'm not on edge right now. I don't want to put up with this shit.

Besides, Hobbs has a history of lashing out—at me, at others—every time he doesn't live up to his own hype and I'm sure as fuck not going to take his shit. Not with my frustration mounting and with him playing the whole game after making errors left and right.

"Back the fuck off."

"I'm doing you a favor and ignoring what you said." I fist my hand in his shirt and yank him up to a standing position. "I'm going to chalk it up to you being too young and too stupid to realize it doesn't matter if a fucking meteorite hits the field and causes you to lose, that you are the goddamn leader of this team and so you take responsibility for the loss." I give him a shake. "You're good, Hobbs. Maybe too good for your own damn good, but you keep this shit up and no one's going to want to touch you with a ten-foot pole. Lose with grace. Win with humility."

I push him back down, shake my head, and point to all of our teammates standing around in various states of undress watching us. "You owe them all an apology. It's their respect you need to earn before anybody will give you theirs."

And without another word, I storm out of the locker room and back onto the field.

The custodians are busy cleaning up the mess the fifty thousand fans left behind when I hit the turf. There are some media still shooting the shit. There are people when I don't want there to be people, but there is no practice field here for me to go to and I sure as shit am not going back into the locker room.

So I glance around for Raptor's personnel.

I ask them to find Steve on their radio for me.

I tell him I'm ready to run my drills.

Chapter
SEVENTEEN

Brexton

THE NEW YORK RAPTORS ARE ON THE FIELD IN FRONT OF ME. THEY'RE running drill after drill with both Justin and Drew taking their turns throwing passes. Coaches congregate in the center and talk about who knows what.

The sounds of helmets knocking and cadences being called out fill the air as I shift on my feet and take it all in.

If anyone asks me, I'm here for my client, Whittier. He's a punt receiver currently having some issues with the special teams coordinator, and I'm here to smooth things over.

In my head though, I'm still trying to get over that kiss from Drew the other night, our flirty texts, and possibly, *maybe*, I'm a little desperate to see him again.

"Did you come to see how being an agent is done?" a voice says to my right. I don't turn to show the owner of the voice, Finn Sanderson, an iota of interest.

"Look what crawled out of the gutter and decided to see the light of day?" I say in the cheeriest of voices as in my periphery, I see him step beside me.

"What is it about you Kincade women, huh? Is hostility a family trait?"

"It goes hand in hand with our greatness." I slide a glance his way and smile.

"Greatness, huh?" He chuckles. "It must be hard at night to fall asleep with all of those lies you tell yourself running around in your head."

"You mean kind of like the ones you tell your clients?" I shift so I face him.

"You'd think this schtick would get old. Do the four of you practice in your weekly office meeting? Is there a prize that goes to the sister who gets to use it that week?" His voice is sarcastic yet playful.

Kind of how it always is between us.

Do I like the douchebag? Not really. But he does provide entertainment from time to time. I'll give him that much. I still think he's a total asshole for what he did to Chase, but if she's over it, then I am too.

"Yes, that's exactly right, so thanks for showing up to let me win this week's contest."

"Glad to be of service," he murmurs before we both fall silent for a beat as the team runs another series of drills, each of the three quarterbacks getting a chance to show off their talents. "I'm assuming you're here for Whittier?"

"News travels fast."

"No news. Just assumptions after that fight he got in with the coordinator at the last game. Fighting with your coach is never a good thing."

"That's one thing we can agree on."

We stop talking as a crowd of players comes closer. Is it stupid that my stomach flip-flops when I see Drew in the group? I try to remain nonchalant behind my sunglasses, but there is the slightest of moments when Drew is drinking his water that he looks straight at me and grins. It has that part-smirk, part-knowing feel to it that says he knows what my lips taste like. He knows that we have a secret.

He's thinking about our kiss too.

And it's everything I need to know to put my restless mind—and heart—at ease.

"So what are you going to do about him?" Finn asks with a slight lift of his chin toward Whittier since players are still nearby. "Trade him? Coddle him? Tell him to suck it up?"

"All of the above?" I shrug. "It depends. I have meetings with Los Angeles and they're interested in him. From what I hear, they're going through a rebuilding year so they're hungry for a lot of positions right now. A QB, some defensive backs"—I gesture to the players—"O-line. So maybe I'll feel out what management here at the Raptors thinks and go from there."

"Huh," he says and mimics my posture with his arms crossed. "I was convinced you were here to steal one of my clients. You're a Kincade. There's always an ulterior motive with you guys when it comes to me."

I roll my eyes and laugh, but refuse to admit that he's right. "The funny thing, Sanderson? Even though you're typically an asshole and your manners need a *lot* of work, I don't mind you as much as everyone else does. In fact, I look forward to these bantering sessions to keep my comeback game in check."

"Is that cold heart of yours thawing some?" He chuckles. "Or is this your way of trying to thaw mine so you can steal one of my clients?"

"You do have eight or nine clients on this team. Are you really going to miss any if I steal one?" I ask playfully.

"I can draw some conclusions."

"Draw away." Drew makes a flawless pass that is so pretty it's ridiculous. *God, he's sexy when he does that.* Hobbs throws a second and it's just as pretty, but not as perfectly placed.

"It's Hobbs," he says after a beat. "That would be the biggest bang for your buck. He's a rising star, hot-shot rookie who everyone is talking about. If you were a smart agent, that's where you would look."

"Are you trying to unload him?" I ask through a laugh. "Because that sounded like a sales pitch if ever I heard one. What you forgot to add is that he's young and cocky and you're not doing your job properly as his agent to explain to him this is a game of longevity versus a balls-to-the-wall mentality."

"See? That's where we differ in our thought process. I say take all you can get while you can get it. Look at Bowman. He's been doing this how long and rarely touches the field. Most guys would rather have their moments short and glorious instead of long and hidden in the shadows."

"He's good though," I murmur as he connects another flawless pass.

"He's incredible," Finn agrees.

High praise coming from another agent. Praise that I agree with. *It just seems so wrong that Drew isn't even a starter.*

"Why doesn't he ever get a chance, Finn?" I speak my thoughts out loud. Kiss or no kiss, I can be objective when it comes to the amount of skill Drew has.

"He did have the chance and was doing great with the Tigers. At the beginning of his second season, he was in a game where he crashed hard. I mean, he didn't look like the same player out there. Passes wide, balls dropped. He was playing under the name Drew Hemmings—his grandmother's maiden name—but someone made the connection to his dad somehow. Fucking bloodhounds. They started posting shit on social media, hinting that he was trying to throw the game like his old man had. It caused quite the controversy at the time."

I stare at Finn for the first time and shake my head. "I don't remember any of that." But if Drew was fresh off the draft, then that means I was in my second or third year of college and was preoccupied with all good things that come with it—studying, partying, boys, and training.

At that point, I had written him out of my life, so why would I have paid attention, let alone to someone with a different last name.

"Anyway, the Tigers brushed the Internet fodder under the rug, moved him to second string while they secretly ran an investigation into whether he did it or not, and when he emerged free and clear from any wrongdoing, he dropped Hemmings and used Bowman."

"How do I not know any of this?"

"I'm good, what can I say?" His smile is quick and highlights the lines at the corners of his eyes. Can't say he's my favorite of agents, but he knows sports inside and out—football especially. So much so that I trust what he's saying as truth without having to look it up. He may be a shark, but his reputation for being knowledgeable is undisputed. Too bad he was an ass to my little sister, Chase, when they dated or I just might like the guy a bit more. "Plus, it was right before the player's strike so timing helped him at first with the accusation and then hurt him when he was cleared, because the whole thing was overshadowed by the walk-out."

"So he was cleared, then?"

"Mm-hmm," he murmurs as he winces when one of his players misses a pass.

"And he was what? Then put back in the starting lineup when play resumed?" I ask as I try to make sense of all of this.

"No. Not sure why. He played out his contract on the sidelines. More of the same when he was traded somewhere else for a few years. Now here."

I nod at what he's saying but my eyes are fixated on Drew. "So he's relegated to second string forever then?"

"Your guess is as good as mine, but his agent is Longmire. I mean, how hands-off can you get? It's akin to not having an agent at all."

"So no one's fighting for him is what you're saying."

"Correct. But it sounds like you might be looking to throw your hat in the ring on that fight."

If he only knew.

"I'm always looking to throw my hat in the ring. Question is, is the player willing to fight alongside you?" I murmur more to myself than to Finn as my thoughts are preoccupied with the data dump of information he just provided.

And as if on cue, the general manager of the Raptors heads out of the tunnel and motions that he's ready for our meeting.

"She's been summoned," Finn murmurs and laughs.

"I have." I pick up my briefcase leaning against my leg. "Make sure to look after my player for me."

"Whittier?" he asks.

"No, Hobbs," I say, making sure to get the last laugh.

Chapter
EIGHTEEN

Drew

SHE'S NOWHERE TO BE FOUND WHEN I LEAVE THE LOCKER ROOM.

That's probably a good thing, because the way she looked in those jeans and heels is just as devastating as the confusion over how she makes me feel.

But Christ, her kiss . . . I may have been more than buzzed at the wedding but the memory of it has lingered like it did all those years ago. It was like lightning in a bottle, and I've never wanted anything more than to open the lid and see what it feels like to let it loose.

I glance toward the practice field, the parking lot, and over where Manny is talking to some people, but she's fucking gone.

I'm a tad wounded that she didn't hang around to see me, but then again, that's not the smartest of things to do.

Not here.

Not with eyes watching.

Not with—

"Hey there."

And there she stands, with her hips resting against a pony wall, her feet crossed at the ankles so the red sole on the nude heels she has on shows, and a smile a mile wide on those gorgeous lips of hers.

It takes mere seconds in her presence to have me question my masculinity. Women are supposed to get butterflies, not men . . . and yet the sight of her has excitement turning over in my stomach.

Just like it did all those years ago.

"Nice shoes." *You waited for me.*

"They seem to get the job done." A sly smile lights up her face as her eyes take me in and my mind wanders to all the places she can wear those while getting a different job done.

"What are you doing here?"

"I thought we had some unfinished business to discuss."

"Like?" I play coy.

"Like the merits of loving mustard as a condiment."

"We're still on that?" I ask, and then glance down the corridor to where some of the guys start laughing before looking back to her. It's weird to have a woman in this space who gets what I do and who isn't intimidated or enamored by the trappings of this industry.

"We are." She shrugs shyly. "Or we could move on to discussing other things that deserve merit."

"Such as?"

Her tongue darts out to wet her lips and the action has my full attention.

Does she have any idea how many hours I lay in my bed the other night thinking about that mouth? Wanting that mouth? What I'd do to that mouth?

"Such as unfinished kisses." She purses her lips as her eyes meet mine. "Such as finishing what we started. Such as following through on promises made."

I take a step toward her but the little shake of her head tells me not here, not now.

"That's a lot of unfinished promises."

"It is," she murmurs.

"And what do you propose we do about that?"

"Oh, the possibilities," she teases and the throaty laugh that follows has my balls drawing up at the sound. "I'm free later if you'd like to discuss them."

"I like the sound of that, but I have things already planned that I can't get out of." I glance over my shoulder at the laughter coming from where the guys are heading toward us. "It's Laughlin's birthday. We're all taking him out to Top Golf for a little competition and a drink or two."

She nods. "That sounds like trouble."

"Could be. Perhaps." I itch to reach out and touch her. "Tomorrow maybe? I have training but after?"

She hisses in dismay. "I can't. I have plans with someone who's here from out of town."

Our eyes hold across the short distance and anticipation dances in the air between us.

"And I'm traveling after that." I chuckle. "It's been ten years, I guess another day or two won't hurt."

"Guess not." She angles her head to the side. Fuck me. She looks like the perfect mix of siren and saint, and I want a piece of both.

I'm having a hard time wrapping my head around the fact that she's here in front of me. How exactly did this happen?

"Hey, Bowman. You ready to get your ass kicked?" Hanover asks as he slaps me on the back. "Oh, hey, I didn't see you there, Brexton. Sorry."

"Hey, Hanover. Great game on Sunday," she says, referring to his three sacks and one interception.

"At least I'm good at something." He laughs. "Because golfing ain't one of them. I'd invite you to come along, Kincade, but I have a feeling it's going to get U-G-L-Y and I'm not talking about this guy's mug."

"Thanks for the invite, but I've got work to do," she says.

"All work and no play makes for a boring life," Hanover says. "You need to help her with that, Bowman."

"Me?" I cough. "How exactly should I do that?" I ask but I already have plenty of ideas.

"You're a smart boy, you'll figure it out." He winks and then shouts down the hallway. "C'mon, assholes, time's a wasting."

The two of us watch him walk away and when I turn back to face her, that smile is back on her lips. "What?" I ask.

"You're a smart boy, Drew, you'll figure it out." And as she walks away giving me a gorgeous view of her backside, her laugh echoes off the concrete around us.

Fuck, yes. I will.

Chapter
NINETEEN

Drew

"Have another drink, Bowman."

"Nah, I've got somewhere I need to be," I say and glance at my phone. It's almost midnight. I've been sitting here all night laughing with my friends and teammates but my mind has been somewhere else completely different.

It's been on Brexton and that little challenge she laid down for me to figure it out. It's been on the curves of her body as she walked away from me. And it's been wondering how in the hell I've let a woman own my thoughts when I've never let one interfere like this before.

"Somewhere you need to be? Seriously?" Hanover asks. "It better be some good-ass pussy if you're leaving us for it."

All I give is a smile and a chuckle.

Let them sit on that.

"Later, guys." I throw a peace sign up as they groan and throw their balled-up napkins my way. Then the names follow that have me shaking my head and laughing as I set my golf club down.

"Seriously, Bowman? You're going to leave just like that?" Laughlin slurs.

"You know I love you, brother." I bump my fist against his. "But I've gotta go."

Another round of protests sound off, but I keep walking. I'm just about out of the door when I hear, "Hey, Drewski?"

I don't hide my sigh or the fact that I don't really want to talk to Justin right now. In fact, other than talking to him on the field when I have to,

I haven't said shit to him since he ran his mouth at me after the game the other day.

"I'm not in the mood, Hobbs." I want to leave, to keep walking out the door, but I stand there and wait for him to start some shit. Clearly, he needs to reassert his precious fucking ego.

"Look"—he holds his hands out in front of him in surrender—"I come in peace." He laughs nervously before glancing over his shoulder where the suite suddenly gets awfully quiet, as the guys all stand and watch whatever is about to happen.

"And?"

"And I apologize, okay? I already did to the rest of the team, but you weren't there so I wanted to say it to you as well." His Adam's apple bobs as he swallows. "I'm sorry."

I nod as I chew the inside of my cheek and contemplate if any of the guys put him up to this. It's been chillier than the polar ice cap in the locker room the past few days, but deservedly so. Hobbs needs to grow the fuck up and if they're not going to put him in his place for acting like a prima donna, then I will.

"So, apology accepted?" he asks.

"Step up and lead the team, Hobbs."

He nods and then lowers his voice. "It's my family, man. They're on the West Coast and I'm here and fuck, man, it's not easy."

It's in moments like this I'm reminded of how young he really is. Twenty-three years old and still figuring his shit out.

"Everything okay with them?" I ask, wondering where this sudden homesickness is coming from and when he grimaces, it's slight but there, I know the answer before he speaks.

"My mom's sick, and it doesn't matter if I have all the money in the world because I'm still here and she's still there."

"Which is why you want to move to California."

He nods.

"I understand where you're coming from," I say and do. Regardless of the rocky relationship between my father and me, playing for the Raptors has afforded me the opportunity to be near him physically. My resentment of him and what he did to our family may be strong, but a part of me acknowledges his illness is a death sentence. The same part of me doesn't want to look back on any time and regret that I wasn't near.

It's a constant balancing act mindfuck. Resentment against regret. Obligation versus love. Bitterness vying against forgiveness. The need to know he's proud of me against needing to know the truth about what happened.

A battle I wouldn't wish on anyone.

"What do you mean you understand?" he asks.

"I just do." I meet his eyes. "If Finn isn't going to find a way to get you to California, find an agent who will. Remember, they work for you."

Chapter
TWENTY

Brexton

I STARE AT THE PHONE IN MY HAND AS IF IT'S GOING TO GIVE ME answers, but yes, the doorman did just call and ask if one Drew Bowman can come up to my apartment.

And then chaos hits as I run to my bedroom and change my shirt. Then realize I have to change my bra because the black bra under the white tank top doesn't look right. I spritz body spray in *all* places, dry shave my legs in a desperate attempt I know I'll regret later, pinch my cheeks to add color, fluff my hair . . . and am completely out of breath by the time the doorbell rings.

I blow out a long, calming breath as anticipation hums through my veins.

Or at least I try to.

Drew Bowman is on the other side of that door. Does he have any idea how many nights I lay awake as a teenager hoping, wishing, wanting this scenario—for him to be standing on the other side of my front door and be there for me—only to be crushed because it never happened?

I put my hand on the knob and let it swing open.

And there he stands. Drew is leaning against the wall opposite my door. His hands are shoved in his pockets and when he sees me, a crooked smile plays across his lips. The same crooked smile I swooned over all those years ago is even more devastating now when accented by a little scruff, eyes full of desire, and a body made to sin with.

"I'm guilty," he says raising one hand and breaking the stretch of silence between us.

"Is that so?" I ask, and he nods. "Guilty of what?"

"Everything." He shrugs.

"That's a broad statement."

He purses his lips and nods again. "It is."

I don't hide the smile seeing him brings. "I get the feeling you're coming to me drunk again. This is becoming a thing, Bowman," I tease. "Should I be worried that you're standing here tipsy?"

He shakes his head yes but then says, "I'm not drunk," while his eyes roam the length of my body.

"No?"

"I only had one shot."

"Only one?" I ask, fascinated by this peculiar conversation.

"Mm-hmm. I have my reasons."

"And those are?"

"We'll get to those in a second." He pushes himself off the wall and steps into my personal space. He smells of soap and sandalwood and all I want to do is reach out and touch him. "Aren't you going to ask me in?" he murmurs.

"How did you know where I lived?"

He quirks an eyebrow. "The same way you found me." My eyes flicker down to his lips and then back up to his eyes. "I lied."

"About what? How you found me?"

"No."

"Then what about?"

"I had two shots."

"Thank you for clarifying." I chuckle. "Why two?"

"The first one was because I've been trying to tell myself that this is a shit idea. I've talked myself out of it every which way because there's too much history. You're Bratty Brex and I'm Dreadful Drew but fuck, Brex, all I can think about is the taste of your kiss. The way I wanted it way back when you'd strut by in your bikini, so I decided I needed a shot."

"I assure you, I didn't have anything to strut back then."

"I beg to differ," he murmurs as his eyes dip down to where my nipples aren't doing a very good job of hiding beneath my tank top.

"Wait? You wanted me? You could have fooled me by the way you hesitated during spin the bottle that night."

"I was a fool." He shrugs sheepishly. "Young and dumb and not prepared for what you hit me with that night."

"Really?" I ask and hate how there is so much awe in the sound of my voice.

"Really." Our eyes hold for a beat as our desire builds.

How is this even happening? How after all these years later, are we standing here like this, both wanting the same thing?

It's crazy.

It's surreal.

It's perfect.

"You said two shots. What was the second one for?" I ask for some stupid reason, as if his intent in being here wasn't already known.

"The second shot was because I was sitting in the bar across the street trying to work up the courage to come up here."

His confession startles me.

"Why do you need courage?"

"Because there's something about you, Brexton Kincade, that makes me nervous."

"*You?* Nervous?" I spit the words out almost in relief as if knowing it will calm the racing of my pulse and ease my own anxiety.

"Mm-hmm." He reaches out and tucks an errant piece of hair behind my ear, resting his hand on my shoulder when the task is done. My body hums beneath the warmth of it, begging to know what comes next but patient enough to wait to find out. "Before, we were young and that first kiss was—*wow.* Way too much for a sixteen-year-old to decipher . . . and now? Now there is so much more baggage and I don't want to unpack it all. *I just want you.*"

I reach out, put my finger into his belt loop, and pull him into me. "You told me the past was the past, Drew."

And it's not like it was unexpected—his lips meeting mine, me yanking him into my apartment, then kicking the door shut behind us—but holy hell, it feels new and exciting while old and comfortable at the same time.

The one thing I hadn't anticipated in all of this was the desperation that owns me. The need to touch him everywhere, the necessity of it, but not wanting my lips to leave his.

And I know he feels the same way because we don't speak, we don't ask, we just act. With hurried hands and shuffling feet, we leave a trail of clothes on the way to my bedroom—shoes, socks, shirts, pants—until we stand at the foot of my bed.

It's only here that we slow down for a beat. It's only now with heaving chests and bruised lips that we stop to look at each other for a moment.

This is Dreamy Drew before me, and he's even better than my teen-age heart could ever fathom him to be.

He reaches up to frame my face and with his erection pressing against my lower abdomen, presses his lips to mine again. The kiss is long, slow, and tender. The kind that draws out every last ounce of desire while simultaneously heightening it. The type that makes you weak in the knees and aching in all the right ways.

The kind teenage girls dream of but then realize when they get older are only things in romance novels or movies.

Or so I thought.

Until Drew.

Because he worships my mouth with an unrivaled reverence. He's heating my body to the point that I can't wait to burn.

And oh, how I want him to make me burn.

But he takes his time lighting the wildfire. He blazes a path with his mouth down the line of my neck and his fingertips trace over the peaks of my breasts. Little fires everywhere. Tiny sparks waiting to ignite.

Needing to touch him in turn, I slide my finger beneath the waist-band of his boxer briefs to find him hard and ready. His hiss at my touch is all I need to circle my fingers around him as best as I can and stroke his length.

His kiss falters as he revels in the sensation. My own gasp follows soon after when he pushes down my panties and his fingers find their way between my slit. My thighs tense as he brushes a thumb over my clit before tucking a finger inside of me.

"Drew," I moan as he continues his onslaught of bliss a few more times before laying me down onto the bed to pleasure me properly. His knees press mine apart as he watches his fingers work me over.

In.

Out.

A quick rub over the hub of nerves at the top.

The scrape of his stubble as he leans forward and takes the peak of my breast into his mouth.

The look in his eyes as he watches my arousal coat his fingers the more he pleasures me.

"Drew." His name is a drawn-out whisper emitted between clenched teeth and a delirium of desire.

"You're not getting me until I get you, baby," he murmurs. "Not a chance on your life I'm going to miss watching you come undone."

And those words mixed with his deft actions do just that. They slip and slide and rub and pleasure until my vision goes white and my body turns hot, as it bursts into a million splintered pieces.

My hands grip his hands, then the sheets, as my back bows, and my breath holds, and every sensation becomes my focal point.

He stays perched between my legs. I know he's watching me. I'm more than aware of it, but I'm so lost in my orgasmic haze that I don't care. It's only when the waves of pleasure turn to ripples that I'm able to crawl out from beneath its blanket. I find him sitting there like a Greek god watching how my muscles pulse around the very tip of his cock that he's jacketed up and rested against my slit.

"You're gorgeous," he murmurs, his eyes finding mine. But there's something about the way he says it, and the intensity in his eyes, which makes me feel shy. It strikes me funny in the moment. I'm laid bare after completely coming undone by his hand and his cock is lined up to take me, yet two words and two intense blue eyes have my cheeks heating.

My smile in return is fleeting because he chooses that moment to slowly press his way into me. And *good God*, does he feel exceptional as my body stretches and burns blissfully until he fills me completely.

There's a strangled moan that echoes around the room. It could be mine, it could be his. I don't know. I'm so lost to the feeling of him when he begins to move inside of me that all thought, all reason, is completely lost to it and to him.

His hands grip the insides of my thighs and hold me still as his hips thrust, punctuated with that satisfying slap of skin against skin.

We move in sync. Two bodies vying for the same destination.

Two people needing a connection.

Two lovers desperate to give each other release.

It's a battle of wills, a combining of libidos, and an intertwining of bodies, as sensations rule and passion lights a fuse that have us gripping and groping and moaning and groaning.

"God, Brex," he says as his head falls back and the tendons in his neck grow taut while my body begins to tense. "I can't—you need to—*fuck* . . ." The last word is a drawn-out breath as he urges me on and lets me know he won't last much longer.

My breath quickens. My pulse races. My mind focuses on the man between my thighs while my body reacts to the pleasure he gives, and within seconds I'm crashing over the edge into oblivion.

And while I'm lost in every single sensation he's evoked within me, he loses himself to his: head thrown back, hands gripping tight, lost in the moment.

It's erotic as hell to watch.

I want to do it all over again just for this moment—to see him like this.

To know that I can do this—make him feel, want, and desire—just as he has me.

Chapter
TWENTY-ONE

Drew

My heart races and my body is still alive with sensitivity as I slowly slip out of her, but Christ Almighty, I can't stop staring at her.

Cheeks flushed, body tempting me to sink back into it again, and those eyes of hers. The hazel ones that look up at me from beneath thick lashes, drugged with desire, lure and tempt when I've already been won over.

How is it possible? How do I already want her again when my pulse hasn't even settled down yet? How does this make any sense?

I fall onto the bed beside her in a less than graceful manner but she's still breathing hard too, so I'm good.

Hell, I'm better than good. I'm fucking fantastic.

I close my eyes for a beat and when I open them, I take the moment to look around her room. It's no-frills but then again, I'd expect nothing else from her. There are light tans and dark browns mixed with light walls. It's way too clean but again, it's Brexton.

"You know this is backward, right?" she asks, breaking the silence. "You're supposed to go on dates first, then sleep together."

"True, but I've been dating you some way or another my whole life." I chuckle and turn on my side so I can see her.

She's staring at the ceiling, and I take in her profile. Straight nose, lips a little swollen from mine, hair fanned out on the pillow all around her.

"What's that supposed to mean?" she asks.

Yeah, Drew. What's that supposed to mean?

I shake my head into the pillow and laugh to cover the words that almost came to my lips.

The ones that can't be real.

The ones that don't make any fucking sense.

How can I already think maybe I've been looking for a little piece of her in every woman I've dated? How can I know that when honestly, I barely even know the woman she is now?

And yet the thought was there, on the tip of my tongue. The epiphany so very clear.

Thank God I didn't say it out loud.

"Nothing. It was just—" I try to distract. "I guess maybe we've been avoiding each other because we knew this would happen. That damn kiss in the Keys set us up for it." I smile as she turns on her side to look at me.

Half her face is hidden by the pillow but the rise of her breast and the curve of her hip are visible in the soft moonlight filling the room.

"Maybe it did," she murmurs and then smiles softly. "I'm glad you took those two shots tonight, Drew."

"Really?"

"Mm-hmm." She reaches out and runs a hand down the length of my cheek. "If that's what it took to get you to show up on my doorstep, then I'm glad you took them."

I itch to reach out and touch her too, but I hate the feeling in my chest. The one that I don't understand or care to. The betrayal that's wound around it from being here—*with her*.

I offer her a shy smile to mask all the shit I don't understand.

And instead of words, I lean forward and press my lips to hers, preferring to get lost in her again, rather than to figure it all out.

There will be time for that.

But not here.

Not now.

I'll do anything to keep the outside world at bay for a little bit longer, because this is the first time in forever that I've found reprieve from it all.

With her.

Because of her.

And fuck if I'm not going to hold on to it and not let go for the next several hours.

Chapter
TWENTY-TWO

Brexton

STANDING AT THE FOOT OF MY BED, I CAN'T STOP STARING AT DREW IN the mid-morning light. He's sprawled out sideways across the sheets, the comforter covers his ass and below, but his broad shoulders are bare, and his arms are tucked under the pillow that his head is buried in.

I swear my heart skips a beat. One I don't want it to skip, because I'm more than surprised that he stayed the night.

It's not like we had a one-night stand. I mean, we do in fact know each other—*sort of.* So there shouldn't be a walk of shame or any moments of awkwardness this morning when he leaves. After all, we didn't exactly fall asleep after that first time. It was almost as if each time our lips met, we couldn't stop until we'd connected once again. Until we thought we'd gotten our fill of each other only to learn we hadn't.

It's never been like that for me with someone before, and I'm not quite sure what that means.

Are we simply a match striking, igniting, and then waiting to burn itself out? A foregone conclusion that we were going to sleep together before identifying that it was enough?

But as I stand here studying him—the scar on his shoulder blade, the defined muscles, his thick lashes against his tanned cheek—I settle in with the thought that this feels like it could be the start of something good.

You've sworn off men, Brex.

But this isn't just any man. *This is Drew.*

And while I may be looking at him right now—grown-up Drew with his incredible body and quick wit—long ago I liked all the things that still seem to be the same. Sure his features are more mature now, but there's the lopsided grin that's part sheepish, part seduction that wins me over every time. There's that impish look in his eye before he shakes his head when he knows you're right but can't admit it. There's the way he narrows his eyes slightly before he fades into deep thought.

I've seen little glimpses of that teenage boy I once knew—the playful and funny side to him—and I'm pleased to admit I'm more than enamored by the man he's grown into. His passion for a game that seemingly has screwed him.

The way he showed up here last night even if it took two shots.

And yet, my subconscious complains to shut my heart out and to listen to my head. Things like this don't happen to me. They're never this easy.

The other shoe always drops.

And more often than not, it's heavy and destructive when it does.

"Hey," Drew murmurs in a sleep-drugged voice. It's made to sin with and pulls me from my thoughts.

I take my time dragging my gaze up his body until I meet his eyes. "Hey."

"Don't look at me like that, Brex." He chuckles with a subtle shake of his head as I cross the room. "There's no way you can possibly be up for another round."

I crawl onto the bed beside him, and when he turns onto his back to follow me, I straddle his hips over the comforter between us. "Mentally, yes." I wiggle my hips playfully. "Physically, give me a minute or two."

He belts out a laugh as his hands find their way beneath the oversized T-shirt I have on. He hums when he finds my hips bare and without panties. "I hear what your lips are saying, but this body is tempting me with something altogether different."

Our eyes meet, the smile on his lips crinkling lines at the corner of his, making him even sexier. "Thank you for coming over last night," I murmur and lean down and press a kiss against his chest. I have the strongest urge to lay my head there and hold on to him—almost as if I need to cherish this moment because it won't happen again.

It's a silly thought but one that plagues me nonetheless.

"Thank you for letting me in the door."

"There's coffee on, if you want any to help wake you up. Or I have shots if you feel the need for more courage." I wink as that smile of his widens.

"No shots are needed. But coffee? Coffee is always welcome."

"What time is your flight?" I ask, more than familiar with the out-of-town-game travel schedule.

"In a few hours. I should get home and pack," he says but makes no movement to do so.

Our fingers link on my knees, and I can't break my gaze from them. He's really here, with me. *In my bed.* And it feels so *normal* to be talking like this. "Should I be stupid and ask what's next?"

He's silent and, when I don't look at him, he squeezes my fingers until I meet his gaze. His eyes are full of the same hesitant confusion I feel, and it's comforting to see. "You always did need to have the next ten steps planned out in front of you. Glad to see some things never change."

I roll my eyes. "That's different."

"No, it isn't. You can't plan for shit like this, Brex. A chance meeting after all these years. Good chemistry. Incredible sex." He shrugs, and that shy smile on his lips owns me. "Why don't we just see where it takes us?"

"Which is . . ."

"Stop." A soft tug on my hands. "It should be enough for you to know that I didn't bolt out of here early this morning because I thought things would be awkward. I stayed. I'm here."

I chew the inside of my lip and nod, realizing that I'm coming off as needy right now. I just don't want another broken heart. But I can't say that. I can't tell him that my planner brain is already those ten steps ahead and wondering what-ifs.

"You did. Sorry. Planner brain, here."

He tugs on my hands so that I lean forward and when I do, he wraps his arms around me and pulls me to his chest. The same thing I had wanted to do moments before. To say I don't swoon when he rests his chin on the top of my head is a lie.

He squeezes me against the firm warmth of his chest. "Quiet that brain of yours, Kincade. If I was going to run, I would have done it while you were still sleeping."

Chapter
TWENTY-THREE

Brexton

"YOU'RE HERE LATE."

I glance up from the conference room table where I have contracts laid out in various stages of review to find my dad standing in the doorway. The formidable Kenyon Kincade in the sports management world is also an attentive father and the biggest softie in the world.

"Just catching up on some things."

"I wasn't aware you were so busy. Do you need me to have your sisters help some with the load?"

"No. I'm good. With Lennox in London now," I say mentioning my younger sister who recently made the move across the pond to be with her love, "I'm just trying to wrap up some of her deals and integrate some of her clients into mine."

"Thank you for helping with that."

"Of course. She'll owe me big time." I grin.

"As in introducing you to some hot British guy type of owe you or something close to that?" He rolls his eyes.

"You catch on quick for an old guy," I tease.

"Funny." He glares at me before that smile lights up his face again. "You're all good then?"

"I am."

"I can wait for you until you're done so you're not alone?" He winks and I offer him a soft smile in return. I'll never live down the scaredy-cat reputation I had as a kid.

"I'm fine, Dad."

"Okay then. I'll make sure Scott knows you're up here though," he says of the office building's lobby security officer.

"Thank you."

"Good night then."

And just as he walks away, I ask the question that has been circling in my mind since that first night I saw Drew. "Hey, Dad?"

Or maybe rather the question I'd been working up the courage to ask him and, since we're the only ones left in the office, now seems to be the perfect time.

"Yeah, honey?"

"What's the real story behind Gary Bowman?"

My father does a double take as his feet falter and his expression reflects surprise. "Gary Bowman?"

"Mm-hmm," I murmur as his eyes hold mine, searching for an answer to a question he's yet to ask.

I hate that my palms are suddenly sweating as I question whether or not it was smart to open my mouth, but there's no taking it back now.

"That's a name I haven't heard in a while," he says.

"I assumed."

"Where's this coming from?" He steps back into the conference room, his expression pensive.

"I was dealing with the situation with Whittier and the Raptors and I ran into Drew. He's their second string QB."

He nods slowly. "I know."

"Did you keep tabs on him after . . . everything?"

"I keep tabs on everyone." He angles his head to the side. "Was he cordial to you?"

I nod. "We spoke."

And I give pause over the fact that I don't tell him any more. The question is, why is it instinctual to keep what's going on with Drew so close to the vest?

Is it because I don't know where things are headed between the two of us and it's premature to say anything in case it fizzles and dies out? Not saying anything would save me from yet another round of *Brexton is the soft-hearted sister* teasing.

Or am I keeping mum because Drew scares me? Whatever this is between us is so effortless thus far that I'm afraid to jinx it. And without knowing the whole story of Gary Bowman's scandal and the role my father did or didn't have in it, it possibly means my father might disapprove of us seeing each other.

My father eyes me in silence for a beat. "You spoke?"

"Briefly." I shrug. "It was weird."

"Weird how?"

"Weird as in our families were inseparable and then in a short period of time, we went from that to basically acting like the other never existed." I lean back in my chair and cross my arms over my chest. "Case in point. Why do we work in the same industry and yet that's the first time Drew and I have crossed paths?"

"I'm sure your sisters have seen him on occasion," he says and I wonder if that's true. And if they have, did they talk to him or pretend as if they hadn't seen him to avoid the awkwardness?

"Have you?"

"Me?" he asks and I nod. "A few times but I've kept my distance out of respect for him and his family."

"What does that mean?" I ask with a disbelieving laugh.

He shrugs. "It means everything was very sudden. The accusations then your mother's passing. There was never closure on any side, and it's not my place to initiate it or put Drew in the position to feel like he needs to answer for his father. So . . . I've made sure to keep my distance."

I stare at my father and consider his very diplomatic answer. I need to know more. Need to know if what Drew and I are doing is going to upset some fragile balance I didn't even know was a thing.

"Did Gary throw the playoff game, Dad? That's what the accusations were, right? That he was gambling on the game and threw it on purpose to win big."

My father nods slowly. "That was the supposition, yes."

"Did he do it?"

He twists his lips and sighs, his expression pained. "I don't know."

"You two were inseparable. You had to have known."

"I don't. No one does, really."

"So he just walked away from the game, from your friendship, and has never talked about it since?"

"Pretty much."

"That's weird. Even you have to admit that it looks shady," I say.

"To you and me and the public, yes. To him and his reasons, maybe it was logical."

I grit my teeth, frustrated with my dad's sense of fairness. It's a blessing and a curse the way he gives everyone the benefit of the doubt. Sometimes you just want him to take a damn side.

"Football was his life. Even I remember how much he loved the game. Was there an investigation? What was the conclusion when it was over? Did—"

"He just up and walked away, Brex. There was nothing to investigate if he wasn't playing."

"Since when is that the case?"

"Since maybe that was the terms of him walking away?" He lifts his hands. "No one knows, but that's what seems the most likely."

"You don't know?"

"No one does."

"Humph." I breathe out a frustrated sigh. "That makes him sound guilty."

"Or it looks like he didn't want to drag his family through the mud because of it."

I chew the inside of my lip and stare out at the lights on the skyscrapers around us. "But why'd he cut you off? You were his best friend. Our families were . . ."

"I don't know. Shortly thereafter your mom passed, and our life fell apart, so I didn't have the energy to try and worry about him when I was worrying about the four of you. I probably should have and that's on me. And maybe I was pissed. Our circumstances were a lot more life-altering, and Gary was so involved in himself that he didn't cross the aisle to see how we were."

I snap my head over to him, surprised by his words. "That's a reasonable way to feel considering we lost Mom while he only lost his job."

"It was his life, Brex. The man lived and breathed football. It was everything to that family—including Drew—and so in a sense they went through a huge loss too."

"So you never talked to him again?"

"I tried for a bit, but it was one-sided."

I mull over my father's words and try to figure how they play into Drew and the man he's made himself into.

"Wait? Why did you ask if Drew was cordial? Did you think he wouldn't be?" I ask.

"Some people don't like reminders of the past. You're a reminder," he says in a measured tone.

"There's more there."

My father's sigh fills the room. "Drew came to me . . . *after*. He was all hot under the collar. Accusing me of things. I don't remember the whole of it other than the fact that he was angry and all over the place with what he was saying."

"Why was he angry at you? Did you have any part in it?"

"No. I didn't even know Gary was gambling. How would I have been privy to him trying to throw a game? I mean, when we were in the Keys he was super stressed over something, not acting himself, but I just chalked it up to the mounting pressure for him to perform in the coming season. I never thought he was gambling or anything like that."

"But Drew confronted you?" I meter my reaction and the shock hearing it brings me.

"He did." His eyes go dark as he remembers. "He was seventeen or eighteen and fuming. Looking for answers as to why his life irrevocably changed. The kid idolized his father and seemed so damn lost trying to understand what had happened just like we all were. I just figure Drew needed answers, so he came to the only other male figure he could trust."

"But you gave him nothing."

"I had nothing to give him but a shoulder to lean on and an ear to listen. He wanted neither."

"And you haven't spoken to any of them since?"

"I have not." He looks out to the city beyond, lost in thought for a beat, a soft smile on his face.

I try to fathom how that happens. How two families who are like one, simply disintegrate at a time when they needed the other the most.

But then again, isn't that what we did when my mom died? We closed ranks and took care of each other. Isn't that what happens?

To Drew, a part of his life died that year too.

"The past is the past. What happened is what happened. We don't talk about it, we don't pick it apart. It's history for a reason." Is that why?

Does he still carry that same anger? And if he does, what can that possibly mean for us?

Chapter
TWENTY-FOUR

Drew

9 years earlier

"Who was that?"

I look over to my dad standing in the doorway of my bedroom, shake my head, and sigh. "USC."

My dad nods but doesn't speak. I'm sure the defeat that owns my posture says it all. Another rejection. Another hollow explanation about how my stats are incredible but . . .

"He said I was *a gamble*." I chuckle but it lacks amusement. "That's an apropos choice of words, don't you think?" I ask, baiting him. I'm pissed and hurt and defeat is starting to wear me down. "A gamble. Wonder why he used those words? The same goddamn words almost every other coach has said to me in some way or another over the past few weeks."

I roll my shoulders and shove up off my bed as it really hits me. My dream school. The same one that recruited me eagerly a year ago as a freaking junior, made all kinds of promises, now is treating me like I'm some run-of-the-mill quarterback who doesn't deserve their time.

My dream school . . . now gone.

"I told you football was a pipe dream, Drew."

And I don't know what it is about his comment—the passiveness in his voice, the underlying disapproval, *something*—but it sets me off.

"A pipe dream?" I turn and shout at him. "A pipe dream?" My voice screeches. "Here I thought you were going to be disappointed in me, and instead you're telling me I need to give up the one thing I have?" I meet his eyes and feel like the man I once knew is no longer there, lost in this hell we've been living in for the past six months. "I don't understand you any-more. Not a fucking thing about you, Dad."

"Watch your tone with me."

I laugh. "That's funny. You think I give a damn about what you think of me? You walked away from this game—from everything you loved—and we've never been the same since. None of us! Not Mom, not Maggs, and sure as fuck not you!"

He doesn't flinch at my accusations, nor does he move from his spot in the doorway, almost as if he's standing there willing me to use him as my punching bag. "It wasn't everything I loved, Drew. You guys are what I loved. *Who I love*. You guys are—"

"Sure could've fucking fooled me. You're a ghost around here. The minute you stopped playing you became a shadow of yourself, and fuck if all I want is my old dad back."

"I understand you're disappointed, but there are other things in life than football, son," he says evenly.

"Like what?" The pitch of my voice is such a contrast to his. "Because my old dad wouldn't have uttered those words. He would have told me that I'm talented and that we'd move heaven and earth to give me a chance. He would have pushed me and encouraged me and told me to never give up until I get what I want. I would have been able to look up into those stands and see him there being proud of me, but instead, *he's* hiding at home like a guilty coward I know he isn't. He would have told me that he's proud of me for following in his footsteps, so I could try to be just like him." My voice breaks and I fucking hate that a tear has slid down my cheek in anger.

He doesn't give me the fight I'm angling for. The same fight I've wanted since that day he stood in our house almost a year ago and told us he was walking away from the game our family had been built on. He just stands there staring at me with indiscernible emotions written all over his face.

His silence is almost as crippling as his complacency.

"Screw you, Dad. Screw. You." My body vibrates with anger and I try to fathom how this is our life. How he became *him* and I became me, and how I've grown to resent him so damn much.

"Everything will work itself out. It will—"

"You're damn right it will," I shout and shove a finger in his direction. "Because I'm going to do this on my own." I think of the form saved on my computer that will allow me to legally change my name. The one I'd filled out in a brash moment last week when I wondered if it was Bowman that was holding me back. If it was *his* name that people were seeing instead of my talent.

Now I know.

I turn to my dad and look him in the eyes—needing to see his reaction when I utter the words of betrayal. Hoping that they will spark a reaction that will give me an ounce of insight into what the truth really is.

"I'm going to do it without your name with its shame and stigma attached to me."

But he doesn't flinch. He simply nods and turns and walks away.

Because that's all he's good at now.

Walking away.

Chapter
TWENTY-FIVE

Drew

"I'm glad to hear you're doing well."

I walk to the other side of my hotel room, one arm tucked under the other one, and look out the window to the rainy sidewalk of Seattle down below.

Maggie inhales a shaky breath. "*Well* is kind of overshooting, but I'm doing what I can."

I close my eyes for a beat and hate that I'm feeling like I'm on top of the fucking world while she's suffering through withdrawal.

"I'm proud of you, Maggs."

"I'm not." There's a brutal honesty to her voice. One I hate to hear—because I know she's going through hell—yet love to hear because it means she's sober.

"Have you talked to Charley?" I ask.

"No. I need—I need to be better before I can. It's rough right now and she . . . Christ, she doesn't fucking deserve this."

"You're right. She doesn't. But neither do you."

There is silence as she digests my words. "How am I ever going to beat this, Drew?" Her voice breaks and it kills me.

"With a lot of help."

She sniffs and then I hear someone talking in the background. "I have to go. My time is up."

"Okay."

"Tell Charley I love her."

I nod even though she can't see me because I have a huge lump in my throat. "Of course."

"I'm afraid I won't be able to be the person you want me to be, Drew."

"I just want you to be you, Maggs. Just you."

There's another sniffle and then the call ends.

It's my sigh that fills the hotel room.

She used her first call in three weeks to phone me. I'm not sure how I feel about that. If I should think of it as a burden that I'm the stability she looks toward or a blessing.

Regardless, I know I feel like shit. Nothing about this feels good.

And it hasn't in the longest time.

I feel like fear is what we Bowmans live in.

I look at you and see one of the most gifted and talented quarterbacks I've ever seen, but the man beneath is too goddamn afraid to step into the limelight.

While I may have been drunk at the McMasters' wedding, those words of Brexton's have stuck with me.

I can't shake them loose.

The worst part?

I'm embarrassed by them.

Does she think less of me because of it? Does she see these other starting players and wonder what they have that I don't?

"Christ," I mutter and run a hand through my hair.

One fucking phone call from Maggs, and I'm already doubting if the high I've been on for the past two days since I've left Brexton's bed is real or not.

Maybe more like warranted or not.

Tapping my cell phone against my chin, I debate whether or not I should call her. Have I wanted to? Of course. Have I worried that everything was just too goddamn perfect and if I call her I'll realize it wasn't? Most definitely.

"Quit being a pussy, Bowman. Just call her."

With a shake of my head, I pull up her contact and dial.

"Hey, you," she answers on the second ring. Fucking hell, my balls draw up at the rasp of her voice.

"Hey."

"How's Seattle?"

"Rainy."

"Forecast calls for clear skies for the game tomorrow though."

"You keeping tabs on me, Kincade?" I ask and chuckle.

"I do happen to have clients on your team, you know."

"I do indeed."

The line falls silent for a beat as I realize I had no real reason to call, and now I don't really know what to say.

"Did you need something?" she asks.

"No. I just . . . I don't know." I chuckle and feel like a complete idiot. "When can we see each other again?"

"I like the way your mind thinks."

"You do, huh?"

"I do. In fact, I was sitting here looking out of my office window thinking way too much about the other night."

And I can picture her in some high-rise building with her heels on, her long legs crossed at the knee, and her hair pulled up off her neck.

"Hopefully they were all good thoughts."

"Mm-hmm. More along the lines of *want to do it again* thoughts."

"Is that so?" I ask as my body hums at the prospect.

"It is."

"When can I see you again?" I ask. "I get back into town on Monday morning."

"Why did I know you were going to say that?"

"Why?"

"I leave Monday morning for the Midwest for meetings."

"Can you tell those corn-fed Midwest boys you have other plans?"

"This time it's a female gymnast, but I can tell her."

I laugh and even when the sound dissipates, my smile remains.

That's what she does to me.

"When do you come back?" I ask, clearly desperate to see her again.

"Friday morning," she says and I groan. "Let me guess, you fly out Friday?"

"Yep. Miami."

She sighs. "Is this where I say good things come to those who wait and then we both pretend like we're okay with waiting?"

"I'm not okay with it," I deadpan.

Her laughter fills the line. "That makes two of us."

"Good to know."

"Sunday night when you get home from Miami then."

"Such the planner."

"Always." She laughs. "So, tell me about your day."

"Do you want the long or the short version?" I tease.

"Long version. I like to hear your voice," she murmurs and wins over another piece of me.

So I talk about the flight here to Seattle. How we ran game prep drills today once we got here, and how I think Klingerman hurt his knee while running a play. She gave her two cents on how this isn't a good time for him to be hurt since he'll be up for free agency next year, and I suggested he may retire.

"What about your day?" I ask when I've run through the paces of mine. "What hot new athlete are you chasing after now?"

"It's quite the opposite actually," she says. "I had to have the conversation with a long-time client that it might be time to hang up his skates."

Her words are like a gut punch to me—words every athlete fears hearing. "That couldn't have been easy."

"Which is why I'm already on glass number two of wine." She blows out a sigh. "And it's never easy, but I'd much rather have my clients go out on top and happy than on the bottom with their reputation tarnished for holding on too long."

"How'd he take it?" There is silence on the other end of the line and then a sniffle that just adds to the twist in my gut. "You okay?"

"I'm fine. It's just part of the job. On the plus side, I negotiated a kick-ass endorsement deal for a female soccer player today that will help compensate for the crap wages she gets paid simply because of her gender."

"That's a definite plus."

She continues, telling me about her day.

Snippets.

Little pieces of our daily lives shared and listened to. Parts of ourselves offered up and accepted.

It's the first time I get a glimpse of what it would be like to have more with Brex. Having that person to talk over the day with, even if it is a bit like sleep, play, repeat, it's my job. And normally, I have no one to discuss it with.

Yet, with her, it feels natural.

Hell, I'm not a stranger to dating or just plain sleeping with a woman to pass the time. I've done sex without commitment on occasion. I've casually dated. But with Brexton, what I can't quite put my finger on, is how it feels so effortless when it should be the exact fucking opposite.

It should be complicated and troubled, because isn't that what I was told her family was? Isn't that all I've known since the day *he* walked away from the game?

And yet the mere thought of her has a smile on my face.

The sound of her voice makes me want to be with her.

And *that* feels so fucking right.

Chapter
TWENTY-SIX

Brexton

"You're working on a Sunday *and* you're watching football?" Chase asks when she walks into my office. "Do I need to check your forehead for a fever?"

I lift my middle finger in the air but don't bother looking up at her. "One, I'm catching up before I leave for Iowa tomorrow. Two, I'm always working. And three, since when is it weird for any of us to watch sports. Last I checked the sign on the door said Sports Management," I say, stretching the last two words out like I'm speaking to a child. She offers me a middle finger in return. "If you'd like to know, I'm watching to make sure Whittier doesn't fuck up again with the added bonus of checking in on Hobbs."

"You mean the man who's already thrown two interceptions? That one?" She perches her hip on my desk and I look up to meet the eyes of my youngest sister. She's in yoga pants and some cute tank top, looking flawless without trying as per her usual.

"Yes, that Hobbs."

"Any leeway with him? I haven't seen anything new on the weekly status reports."

"Because those reports are annoying."

"And yet they keep the pulse of everyone and everything."

"Spoken by the rule follower," I tease, because while we're all disciplined, Chase goes that extra mile to follow every rule to a T. When she just stares at me, demanding an answer, I continue. "There is nothing to report. I'm trying and he's denying."

"So no Hobbs yet? Then who exactly is putting that extra pep in your step?"

I meet her eyes and roll mine. "No one. I'm just in a good mood is all."

"The only thing that puts you in that good of a mood is some good old-fashioned sex."

"Whatever. Speak for yourself." I wave a hand at her. "Go away while you're at it. I've got work to do."

"Rumor is that you were kissing some man at the McMasters' wedding." My expression must fall because her grin widens and eyebrows lift. "What do you have to say about that?"

"I'd say a kiss is a kiss. Nothing more, nothing less," I lie on the fly as I think of all the wonderful things that Drew can do with his mouth.

"So you what? Found a groomsman to get hot and heavy with in the bathroom?" she teases.

"Not a groomsman. Another guest, if you must know. We'd both had a few drinks, danced a bit, and then we kissed. Is that a crime?"

She throws her head back and laughs. "When you pull the *is that a crime* bullshit, we all know you're lying."

"Go away, Chase." I wave a hand at her. The last thing I need is her meddling nose in my business.

"So it was more than just a kiss, then?"

So much more than just a kiss. The night with Drew comes back in snapshots. Him at the door. Him hovering over me. Him sinking into me.

"Did you plant spies there? Jesus." I laugh.

"Nope. More of a friend of a friend kind of thing." She scrunches her nose up. "Too bad they're shit at spying or I'd know who the Wedding Kisser is."

"There is no . . . *him*," I say refusing to dignify her stupid nickname. I slide a printed contract to the side of my laptop, trying to end the conversation. "Go away."

"Why won't you tell me?" she asks in her most annoying little sister voice.

"Because it's none of your business, *Tattletale*," I say, using the nickname we used to call her just to upset her when she was little.

She used to be so desperate to be a part of whatever the rest of us sisters were doing, and she tried to get us in trouble when we wouldn't let her.

"Oh, geez. You're reaching deep with the insults using that one." She rolls her eyes, unfazed, and I level her with a glare.

"Since when do any of us tell *you* anything?" I continue, trying to deflect. My little pain-in-the-ass sister. I love her to death, but she's notorious for running straight to everyone else and gossiping.

Or trying to get one of us in trouble.

"Ohhh," she chides. "It must be *really good*. Or he must be *really wrong* in all the right ways if you're afraid for Dad to find out."

"I'm not afraid for Dad to find anything out." I start typing on my keyboard to try and show her I'm busy.

"You're such a liar," she goads and then sighs. "Guess it's time for me to go work my sources and find out who exactly the Wedding Kisser is."

"Have fun with that," I say as she turns and heads out of my office.

Then I silently wonder if anyone I know—or she knows—saw Drew kiss me.

She grins at me before stepping into her office and I immediately grab my phone and change my passcode.

She's a little shit.

I wouldn't put it past her to "accidentally" check my texts.

The last thing I need is for her to see the heavy flirting going back and forth between Drew and me.

She wouldn't be able to keep anything that juicy to herself.

Chapter
TWENTY-SEVEN

Brexton

"KSM. This is Brexton." I move the pile of papers on my desk and rap them so their corners square up.

"Brexton. This is Justin Hobbs."

I stop mid-motion, surprised to hear from him, considering he hasn't returned any of my calls thus far.

"Justin. Hi." I grab a pen and my notepad. "What can I do for you?"

"That's what I like to hear," he says and chuckles. "A woman who knows she's—"

"Don't mistake the fact that I want you as our client to mean that I won't put you in your place for being crass."

He whistles softly. "Nothing wrong with a woman who can grab a man by the balls and give them a good twist."

I'd like to twist them, all right.

"You called me. Now, what can I do for you?" I ask trying to get him to focus.

"I'd like to talk with you about representation," he says, and I nod even though he can't see it.

"What about it?"

"What you can bring to the table for me."

"The table is set differently for every athlete, Hobbs. I need a bit more than that to know what we're talking about. Are you looking for a long contract, more money, a specific team? I mean, I can bring a lot of things to the table, but that doesn't mean you're going to sit down and eat."

"I have a big appetite."

Clearly, and not that I'd ever say it out loud, but Finn's done a decent job satisfying Hobbs's hunger. Besides, Justin's barely into his professional career and he's already playing the agent-game. I'm beginning to wonder if Justin is just one of those guys who's never satisfied.

I guess it's my goal to see if that's true or not.

"I'm not a miracle worker but my track record speaks for itself."

"I've researched and am well aware."

His sudden change of heart to talk after blowing me off for the past three weeks means he either had a fight with Sanderson or he's playing the field without any real intention of making the switch over to KSM.

It's a conundrum. My gut instinct is to tell him to take a hike and that I don't need him. My sense of responsibility to my family and our company has me biting my tongue because isn't this what my dad asked of me? To land Justin Hobbs as a client? His experience in the industry has him thinking that if the rising star comes our way, other football players will wonder why he made the switch and follow suit.

It's all about visibility and catching the brightest stars. It's about securing the future of KSM for my sisters and me. It's about sticking to my word.

So I grit my teeth and grin and bear it. Or at least I try to.

"I think it's best if we speak face to face," Justin says.

"Agreed. What works best for you?" I ask as I pull up my calendar on my computer.

"I'm in Florida. Practice tomorrow. Game on Sunday," he says. It's not like I didn't already know where Drew was, but I don't say a word.

"And you're telling me this because . . ."

"Because if you want my business then you'll come to me."

I have to keep my mouth shut, when all I want to do is tell him that no self-respecting woman would do just that. But I have to.

This is business, after all.

"Let me be clear on one thing. I'm not a fan of wild goose chases, Justin."

"Noted."

Silence stretches as neither of us want to bend our wills, especially considering he'll be back in New York less than thirty hours after the game. Wouldn't it be easier to meet then?

But that's not how Justin plays. I know that much.

He likes the trappings of fame. The entourage. The people who come at the snap of his fingers. People chasing after him for his business.

That's the only way this is going to work. My satisfying his need to be sought after.

The problem? I'm already committed to being in North Carolina on Sunday.

"Give me one sec," I murmur as my fingers fly over my keyboard and I check flights. I can be in Miami by five p.m. today then leave Saturday for Chapel Hill.

"I'll be there tonight. We'll talk then."

"Tonight?"

"You said if I wanted your business I needed to come to you."

"Responsive." He chuckles. "You have no idea how much I like that."

I ignore the innuendo and the suggestion I hear in his tone and say, "I'll be in touch."

The bright side in all of this? I might land the client I've been chasing. Even brighter? Miami means there's a chance of seeing Drew again.

And yes, I'm fully aware that that means I'm chasing after a man.

But I'm just going to pretend that I'm not.

Chapter
TWENTY-EIGHT

Brexton

"That's what I require in order to sign with you and be under KSM management."

"So that's the ultimatum huh?" I ask. "I need to get you traded to the Los Angeles Chargers or Rams and then you'll transfer your representation over to me?"

"Simple, right?"

I all but laugh as I meet his eyes across the table in the back corner of a small Cuban restaurant I decided on. It's crowded enough that there are people around in case Justin decides to get handsy but not too loud where he can't hear me.

The fact that I even had to navigate those boundaries says more than enough about the character and reputation of the man sitting across from me.

I shake my head. "You're asking the impossible. There's no way in hell any management team is going to listen to me, let alone negotiate with me on your behalf, when they already know you're represented by someone else. It's unethical and frankly kind of shitty for you to ask me to consider it."

His nonchalant shrug and unapologetic smile grates on my nerves. If he's asking this of me before I'm his agent, I fear what he'd ask once I am.

Especially since I'd have already broken rules for him.

"I prefer to call it dangling the carrot to see how hungry you are for it."

"I don't like carrots," I deadpan. "In fact, I hate them." I lean across the table. "What I prefer are athletes who are straightforward and without bullshit. That's the kind of thing that excites me, Justin. Those are the athletes I like to fight for."

He stares at me with confusion etched in the lines of his face, almost as if he can't figure out if I just insulted him or not. "Isn't this the part where you as an agent are supposed to be showing me just how good you really are?" he asks over the top of his beer bottle.

"No, this is the part where I tell you that you're asking the impossible. Like I told you on the phone, I don't like games and, frankly you're playing one right now. Without that little thing called a signed contract, I literally have no authority to act on your behalf. I can bring you up in a casual conversation, I can mention you to the general managers when discussing possibilities, but as far as flat-out asking, it can't happen."

"So then you're saying you don't want to sign me?"

"No, I'm saying that no one client is worth risking my reputation. Once word got out, team management would shy away from me, other agents would think I'm always out to steal their clients, and other athletes would question my integrity. You're good, Hobbs, and would be a great addition to KSM, but not with that being the cost."

Justin blows out a steady breath and shakes his head, no doubt stumped why I'm not bending over backward for him like I'm certain he expected I would.

An awkward silence settles between us as the server clears our plates, and while I try to figure out how to salvage this business meeting. When she leaves with dishes stacked on her forearm, I ask, "Why California? As an agent, I have to tell you that your strengths are best suited to teams like the Raptors over the Chargers, Rams, or even the 49ers."

"I've got my reasons," he says as our eyes hold. I don't back down from the stare. He needs to know I'm not intimidated by him in the least.

But while he's being stubborn, I'm sitting here doing mental gymnastics over the epiphany I just had.

Getting Justin to California opens up the starting QB spot that Drew could easily step into. That would create the opportunity he's been waiting for. It would finally give him a chance.

And while that scenario is as perfect as perfect can be, it doesn't address how I could ethically make it happen.

It's a line I can't cross.

But I decide to play Justin's game, to feel him out, and see if there is a legitimate interest in my representation or if he truly is playing me. "So say, perhaps, I could pull this off and get you traded, how do I know you're not bullshitting me? How do I know that I'm not going to be doing all this work, get things lined up for you, and then you'll turn around and have Finn take my work and own it as his own?" I ask as his eyes widen. "I mean, I'd be the one working without a contract. All I have is your word that you'd actually sign with me."

"Are you saying you don't trust me?"

I lean onto my elbows on the table and lower my voice. "I've dealt with a lot of players over the years. While I may be out chasing after and for you, you're only out for yourself. That makes it pretty damn easy for doubt to fester."

Justin takes a long sip of his beer and then leans back in his chair, lips pursed for a moment. "Then how do we get around this, Kincade?"

"Why did you call me, Justin? What made you pick up the phone?"

"I was told you were one of the best."

My eyebrows raise. Not because he's speaking of me, but that feels like the most honest thing he's said all night. "By whom?"

"Drew Bowman." I measure my reaction to his words. "Shit, the way that fucker defends you, you'd think he has a thing for you."

"That's ridiculous." I bark the words out.

"Stranger things have happened. Just don't tell your boyfriend or he might get jealous of all this extra attention." He winks.

"My *boyfriend*?"

"Yeah. Drew said you had a man already and that I couldn't poach."

I nod, confused and amused. *Poach?* "I'm flattered, Justin, but one, you are way too young for me"—I laugh quietly to soften the blow—"and two, I never date clients or potential clients. It's not a line I cross."

"All lines get crossed at some point." He chuckles. "Just like the one you'll figure out how to cross to get me traded."

"It's not the same. It's—"

"I'm sure you'll figure something out."

I emit a resigned sigh as my mind races over a conversation I'd love to have been a fly on the wall for and a trade I can't technically negotiate.

"I'm sure I will," I murmur.

"Los Angeles, Brexton." And it's the last thing he says before he balls his napkin up and tosses it on the table before excusing himself and walking away.

My sigh follows soon after.

He's already proving to be difficult and he's not even my client yet.

Chapter
TWENTY-NINE

Brexton

THE BASE OF THE CLUB THROBS AGAINST THE WALLS AND FEELS LIKE it's a second heartbeat in my chest.

It's the last place I expected to be tonight, but I needed to put myself in check. I'm in Miami for work. Sure I slept with Drew and want to again, but reaching out to him while I'm here felt needy and stalkerish. In an attempt to keep my overromanticized heart in check, I texted one of my college girlfriends who now lives in Miami.

And now we're here at Club Cerulean where the drinks are strong, the men are deliciously hot, and the music is on point.

It's the perfect place to let my hair down and just breathe. It's a chance to let loose and remind myself that man or no man, I can have a great time.

"You ready to hit the floor again?" she shouts above the beat.

"Yes. I need some air though, first." I fan my hand in front of my face as if it's actually going to help cool me off.

"'Kay. Let's head to the patio for a minute. Then we'll dance our asses off."

We push our way through the crowd and just as we hit the exit, I run smack dab into Dax Conway, the Raptor's tight end.

"Kincade? What the fuck are you doing here?" he asks as he wraps his arms around me in a brotherly yet drunken hug that I gently extricate myself from.

"Work. Meetings." I push against his chest when he steps in closer and he just laughs.

"Hey. Look who I found!" Dax says as he turns to about seven other players. As I wave in greeting to all of them, Drew walks up, his feet faltering when our eyes meet.

Shock and confusion blanket his face and then if I'm not mistaken, hurt follows right after it.

"Hey," he says in a flat tone as his eyes hold mine. They ask questions I don't understand but I just smile softly.

"Hey," I say in return, our gazes holding longer than is normal before I break away and introduce Lisa to everyone.

"Fancy meeting you here," Justin says as he barrels up behind Drew and whistles, long and low. "Earlier you were all businessed-up and now you're dressed to fucking kill, isn't she, boys?"

I ignore the scrape of Justin's gaze up and down my body. His objectifying me. And it's not that I don't care, but rather I'm too busy noticing the clench of Drew's jaw and the fisting of his hands.

I'm definitely not privy to something that has transpired between the two of them but I have an inkling that it most definitely had something to do with me.

"*Earlier?*" Drew asks Justin, ignoring me.

"Yeah, bro. She took me to dinner. Wined and dined me." He winks and slaps Drew on the shoulder. "I can't help that I'm irresistible."

"I'm surprised your ego fit through the door," I say with a saccharine-sweet smile. "And for the record, some meetings, Hobbs, are supposed to remain private." I give him a nod and a stern look and only hope when I turn to Drew that he understands what happened.

Hell, supposedly he gave Justin the push to call me, after all.

Drew gives me a slight lift of his chin but breaks eye contact when Dax says, "Come join us. We have bottle service up top." He points to the lounge area above the dance floor that looks down onto it.

"No, we're good—"

"C'mon, Brex. Don't be such a stick in the mud!" Lisa says as Dax puts an arm around her and she giggles. "These guys will protect us."

Is this the time for me to remember that Lisa becomes the giggly airhead around men when she wants their attention? How did I selectively forget that when I texted her to go out tonight?

Maybe because it only makes a difference now.

Only when I have to sit within feet of Drew and not touch him. Only now that the feel of him is at the forefront of my mind, and my blood is all but singing with unsated desire.

"Thank you for the offer, but I normally don't mix business with pleasure."

"C'mon, Kincade," Justin says. "Don't be such a prude." He tugs on my arm as if we're old college buddies when we're not. "What's the worst that can happen? A bunch of professional football players protect you from some assholes?"

"You mean from someone like you?" Drew asks as he bumps Justin's shoulder with his before heading up the stairs after everyone. He turns back to the two of us, absolute indifference on his face. "You coming?"

Do you know how hard it is to sit across from someone and not show that you know them, want them, and are reliving their touch?

I know that Drew does. Because every time I risk a glance toward him, our eyes meet fleetingly, and he conveys what seems like the same desperate desire that's owning my body right now.

To make matters worse, every time he passes behind me to talk to a teammate, he touches me ever-so-slightly—a hand across my ass, a fingertip across my shoulder, the heat of his body simply standing there.

It's like he keeps adding kindling to a fire I know we can't stoke.

He'll be under team curfew at the hotel, and there's no way in hell I'll be the cleat chaser getting caught sneaking in and out of the room. Talk about ruining my professional reputation.

So instead we're relegated to this. The taunt and tease and tempt without anyone noticing.

It's devastating to my senses while simultaneously being the most seductive foreplay I've ever partaken in.

A glance here. A touch there. The dart out of a tongue to wet his lips. Eyes telling me what he wants to do with their flick down my body.

And yes, sure we may be laughing and having separate conversations with his teammates, but we are one hundred percent aware of each other at all times.

My phone vibrates in my purse at my side. When I glance at its screen, I fight my smile.

Drew: Meet me in the middle of the dance floor. It's dark and crowded and no one will see.

I glance up to see Drew staring at me, eyes intense, intent clearly etched in the lines of his face.

Me: You dance?
Drew: If you consider my hands on your body dancing, then yes.

He offers me the sexiest smile from his place in the corner as I rise from my seat beside Dax and Lisa, who are in a heated discussion about who knows what.

"Hey?" she asks.

I smile. "I'm fine. I'm going to catch some fresh air. I'll be back."

"You sure? I can come with you," she offers but makes no movement to grab her purse. An empty promise I was counting on.

"I'm good. Stay. Enjoy yourself."

Drew was right. The dance floor is packed and with the strobe lights over the darkened room, it would be clearly impossible to figure out who is who among the crowd of bodies.

It takes me some time to make my way into the center of the space. Bodies are moving to the Latin beat, hips gyrating, arms thrown up in the sky, as they lose themselves to the beat.

And it doesn't take long for me to do the same. To move to the music and wait with burning anticipation for Drew to find me.

To touch me.

To kiss me.

When his hands slide around my midsection and the heat of his body blankets me from behind, I don't know how to react. My body's so taut with anticipation while being so ready for him, that all I can do is sink back against him and close my eyes.

We begin to move. It's not him or me, it's just us moving together.

His hands on my abdomen. My fingers lacing through his. My body reacting to his.

We don't speak. We'd never be heard above the music. Instead, we communicate with our bodies. With touch and feel and fingertips and silence.

His teeth find an exposed part of my neck and they scrape against the sensitive skin there before lacing it with an open-mouth kiss to ease the sting.

It's fire and ice.

Fans are flamed.

Tinder slowly ignites.

Every part of me aches for his touch. *For him.* For what I can only hope is to come. But when I try to turn around, he keeps me in place. He holds me so I have no choice but to be aware and acknowledge the incredible way his body feels against mine. The heat of his chest against my back, the hardness of his cock pressed to my ass, the possession in his hands as they run up and down my sides.

Each touch is an assault to my senses.

Each touch is a temptation I can't wait to get lost in.

Our hips move in sync to the pulsating beat. Bodies bump us from all sides, but I only feel his. I only want his.

Need becomes desperation as his hands map my lines. Down my hips, gently toward my front and over the apex of my thighs, before running up so that his thumbs brush just beneath the curve of my breasts—before starting their torturous course all over again.

This time when I turn, he doesn't stop me.

Our mouths find each other immediately. We're a clash of lips and tongue and need and greed. His groan is my gasp for breath. His touch is my drug of choice. His taste creates an addiction all on its own.

But as the beat reaches a crescendo, all I can process is that this isn't enough—it'll never be enough—because even when our hands are on each other, I still crave more.

The crowd we're in the middle of feeds the frenzy we feel.

Our bodies move as our tongues connect over and over again. As the desperation edges with necessity. As reason gives way to greed.

As sanity loses the battle against lust.

Chapter
THIRTY

Drew

I NEED MORE.

Her lips on a dance floor. Her body against mine. People around us. *More.*

I've waited almost two goddamn weeks to see her again, and it's like some cruel joke that I can touch her but I can't have her.

So much more.

This is akin to putting a Band-Aid on an open wound. It'll help momentarily, but it's not going to stop the onslaught in the long run.

How can I get more?

Brexton gently tugs my bottom lip as I search for a way to feed the desire. To ease the ache in my balls and the fervor to have her own me completely.

I move my hand between our bodies and slip my hand inside the hem of her skirt. It's not a smooth or particularly pretty move, but when my fingers find purchase—her slick, warm, wet slit—I all but come on the spot.

I try to focus. On the beat of the music. On her fingers digging into my shoulders. On how to pleasure her. But I'm fucking oblivious to anything but the feel of her coating me as I work my fingers back and forth.

Fuck. I was wrong.

There is no lessening desire when it comes to Brexton. There's no having a taste to tide you over till the next time. There's only adding to it. There's only lightning striking and taking you for its ride. There's only temporary pleasure before you need her again.

And fucking hell do I need her again. "Come," I tell Brexton. I pull my hand from between her thighs before tugging on her hand, without an explanation, and leading her off the dance floor toward the back of the club.

Should I be worried about the guys seeing us?

Yes.

Am I?

No.

I only have one thought on my mind, one person I care about.

Brexton, in that sexy-as-hell outfit that highlights her perfect ass and every curve connected to it.

Brexton, whose lips taste like wine and whose kisses are an addiction all on their own.

She stumbles behind me through the dark hallway as I look for anyplace, anywhere, that we can go.

"What? Drew? What are you—"

I turn and spin on her so that her back is against the wall and my lips close over hers to steal the words from them. There's anger in our kiss this time. A need so violent that I can't put words to it—can't express it—and so kissing her is the only way I have.

"What is your problem?" she asks, hands fisted in my shirt when we come up for air. She has to feel the same way as I do right now.

I can't be the only one.

"What's the problem?" I growl. "The problem is *you*."

"Me?" She laughs.

"Fucking hell. Yes, you." My lips are on hers again. My hands itching to slide beneath her skirt again and touch her skin. "I can't get enough of you and it's goddamn maddening."

She puts her mouth near my ear and whispers just above the throb of the music. "That makes two of us."

I lean back and stare at her—eyes dark, lips curved up in a taunt—and love that she's been suffering tonight as much as I have. And we're on the move again. Down the hall with her hand in mine as I try handle after handle until I reach the employee locker room. The door gives and I pull her inside without a second thought. It's small and stifling, dim and empty, but as long as the door is sturdy and the lock stays, that's all that matters.

She yelps out a laugh as we slam back against it. Our lips branding each other's again as her hands unbutton my pants and my hands pull up her skirt.

"He knew you were here and I didn't," I murmur before tugging on her bottom lip with my teeth.

She mewls out a moan as my fingers dive between her thighs to find her even more wet and ready than moments before and Christ, there's no way I could get any harder. It's already painful enough.

She frees my cock and I groan when she wraps her hand around it and squeezes. "I was trying to keep it professional." She sucks my bottom lip, her breath labored, her nipples hard against my chest. "We're both working. We were both—"

Her words stop as I heft her up so that her legs wrap around me, her back is braced against the wall, and my cock presses at her core.

Goddamn right. That'll make her stop talking about Justin.

"How's this for professional?" I ask as I lower her down and push my way into her.

My body electrifies at the feel of her tight, hot heat.

I'm staggered.

Speechless.

Fucking consumed.

Her drawn-out moan and exposed neck as she leans her head back, overcome with the sensations, are a goddamn seduction in and of themselves.

But I don't need to be seduced. Not by Brex. No. She's already done that. All I need to do is feel.

And when I begin to move, that reality has never been more apparent.

Jesus Christ.

There is no beauty in our sex. No gentleness. No sweet words. There is only pure, unadulterated need. Only desire melding with greed. There is only hunger for more.

Just more.

Of her.

Of me.

Of us.

It's her fingernails scoring my skin. It's her teeth sinking into my collarbone. It's her heels digging into my hips.

It takes every ounce of my control to hold on, to ensure she climaxes.

"Drew," she pants as her breath grows shallow and her pussy tightens. I pick up the pace.

"*Drew.*" Now a moan as her fingers grip tighter.

She emits a strangled cry as she locks her ankles above my ass and bucks her hips against mine.

I can feel her orgasm. Its tight hold around my cock. The way her muscles pulsate around me. The way her arousal drips down my balls.

And fuck. It's enough to push me over the edge.

Not that it would take much though, because I was holding on by a very thin thread, and thank fuck it just snapped.

I lose thought. I forget about being gentle. I can only focus on the tidal wave of fucking sensation that's so hot it edges on painful, and the only way to soothe its singe is to come. I thrust into her a couple more times before I lose all sense of reality, before I become lost to the moment.

To her.

And the last thought that crosses my mind before I lose myself to the madness she's drawn from me is this—*I understand it now.*

I get why men would go to war for this. *Over this.* To save this.

With a shake of my head, I laugh out loud as I drag my lips over hers one more time before setting her down and stepping back to look at her. At her lips swollen, her hair wild, and her eyes alive.

And I worry at what lengths I'll go to do the same. There's something about Brexton Kincade.

And it scares the fuck out of me.

Chapter
THIRTY-ONE

Brexton

I LOOK AT THE TEXT AGAIN ON MY PHONE AND TRY NOT TO BE ANGERED by it.

Drew: I have to cancel tonight. I'm sorry. Something came up unexpectedly.

I type my single-word answer and stare at it for a beat, grateful that tone can't be inferred in a text. Or maybe I wish he could hear it. The disappointment. The sadness. The frustration. I glance around my living room—to the candles lit and the dinner being kept warm—and hate that I deflate before I hit send.

Me: Sure.
Drew: Thanks for understanding.

I read it again and look down at the stockings connected to garter belts on my legs and sigh.

I got dressed up for him. I spent an hour in Agent Provocateur today, and the silk and lace and heels I'm currently adorned in prove it.

I cooked for him—when cooking is something I rarely make time to do.

I planned a special evening, because I wanted to welcome him home from his road trip. He seemed rather upset earlier when he texted about not touching the field and I thought this—me and a romantic evening—might help take the sting out of it.

The funny thing? I'd debated doing this. In a sense it was me putting myself out there for him. It was more than us meeting up to have a quick and randy bout of sex.

It was my way of showing him I wanted more than that.

All that worry, all those pep talks that I needed to go for it, all this planning, and for what? To be blown off? To be put back in her booty-call only box?

My exasperated laugh echoes around my empty apartment as I try to hide how upset I am.

"You're losing it, Brex."

Maybe it was something with his family. But if that were the case, wouldn't he have said something to make him bailing on me more understandable? I know I would.

The needy side of me wishes I would have asked him what it was that came up. The stubborn side of me refuses to.

The first one I refuse to be. Needy can be done in my own thoughts, but never outright. Tears burn in my eyes, and I shake my head as I try to shake the disappointment and my overthinking off. But it's rather hard to do when I'm dressed like this and the atmosphere is set for seduction.

I grab the bottle of wine I had breathing on the counter, kick off my heels, and plop onto the couch without an ounce of grace.

"Looks like it's just me and you," I mutter to the bottle before I take a drink straight from it.

When I rest my head back on my couch and close my eyes for a beat, the first tear slips down my cheek.

I laugh, then I allow myself to be ridiculously pathetic for a few moments.

It's allowed, right?

I mean, I've looked forward to this since we saw each other at the club in Miami. Since the flirty texts we sent to each other while I was in North Carolina and he had a short turnaround to a Thursday night game of the week.

Maybe that's the problem.

Maybe I want more out of this than he does. It's not like that hasn't happened to me before. I read all of the signs wrong with Micah. I jumped all in thinking he was doing the same only to find out later he was bitching to all of his and *my* friends that I was too clingy, too everywhere. I guess me being *everywhere* put a damper on him wanting to be everywhere with other women while dating me.

I sigh and take another long sip of Merlot.

But I know I'm not wrong about Drew. Can't be. I saw the way he looked at me in Miami. I felt the intention in his kisses. I've heard his morning voice through the phone and heard the smile in it. I've read and reread our shared texts and know I'm not seeing something that isn't there. I'm not wishing there to be more when it feels like it's going there naturally.

All of those things suggest there's more between us than just sex. Maybe he's afraid to admit it.

Is that what tonight is all about? Did he realize things were moving too fast and so this was his subtle way of taking a step back and reasserting that this is nothing more than casual dating?

Well, I own the notion that whatever between us is more. I know it is.

I push myself up from the couch, lick my fingers, and extinguish the first candle's flame by pinching them together. The sharp sting is a reminder to me that I need to be careful. That I need to be the one taking a step back. Drew canceling on me last minute is the perfect moment to put my head *and heart* in check. It's the ideal time to realize he was right—that I was planning ten steps ahead versus letting the moment guide us. It's fine to acknowledge that I'm falling for the boy I gave my heart on a platter to when we were teenagers. But we're not kids anymore. We're adults with lives of our own and problems we haven't shared.

In fact, from this vantage point, it's apparent that Drew and I are nothing more than the physical. Sure, I have the lingerie on and a nice dinner planned, but isn't that just window dressing for a booty call? It's not like we had a night on the town followed by this. In fact, we never have. Shouldn't that be more than enough to tell me where things between us stand?

Is that a tough pill to swallow?

I take a drink and nod vigorously. *Of course it is.*

But I think it's exactly what I need to force myself to step back and recenter my priorities.

Chapter
THIRTY-TWO

Brexton

"MAY I ASK WHY YOU'RE ADVOCATING FOR CLIENTS WHO AREN'T yours?" Neil Milton, the general manager of the Raptors leans back in his chair, fingers steepled in front of him, eyes laser focused on me.

We've always had a good rapport. If we didn't, I never would have approached him in this manner, but the opportunity presented itself when he asked for my opinion on several players and so I just dove headfirst into it. Now it's sink or swim.

I was right in my assessment of how a GM would respond to my meddling on another player's behalf. At least I can trust my instincts on this.

What I'm not trusting is why I even brought Hobbs up in the first place when I'm still mad at him for the high-pressure game he pulled when we were in Miami.

And yet Neil asked my opinion and I thought I'd stick a toe in the water with a GM who I have a good rapport with.

"You're mistaken. I'm not necessarily advocating for them. It's more along the lines of showing you how the chess pieces would fall if you moved the King."

He nods as he chews my words over. "But the statement you made about Hobbs—that he wants you—was clear as day."

"I'm simply being upfront with you about the fact that Hobbs approached me. He said he wants to play in California for reasons I'm not privy to."

"Why'd he approach you?" Neil asks.

"He said his agent isn't pursuing the avenue, but that he knew I had connections there and decided to try another means to get traded." I set my pen down and don't back down from his stare.

"Yet he's not your client and you're still standing before me."

"I assure you that being caught in the middle of this is the last place I want to be. I'm standing before you because we have a history and a good working relationship. You asked my opinion about players and while I'd rather stay completely out of this, I decided to be honest and let you know what I've heard. Talk to your players to validate what I'm saying. See what they say. But Justin is telling everyone he has one foot out the door. His immaturity is showing and his teammates aren't happy with it. Besides, I have players on this team. The Raptors' success means their success." I shrug. "The last thing I want is for you to be caught blindsided in his upcoming contract negotiations if Finn Sanderson decides to act on his client's wishes."

"And you expect me to believe that there's nothing in this for you?"

"Like I said, I do have clients on the team as well as one out in California who would be a good fit here in a trade."

"A QB?"

I narrow my eyes and shake my head at him. "Why would you need a quarterback when you have a phenomenal one sitting in the wings?"

"Bowman?"

I nod. "Yes, Bowman."

"Are you representing him now too?" He chuckles.

I shake my head. "No, but I don't understand why the guy doesn't get a shot."

"There are reasons."

"Like something his dad may have done ten years ago that holds no bearing on his career? You mean those kinds of reasons?"

"This is the moment in the conversation where I tell you you're starting to step over the line, Brexton."

I shove up out of my seat and walk to the far end of the conference room, confused and trying hard to keep my personal emotions out of the situation. "Understood, but have you seen him down on the practice field after a game? Have you stopped and watched him in the darkness?

It'll be nine o'clock at night and he's out there working. His arm is a laser. His stats from when he's been given a shot are insane. And from what I've heard from the guys in passing, he plays simply because he loves the game."

"And you've taken all of this away by watching him practice on the practice field?"

"No. I saw him the one time and then looked him up. I was confused over why he was in the dark instead of under the lights and in front of a crowd of sixty thousand."

"And what is it you think you found when you researched him?"

"I found the next leader of your team."

He laughs just to humor me. "Thank you for the advice, but I have plenty of advisors who do that."

"As you should." I round the conference room table, sit on its edge, and cross my arms over my chest. "Hobbs is good but still learning. The mistakes he makes are because he's young, inexperienced, and unwilling to admit that. You can get away with shit like that in college but this is the NFL. You either step up and lead or teams move on. And let's face it, you've lost the last two games because he's not leading properly. From what I hear, the guys respect Bowman. He's not flashy and he puts in the work. They respect that."

Milton taps his pen against the table and scoots his chair back, a surefire sign that this conversation is over and that I've overstepped my bounds. "I hear you, but I'm more concerned where this conversation is coming from."

"It's coming from an agent who sees a talented player going to waste. Nothing more. Nothing less."

"And you've taken it upon yourself to be the advocate for such a player."

I chuckle, not wanting to be trapped in whatever narrative he's trying to create here. "No. I see a team with so many working pieces, so much untapped talent, that it'll be the management who holds them back from a championship, not the players."

"I'm thinking I should be insulted by that." He smiles, but I know I've pushed my luck enough.

"Not at all." I stand and start collecting my laptop and put it in my bag. "As usual, I appreciate the time and your attention."

"As I do your unsolicited advice in regards to clients you don't represent."

"We were just shooting the shit, Neil. Not everything is a negotiation."

His laugh is rich and boisterous as he rises with a shake of his head.

Chapter
THIRTY-THREE

Brexton

"You were at the Raptors' offices today." Drew's voice comes loud and clear through the phone line. My body has a visceral reaction to the sound of it.

Unfortunately, my heart does too.

"I was. I had a meeting with Neil about some things."

"You could have dropped me a text. We could have met up afterward."

"I had another meeting I had to run to right after."

"I see," he murmurs and then silence eats the line. "You didn't return my calls yesterday."

"Again, busy with work." I move to the door of my office and close it. It was so hard not to pick up yesterday when he called, so hard not to call him back after he'd asked if he could see me later, but I had to prove to myself that I could take a step back, for my own well-being. "Did everything end up being okay?"

"Okay? What do you mean?" he asks.

"We were supposed to meet up when you got home from your flight. You canceled. Said something came up."

He sighs heavily and I try not to read into it. "Right. Yes. Sorry. That feels like forever ago already."

But he says nothing more.

"But everything went well?" I ask, needing to know I wasn't stood up for something trivial like the guys wanting to hit a bar for some beers. Not that I care if he did, but just not when he'd previously made plans with me.

"As well as things can be."

"Meaning?"

He chuckles. "Meaning some things are just better left alone, Brexton." And he silently drives a dagger into my heart.

I'm good enough for him to text yesterday to ask if he can come over, or call me and ask why we can't meet up, but I'm not good enough for him to open up to.

"Got it." I nod and hate that I'm hurt by it. But isn't this what I expected after my epiphany the other night? I feel closer to Drew because of our past, the shared history. I feel like I know him when with anyone else at this stage of the game I would be keeping them more at arm's length.

And even knowing all this, I have to acknowledge that our time together hasn't exactly been *get to know you*. It's been more along the lines of *get to know your body*.

So while our chemistry is intensely crazy and I truly like him, right now we're simply sleeping together.

There's been nothing more than that.

And I deserve more than that.

"What's wrong, Brex?" he asks.

"I just have a lot on my mind."

There's a shift in the conversation. In the realization that I'm not sitting here waiting for him.

"Okay. Well, I'll let you go then. I'd love to see you again."

I hate that those words cause an ache and burn within. A bittersweet one that knows I'll give in at some point.

"We'll figure it out." I fake a smile even though he can't see it.

It's a fine line to walk. Not coming off like a bitch—or feeling like I'm being one. I deserve more than being a booty call, being a mousy woman who accepts that this is just sex and never speaks up.

Neither leaves me satisfied completely.

And maybe I just need a few days to figure out if this is what I want.

Then again, I already know the minute I hang up with him, I'll regret the decision and miss him.

"Hey, Brex? Am I missing something?"

No, it's what I'm missing that's the problem.

"What do you mean?" I feign naively.

"You didn't answer my calls yesterday and now you're . . . I don't know what you're doing."

Protecting myself.

Guarding my heart.

Taking care of myself for once instead of worrying about everyone else.

Isn't that enough?

"Look, you're right I could have texted you, but for what? For you to be embarrassed about being seen with me again?"

He sighs. "Is that what you think? That I'm embarrassed about being with you? Are you out of your mind, Brex? I want to show you off to the fucking world but, this—*you and me*—is fucking complicated enough without adding in outside pressure."

I can all but picture him on the other end of the call. His hand running through his hair and the frustration etched in the lines of his gorgeous face.

But I'm suddenly sitting up a little taller as his words hit my ears and I process them. Is he saying what I think he's saying? Is he wanting more but uncertain how to get there?

But why? How? There are so many things I want to say but all of them lower my guard and I can't do that yet. I can't let him in more when I still feel like he's partially pushing me away with this *complicated excuse.*

So I focus on that. On the one thing we need to figure out that seems to be standing in the way in his eyes. "Why is it complicated? *How?* I see only *you* when we're together, I don't understand why it's not the same for you."

"We have a history."

"No. *Our families* have a history. Our dads do. It has nothing to do with us," I say thinking back to my dad's comments. About accusations made by a seventeen-year-old Drew, and I wonder what it is that he thinks happened.

"Like I said, complicated," he murmurs

"Family's always complicated. But at the end of the day, there is something here and I'm not willing to get invested in it if I know I'm going to get hurt before I even start."

"There's never a guarantee on that."

"I know but . . ." I pace from one end of the office to the other, frustrated, and fearful that I might lose Drew before we really even find each other again.

"Brexton." He only says my name but there is so much emotion in it that I know he feels there is something between us too. But he's scared of something, and I don't know how to make him not be. "I'm not embarrassed by you," he whispers.

"I was upset when you canceled on me the other night. I know you had an emergency but it feels like you want me in some areas of your life and not others, and that's hard for me when I feel like mine is an open book. I mean, I get it, we've only just reconnected after years. But to me, there's a different level of closeness because we *did* know each other years ago. We were friends. Are friends."

"So you've told your family that we're seeing each other then?" *Not a chance.* I hesitate and he knows why. "You haven't, have you?"

And he's got me. What I'm judging him on, I'm doing the same thing.

"I haven't, no," I admit.

"Why not?"

"I don't know why I'm afraid to. It's almost like I fear that if I do, they'll make fun of me for falling so fast for you."

"Which leads me back to that first night at my house when I said we don't talk about the past."

"But the past is who we are, Drew. The past made us and brought us to this point in time . . ." I make a strangled cry that doesn't make me feel any better.

"See? Complicated."

"It is, but in the same breath it's simple. We have our own lives to live. That—the past, our history, our dads—don't get to own us. Dating someone is hard enough and then dating someone who cancels dates on you at the last minute but doesn't explain why is worse. It makes me feel like I'm simply another willing body to you, like I'm inconsequential, and frankly, I deserve more than that." *I'm twenty-six years old. I want more than that.*

"You do, Brexton." He clears his throat and sighs. "You deserve so much more."

"So can you understand that I'm not ignoring you? It's more that I just need to figure things out."

Like how I'm already head over heels for you, Drew Bowman, when every part of me is telling me that it's too soon. That I need to find my equilibrium before I'm so off-kilter I get hurt.

I know there are no guarantees in love. *Love?* Christ. That thought in and of itself is justification on why I need to pull the reins in just a little. Why I need to make sure we're both in this together and wanting the same things out of it.

Chapter
THIRTY-FOUR

Drew

THEY'LL MAKE FUN OF ME FOR FALLING SO FAST FOR YOU.

Brexton's words mull around in my head. Eat at me.

Did she not realize she'd said them?

Were they a slip of subconscious?

But she did say them and they're out in the open. Now I know where she stands—thank fuck for that. I thought I was being a tad crazy over here feeling the same about her.

How does shit like this happen?

How do you meet someone in your teens, reconnect with them later in life, and just fucking know it was meant to be?

Meant to be? Motherfucker.

How is that possible? Why am I thinking along these lines? And, how do I accept that when I've never been one to think like this before?

It's been football. It's been family. It's been surviving.

And now it's fucking *her.*

Brexton Kincade.

And somehow, I need to make it right again.

I slow my pace at the light and jog in place, waiting for the pedestrian sign to change and traffic to stop.

She thinks I'm embarrassed about her. That's hilarious.

Doesn't she realize I lose my fucking mind every time one of the guys makes a comment about her? About the shit they'd love to do to her? Doesn't she know I'd love to let everyone know she's mine?

Because she is mine.

Hasn't she been in some way or another since that first kiss in the Keys?

It's almost as if seeing her again, being with her again, confirmed something I hadn't realized I'd been looking for. Brex's tenacity. Her energy. Her passion for what's right even when everyone else disagrees. Her dry wit, which so many don't understand, and the way she snorts when she laughs too hard. It's damn adorable.

I forgot about her kindness and compassion to anyone and everyone even when they don't deserve it. And I definitely didn't deserve it when we were younger, and yet she gave grace to me anyway. But now that I've seen her, spent time with her, I remember.

Then there's the obvious. Her looks. Her beauty. The surface that everyone can see when they don't have a clue about the shy girl she used to be. How did that girl turn into this incredible woman? The one with such a natural, sexy-as-fuck confidence?

All these things, all these traits, are things I love about her when I've found them lacking in others.

In every woman I've dated, I've been looking for a little piece of her.

"Christ," I mutter and the lady standing a few feet away from me pushes her stroller a little farther to avoid the crazy man talking to himself.

But I hear Brex's words.

I think I understand what she means.

And didn't she state it that very first time? That we're doing things backward. That you're supposed to date first and then sleep together after?

Well, maybe it's time I show her that I heard her.

It's going to kill me to do it—to deprive myself of her—but maybe it's time I slow things down.

Maybe it's time to start things without a drunken kiss.

Chapter
THIRTY-FIVE

Brexton

Drew: I'm picking you up on Saturday. Be ready at 9 a.m.

I STARE AT THE TEXT AND VIBRATE FROM THE THRILL THAT SHOOTS through me.

It's been four days since we talked. Four days where I stressed over whether I said too much, pushed too hard, and ultimately scared him off.

I mean, we have only really been together a few times, and yet . . . I think I needed to say what I said. I needed to put my mind at ease and get it off my chest.

And now this? A cryptic text. A supposition that I'm not busy.

I'm not.

But if I were, I think I'd figure out how to be free.

My grin is huge when I pick up my phone to answer.

Me: A little demanding, are we?

Drew: Someone has to take charge here. Be ready at 9. Plan to be gone all day.

Me: Am I allowed to ask where we're going?

Drew: No.

Me: How to dress?

Drew: A swimsuit. A jacket. We'll be outdoors.

Me: Anything else?

Drew: I can't wait to spend the day with you.

And if the date wasn't enough, that last line right there was.

I feel like a sap as I sit there and stare at it for way longer than I should, but I don't care. We're going on a date, and the giddy female in me can't wait.

Chapter
THIRTY-SIX

Brexton

11 years earlier

"THAT'S SO FUCKING LAME," DREW THROWS HIS HAND UP, AND Dekker and I glance at each other and roll our eyes.

The *fuck* thing is new this trip. Apparently, Drew is a teenager now and that means he thinks he's cool if he says *fuck* a lot.

Dekker has tried it a time or two but then looks around quickly. Mom and Dad would kill us if they caught us saying it.

"What is?" Dekker asks as she props her feet up on the table and grabs a handful of popcorn, dropping some on the floor as she does.

"Look at that poor sap." He points to the college football game on the TV.

"Who? The guy who just threw that Hail Mary for a touchdown?" Dekker asks with a laugh. "You mean, that one?"

"That's beside the point," Drew says as he flops down on the couch.

"What about him?" I ask, desperate to be in any part of this conversation, because Drew might have to take notice of me. I mean, Dekker is sitting on the couch a foot from him with her long legs and almost boobs, while I sit over here looking like a carpenter's dream—flat as a board and rail straight.

"There is no way on God's green earth you'd catch me putting some girl's initials on my helmet like that QB has. Such a sap."

*We all look at the screen and wait for the quarterback to be shown again. And when he is, sure enough there is a "K ♥ J" on the back of his helmet.

"Maybe he loves her," I say.

Drew snorts. "There is no place for that kind of love on the football field."

"Hold on a second," Dekker says in her overdramatic fashion with hands gesticulating as she turns to face Drew. "How can you say that?"

"Easy. I open my mouth and words come out," Drew says

"You're not funny," Dekker counters.

"Yes, I am." Drew pops some popcorn in his mouth and chews annoyingly to irritate us.

"Aren't you the one who had GH painted on your hand for your homecoming game last month?" she asks.

"No. Never," he says, eyes widening.

"That's such crap. Don't lie. I saw it on your social media. You had a GH for Ginnie Huber on your hand."

"I did not." Drew's voice rises in pitch and then cracks, and we all snicker.

"Yes, you did." Dekker throws a piece of popcorn at him. "Who's the sap now, huh?"

"It's totally different."

"How so?"

"She asked me to put it there. It was homecoming. All the football players did it."

"That's the biggest crock of shit," Dekker says and then glances around quickly as if my parents were magically in the room . . . when we can see them in the backyard through the windows. "None of the other players had initials on their hands. I looked."

"You stalked my football team's pictures?"

"I did, and I didn't see a single one," she says, her grin widening.

"Well, you didn't look hard enough," Drew says.

"So you're telling me that out of the blue, Ginnie Huber asked you to write GH on your hand and you just decided to go along with it?"

"I said it was a long story."

"No, you said it was a homecoming thing. Which is it?" Dekker crosses her arms over her chest, more than thrilled to catch perfect Drew in a lie. "Because it sounds like the kind of story where you thought if you wrote GH on your hand then you were going to make it past first base after the game."

"I don't need initials to get past first base," Drew brags and a tiny piece of my heart breaks as I stare at him, wishing I'd get the chance at first base with him.

He's so cute. His hair is longer this trip so that it curls a little over his ears, but his body is changing. Or maybe it's all the weights he's lifting for football, because he definitely has muscles now. He catches me staring and lifts his eyebrows as if I'm in on this harassing that Dekker is handing him.

I just shake my head and avert my eyes back to the game. *Talk about lame, Brex. Staring? And getting caught? You're such a dork.*

"When did you become so arrogant?" Dekk asks.

"About the time you became so lame," he says.

"Lame? You're the one making fun of that player for doing it." She points to the television. "What's next? Are you going to put a GH on the back of your helmet too so the whole school knows you've done the deed with Ginnie?"

Dekker's words make me wince. The last thing I want to think about is Drew *doing anything* with anyone else. I blush.

"Like I'd ever put that shit on my helmet." He snorts and crosses his arms over his chest in annoyance.

"Not even if you were madly in love?" she asks.

"Nope," he says and emits an exasperated sigh.

"You're telling me if it was the only way to profess your undying love for someone that you wouldn't do it?"

"Dekker." Her name is a frustrated warning.

"Well?" she asks.

"Sure. Yes. Of course. That's *exactly* how I'd profess my undying love for someone. A public statement for everyone to see, because I especially enjoy the guys razzing the shit out of me over it just like I am to the dude on the TV right now."

"I'm serious," Dekker adds.

"So am I. Better yet, I think that's the way I'll propose to the woman I plan to marry. Nothing like ridiculous fucking gestures to make the whole moment that much sweeter."

"But you've always said you're never going to get married."

"Exactly," he says with a definitive nod and a chuckle as he drops the remote control in mic-drop fashion before striding out.

He must be frustrated if he's leaving halfway through a football game.

And by the grin on Dekker's face, she knows he may have *dropped the mic*, but she got in the last unspoken word.

Chapter
THIRTY-SEVEN

Brexton

I OPEN MY DOOR AND ALL BUT SWOON AT THE SIGHT OF DREW standing there. He has on a black V-neck, shorts, and a slow, easy grin that slays me from its start.

"Hi."

"Hi," he repeats and holds out some daisies to me. "These are for you."

I emit the giddiest sound, and I'm not ashamed of it as I bury my face into the wildflowers. "Thank you. They smell beautiful." I reach out and grab his hand.

"I missed you, Brex."

Jesus. It's only been minutes and my resolve to keep him at arm's length is already shot. "I missed you too," I say and step into him to give him a hello kiss, but he steps back before I can land it.

"Not yet."

"Not yet?" I laugh, a little confused.

"It pains me to say that. Especially when you're standing there looking like that and I'm standing here missing you like crazy, but you were right that first night."

"About?" I laugh.

"About how we did this all backward. Sleeping with each other before ever dating, and so—"

"Why do I think I'm going to regret saying that?" she groans playfully.

"Believe me. Falling into bed with you is the easiest thing I've ever done. Staying out of it—doing this the right way—is going to be one of the hardest."

"So what are you saying, Drew?"

"I'm saying we are going on our first date. I made myself a promise that it will be the best first date ever. I owe that to you."

My heart melts into the biggest puddle at his feet, and I can't help but smile. "I don't even know what to say."

"Say you're excited to spend the day with me."

"I am. I most definitely am." I take a step closer to him. "Don't I at least get to give you a kiss hello?" I ask coyly.

He looks at me, jaw clenching, eyes laden with desire. "If you insist."

We meet halfway in the middle. His thumb and forefinger find my chin and tip my face up to his while his lips press the softest, most tender of kisses on my lips.

It's the kind that promises things to come. A level of respect that I've never been particularly shown before from any man other than my dad. This is a kiss of gentleness we haven't shared yet.

Of a first we've yet to experience.

～

I glance over to Drew and shake my head, still trying to believe he went to all this trouble.

He's sitting beside me with a headset on and his hand casually resting on my thigh, as the world outside the window beside him zips away. It's gone from concrete jungle to lush green trees. City to country.

If I thought the date in general was a surprise, Drew pulling up to the airport and walking us onto the tarmac toward an awaiting helicopter was even more so.

He smiles at me, and I want to crawl into his lap and just remember this feeling. That he took the time to plan something for me. Perhaps a little over the top, but incredible nonetheless.

And my body is still reeling from that kiss. Odd when we've already slept together, when we had that hot-as-hell sex against the door in Miami—but there was something about the feeling behind it that told me this was more . . . that he is taking the next step toward trying to figure out what it is that we are.

"Are you going to tell me where we're going yet?" I ask, making his grin widen.

"Right there."

I follow where his finger points and it's a massive lake sprawling between a thick forest of trees. Leaning closer to the window, I take it all in. The glistening of the sun off the lake. The boats zipping around on the water. The green of the trees surrounding it.

It looks like summer and relaxation, and when I turn to look at him my grin is wide. "Really?"

He nods. "Do you remember it?"

It's my turn to stare at him for a beat as realization hits me. He's taking me back to our childhood playground: Lake George. Where we'd spend summers and eat way too many s'mores while trying to scare the crap out of each other with ghost stories.

They are the days I remember as carefree and innocent. When laughter filled the cabins we rented, the nights stretched into lying on our backs and staring at the stars, and when my mom was still alive. It's amazing how I still miss her like crazy after all this time, and after seeing the lake, this is one of those times. Memories flood back. The sound of her laughter as I accidentally overturned the kayak we were in one summer. The way she'd sing the Star-Spangled Banner at the top of her lungs when we watched the fireworks explode over the lake on the Fourth of July. Her penchant for sneaking us kids down to the ice cream parlor under the guise of going to get some exercise and then make sure the evidence was hidden from everyone else. How she'd call us into their bedroom so we could have snuggle time that would end up with giggles and tickles.

Thoughts of Lake George are always happy and carefree. *And Drew brought me here today.* Does that mean he's prepared for some of his past to enter the present?

"Are you serious?"

He just smiles as the pilot informs us that we will be landing shortly.

Drew and I stroll down the small main street, our hands linked and swinging together, and the sun overhead. How many nights did I lay in bed on a trip here and wish for this exact thing? How many things had I mentally bartered for this to happen? Not only for Drew Bowman to notice me as more than Bratty Brex, but for him to hold my hand for everyone to see?

It's funny how life changes and even funnier how when it does, some of those simple things still feel so very important.

Like this.

Like right now.

"What is it you remember most about this place?" Drew asks

"So many things but that ice cream place, the one with the huge cones—"

"The ones that we'd see who could finish first but then be plagued by the worst stomach ever?"

"Yep." I nod.

"Your mom loved that place."

"She did." I smile, loving that he remembers. "Laughter. There was so much laughter all the time is what I think of when I remember our trips. That and getting up in the morning, running down to the dock and jumping in the water, because the last one in was a rotten egg."

He nods, his smile growing.

"Fireworks on the Fourth of July. Days spent swimming and nights spent in front of the campfire," I say.

"It was the best, wasn't it?"

"It was." I look over at him, but his eyes are hidden behind his sunglasses. "More than anything, I remember not ever having to worry about anything. Being a kid. Being carefree. And only thinking about what trouble we were going to get into the next day."

He stops in front of a driveway and takes our hands and lifts them to point at the house in front of us. It's a gray clapboard with white trim. There are beach cruisers out front and an American flag waving from atop the apex of the garage's front.

It looks like idyllic, middle America somewhere with its green grass and overflowing flowerbeds.

"Do you remember this place?" he asks.

I shake my head and then stop as I realize this was *the house* we used to stay in. The Kincades stayed in this one and the Bowmans in the matching blue one right beside it.

"Why do I remember it feeling so much bigger? Being so much farther out of town?" I murmur as I take it all in. Memories flood all at once. Drew chasing Dekker through the front yard with the hose. Maggs and I drawing a chalk hopscotch on the driveway. The joint dock that stretched out toward the lake that served anything from being a performance space to a fishing hole to a raceway.

"Because we were little and everything seemed big back then. Add to that, the town's grown so what felt like the outskirts is now the middle of the town." He pulls me against his side and presses a kiss to the crown of my head, as the two of us stare like idiots at a welcome piece of our childhood in front of us. "But the houses still look the same."

"They do."

"C'mon," he says. "Let's see if it's still there."

"If what's still there?"

He tugs on my hand for me to follow. "We're trespassing. *Drew.* We're going to get into trouble." He just laughs and slows his stride when we hit the side of the house. "What are we doing?" I ask in a harsh whisper.

"It's still there," he murmurs, as he squats down and brushes something off the concrete that I can't see.

"What is?" I ask.

"I thought you might like to see this."

And when he moves his hand, I can't help the sound that comes from my mouth or my immediate reaction to drop to my knees and touch it.

There in the concrete are five sets of handprints—one big, four little—all with initials carved into the center of them.

But there's only one set I reach out to touch. There's only one set with the initials CK in the center. *Claire Kincade. My mother.* Tears well and spill over as I put my hands on my mother's. As I find a connection with her that I didn't realize I so desperately needed.

And I welcome the onslaught of fond memories—joy meshed with sorrow, longing, and heartache—on the side of someone's house where there is laughter somewhere inside. I also notice how my hands are the same size as hers.

I stare through the blur of tears, unable to tear my eyes away from the sight of her holding my hands. The mom I miss so desperately and yet in this moment, feel a little closer to.

Drew's hand rubs up and down my back in support as he sits beside me in silence, allowing me to have a moment I never even knew existed.

He gives me as much time as I need, letting my muted sobs turn into hitched breaths, then into appreciative silence.

"Thank you," I whisper as I rest my head on his shoulder.

"No need to thank me. I thought it might be something you'd want to see."

"How did you even remember this? I didn't."

But I do now. How the owners poured concrete and we all waited until the workers left for lunch before running out and sinking our hands into the slowly-drying slab.

"I remember because I was jealous that your mom would do it and mine wouldn't be caught dead getting cement under her nails."

I smile softly, but I'm filled with bittersweet memories. The next closest person I had to a mom was Brenda Bowman. She's the one I needed when my mom died. She's the one I wanted to hold me tight when my tears coated my cheeks and words wouldn't come.

Because with her I would have been able to express my grief, my sadness. I couldn't do it around my dad. He was already devastated enough that I held it in, that I pretended, but there were so many nights I cried myself to sleep, muffling my sobs in my pillow and wishing I had someone to console me. Someone who understood what my mom meant to our family. To me.

We'd already lost so much and then we lost them too.

I wonder what things would have been like if Gary's scandal didn't happen when it did. *Or at all.* Would Brenda have stepped in to be a pseudo mother to us? Would having had her in our lives saved Dekker the heartache and headaches that came with growing up way too fast and trying to be the mom for us?

Such a significant ripple effect—whatever happened. Why the secrecy after all these years?

I won't, can't, let the *what-ifs* spoil this moment. This memory. She was alive here. Warm, loving, filled with joy.

And that has to be enough for me.

"This is the best gift anyone has ever given me. One I never knew I needed. By the blubbering idiot I became, you can guess I loved it."

"I'm just glad it was still here."

I pull out my phone and take a picture of the memory and have Drew take one of my hands fitting in my mom's. "I think we should go before we get in trouble for being here."

"They knew we were coming. I was able to find their number and ask if it was still here."

"You did that for me?" I ask.

He just gives me a shy smile and helps me to my feet in response.

Chapter THIRTY-EIGHT

Brexton

"WHAT WAS IT LIKE AFTER YOUR MOM DIED?"

I look up to meet Drew's gaze from where my head is resting in his lap. The pebbled sand is warm beneath us and kids are still splashing in the water about ten yards away. The beach is still busy despite the afternoon's sun slowly beginning its descent from the sky.

How do I answer that question? How do you explain what it's like to have your heart ripped out the week after your sixteenth birthday so that you fear you'll never feel again? So that you throw yourself into situation after situation—even if that means getting your heart broken time and again—just to prove to yourself that you can still feel. That your heart is still beating when it feels like it died.

I twist my lips and hold those blue eyes of his before speaking. "It was like trying to find a new rhythm that you knew would never feel normal no matter how much time passed. It was like being thrown off a cliff without a parachute and being told to figure out how to land. Even if you didn't think you'd still survive and the pain would be unbearable."

"I'm sorry."

"It was a long time ago," I say and shift so I can see him better.

"But we weren't around for you guys. We could have been."

"Your world was busy falling apart too, Drew."

He physically rejects the words with a shake of his head. "The lake feels smaller now. It used to feel massive when we looked out at it from here as kids."

The sudden shift in topic couldn't be more obvious, and I struggle with how to navigate this. Let him change the subject and brush it under the rug or just flat-out ask him?

The fact that we're here—that we've come this far figuratively and literally—means I have no choice but to ask.

"Why are you so afraid to talk about what happened with me?" I shift so that I can sit up and meet his eyes.

"Talk about what?" He averts his gaze and I grab his hands in mine.

"Your family. What happened. Anything and everything that is keeping me in your blind spot."

He stares at my hands, his shoulders sagging with what seems like the weight of the world. "My dad is sick," he whispers. "The other night when I landed, when I canceled on you, I'd received a frantic phone call from my mom that he'd been admitted to the hospital."

"Drew." I gasp the name out, terrified for him.

"He's fine. It's fine now. He had a reaction to his new meds and I don't know . . . it was total frantic chaos and she needed me."

"Why didn't you just tell me that? Why . . ." I'm at a loss over what to say. Why the secrecy? It shouldn't be that hard to tell someone who's known you for a long time that a family member needs you. *It's what family does.* "All you had to do was tell me."

"I don't know." He traced a fingertip over the top of my hand. "I felt like telling you was betraying him." I open my mouth, and with a shake of his head, he stops me before I can speak. "I know it doesn't make sense to you, but it does to me. No one knows he's sick. Not a soul and it needs to stay that way. And the last person I think he'd want to know is Kenyon's daughter, especially after everything that happened."

I force a swallow as I try to comprehend what it is that Drew thinks my father had a hand in. What did Gary tell his son to displace the blame to make him appear in a different light?

And as much as I want to shout from the rooftops that my father had nothing to do with Gary's scandal, it's not the time nor place to. In this moment, there's nothing I'm going to say to Drew that will undo a lifetime of being told the sky is green when it's actually blue.

My eyes well with tears, and unfortunately, I can't blink them away before he looks up and finally meets my gaze. The problem is the emotion in his—the worry, the confusion, the discord—as it only makes me sadder.

"So is this the battle we face? The rift that will always be between us?" I ask.

The muscle in his jaw pulses as he tries to figure out his answer. "That's why I said from the first night that the past is off limits."

I blink away the tears wetting my eyelashes and shift to stare at the lake beyond. The breeze has put ripples in it while some spots remain still like glass. Just another reminder that we've both been touched differently by the same events.

He scoots up behind me so that his legs frame mine and my back is to his front. His chin finds my shoulder and his arms pull me against him.

"I'm working on figuring it out, Brex. You—this—is unexpected and awesome, and I have to undo years of being protective of shit I don't even know the whole story of. So bear with me and don't let it ruin whatever this is, because just like you needed seeing those handprints today to bring you back, I feel the same way about you." He presses a kiss to my bare shoulder. "There's something here, something worthy of first dates even when we've already had sex."

I slide my hands over his and close my eyes. Sure, the scenery before me is gorgeous and inspiring, but so is the man at my back. I have to have faith that we'll figure this all out.

"You said your dad was sick," I murmur.

"ALS." There is no emotion to his voice but those three letters are devastating in and of themselves. He clears his throat and clarifies further. "Sporadic ALS."

"I'm sorry." Two words he said to me about my mom, and even though I know from experience that they mean so little in the face of loss, I hope he knows that I am sincerely sorry that he will experience such loss with his dad. My knowledge is limited on the disease, but I do know that there is no full recovery from it.

"It's slight right now. The tremors. But it's like jumping over that cliff you were talking about—even with a parachute, you know the end is going to be fast and painful."

I nod, because I understand what he means. I've already gone through the hell of losing a parent and he's diving headfirst into it. The question is, is it better to be blindsided by it or to see it coming at you?

He presses a kiss to my shoulder and unexpectedly begins to tickle me. There's nothing like fingers on a ribcage to break up a heavy conversation. I wiggle out of his arms and laugh like a hyena.

"Stop. Please stop." I giggle as he holds me in place with one hand while letting his fingers dance over my skin with the other. "I'll give you anything, *anything*, to stop."

"Anything?" he asks as his hand stops, his chuckle suggestive. "I'm trying to be on my best behavior here. Don't tempt me."

"Yes. I forgot," I say in my primmest voice. "My apologies, kind sir."

He chuckles and presses a kiss against the back of my head. "How about this instead?"

"What?"

"This." Drew proceeds to draw something on my back with his finger.

"What are you . . ." But my smile is automatic when I figure out what he's drawing. Does he really remember that conversation like I do? The one about initials on football helmets and hands during homecoming and trying to get past first base or is this just some crazy coincidence? He traces the two letters again. *DB*.

What was the term he used that day way back when? *A sap*. Yes. That's it.

"Are you becoming a sap, Drew Bowman?"

"Me? A sap? I don't exactly think that's a word one would use to describe me." He laughs.

"Sap or not, you've got it backwards. It was me who was desperate to have my initials on your hand after that conversation. I was so jealous of Ginnie whatshername. You wore her initials and you were trying to get past first base with her."

Drew throws his head back and laughs. "Damn that Ginnie Huber. I do believe you and I have long since passed first base."

"I still want the initials on your hand," I tease.

"Here," he says and holds out his hand. "It's all yours."

I hold a hand to my chest and feign excitement. "For me? The dreamy football player is going to wear my initials?"

"He is."

I take his hand and trace BK on the top of his hand a few times, a ridiculously silly smile on my face the whole time.

"Feel better?" he asks.

"I'm on cloud nine now."

"Apparently you're easy to please."

"Shh. Don't tell anyone," I say before relaxing back against him.

Is this what it feels like to be with Drew? Relaxed? Mindful of the past, but not disconnected completely?

Of course I still want to know the truth about the past, the answers concerning what ended our dads' friendship, but maybe this is what it feels like for us to move forward? Maybe this middle ground we've found is enough for us so we can find our own normal.

Because isn't that what today feels like? A step in the right direction? The beginning of what could be an us?

The best part? *I truly feel like he wants there to be an us too.*

This has been the most perfect of days in so many ways and as we sit here, I revel in that notion as kids play, moms scold, and dads gripe about all of the crap they have to carry back to the car.

It's so perfectly normal and I love it.

"At the wedding, you told me I was too afraid to step into the limelight—"

"I was just pissed about—"

"He's my reason," he states matter-of-factly. "If I'm in New York, then I'm near my dad. That allows me to help out when things get bad. And I'm not naïve, Brex. They will get bad. I don't ever want to regret not being there."

"You're too good to be second string, Drew."

He chuckles self-deprecatingly. "I know. And maybe I'd forgotten that. Maybe I'd let that get lost in my duty to my family, but hearing you say it, knowing you believe it, has made me realize how much I put aside my own wants and desires."

I meter the surprise in my reaction when I meet his eyes. I want to feel relief over his sudden revelation, yet I know there is often a long distance between the epiphany and acting on it. "What do you plan on doing then?" I ask hesitantly.

He shakes his head, his expression serious. "The Raptors won't get rid of Hobbs. That means in order for me to be QB1, I'd have to be traded to another team. Regardless of how bad I want to be on that field, is that the right thing to do?"

"I don't think there is a right answer in this situation," I murmur.

"Our relationship—my dad and mine—it's complicated to put it mildly. But he may only have a year left for all I know. Is me being selfish something I should own or will it be the one thing I'll always regret?"

I squeeze his hands in response and wonder how hard that would be. To settle for less professionally so you can give more personally.

It can't be an easy thing.

Especially not on a man's ego.

Particularly when you know you're talented enough to make it elsewhere.

So many layers to this man. I'm guessing there are so many more I don't even understand yet.

"Thank you for trusting me enough to tell me," I whisper and dip my head so I can press a kiss to his bicep. "I'm here if you ever need a sounding board. I won't have the answers but at least you'll have someone you can confide in."

His sigh is the only answer he gives.

With his arms wrapped around me, we watch as the sun slowly sets into the trees surrounding the lake. We watch the first twinkling of the stars, the first sigh of night rustling through the trees, and simply enjoy the silence.

Because we have each other.

Chapter
THIRTY-NINE

Drew

"You're not coming in?" She does a double take as I stand outside her door, our hands extended between us.

I try picturing something, *anything*, to rid the image of how incredible her body looked in that bikini earlier. I'm not sure if it's harder or easier on me knowing that my hands have been on every inch of those curves.

"I can't."

"You can't? I promise I won't make you late for your game tomorrow." She smiles coyly.

"You're not playing fair, Brex." My chuckle is strained.

"What's that supposed to mean?"

"It means it's absolutely what I want to do, but I can't."

Her eyes light up with confusion. "Why not?"

"Because this is our first date, and I promised myself that I wouldn't."

"Oh." Her lips shock open into an O, and I have to tear my gaze away from them and where exactly I'd love them to be wrapped right now. "But my imaginary initials are on your hand."

"That doesn't buy you more, *Ginnie*," I say and laugh. But I'm still not stepping inside. "First dates end in kisses. They end in you shutting the door and me going home worrying if I made the right impression tonight."

"You're serious, aren't you?"

"I'm trying to be."

"You made the right impression, Bowman. No need to worry there."

I grin like a fucking teenager. "Good to know."

"Do I at least get a kiss?"

"I've been working hard to earn one all day," I say as I take a step forward.

"You most definitely earned one," she murmurs when I frame her face with my hands and give in to the temptation that is Brexton Kincade.

I'm going to regret my promise the minute our lips touch. The moment my tongue coaxes her lips open. The second her soft moan hits my ears and rumbles against my chest.

Goddamn this woman.

Her kiss.

Her defiance.

Her beauty.

Her compassion.

Her passion.

I have to force myself to drag my lips from hers. To step away.

Because a man is only as good as his word, and I'm about to go back on my promise if she tempts me much longer.

Brexton groans in protest when I physically remove my hands from her body and brace them on either side of the doorjamb.

"I should go," I murmur.

She nods as her teeth sink into her bottom lip and she looks down to my cock, which is hard and pressing against my shorts. Her eyebrows lift.

"I really should go."

Her laugh is throaty when it hits my ears and does nothing to dissipate the desire.

"Thank you for today, Drew. For remembering old memories and for making new ones with me. For talking. For laughing. For kissing me goodnight after our first date and being a total gentleman."

She steps forward on her tiptoes and kisses me again. This time it's slow and sweet and like a pleasurable torture I can't get enough of.

"Goodnight, Bratty Brex," I say.

"Goodnight, Dreadful Drew."

And when she shuts the door, I rest my forehead against it, hands fisted against the jamb, and emit the longest sigh in the history of sighs.

I told her about my dad.

There's gravity to that. An acknowledgment that I just let her in.

A part of me feels . . . relief at the thought. *I'm no longer completely alone.*

The rest of me is terrified. *What if I'm betrayed?*

Chapter
FORTY

Drew

6 years earlier

"Do you think I didn't know who you were, son, when I recruited you?"

I look over to Roger Molleman, general manager of the Tennessee Tigers, and fight down the emotion that's paralyzing me.

"That I don't remember holding you as a baby or tossing the football with you when you were four or five?"

He twists the championship ring around on his finger, and that's all I can focus on. I can't meet his eyes.

"I knew who your dad was and yet I still took the chance on you when the other coaches would have looked the other way."

My hands fist and jaw hurts from clenching it so hard. It drowns out the pain from being sacked more times than I care to count tonight. The aches from the physical hits have nothing on the pain I felt earlier.

On the pain I still feel bone-deep after getting the news.

"And now . . . fuck, Drew . . . after eighteen games of absolute goddamn brilliance, tonight looked like a fucking repeat of what your dad did all those years ago."

Drew, it's your dad.

"Please tell me you didn't throw the game, Drew."

He was in a really bad accident.

I meet Roger's eyes for the first time and shake my head in disbelief. "How can you ask me that?"

His legs locked up. He couldn't control them. The doctors . . . he's been diagnosed with ALS, Drew.

"It's what everyone's going to be asking. You've got a second string QB dying to play and he had no problem connecting the dots and saying it publicly tonight. To the press. He's talking about seeing you with a bookie in the parking lot after practice. He's saying he watched you give him money."

"That's total bullshit, Roger."

"The press is already having a goddamn field day with it and the game isn't even three hours over."

Yes. It will *kill him. I'm sorry to tell you right before your game, but I thought you'd want to know.*

"Do you think I threw the game?" I ask the man who's been my biggest cheerleader since signing with the NFL. "I've played my ass off and my heart out for this team. Eighteen games to be exact. One full season and two more into my sophomore season with the NFL. How dare you stand there and even ask me that goddamn question."

"And yet I haven't heard a simple yes or no from you."

I stare at him, fury raging and pulse pounding. He is the one person I thought had my back. The one fucking person who would believe me, and yet he's asking questions. He's letting the doubt seep in.

After all the blood, sweat, and tears I've dedicated to this team in the short time I've been here, he's still doubting me?

One fucking bad game, and he's already turned his back? What the actual fuck?

My mom's voice is in my head. Again.

Just like it was during the game.

It's on goddamn repeat.

Over and over and over.

Every sentence of the conversation was like the cadence I'd give before a snap.

Every word was motivation.

I used the anger at first. The rage and the fury over her call to make me play like a wild man. To channel it through aggression.

But somewhere around the start of the fourth quarter, it was like the life had been sucked out of me.

Like I had lost everything.

My will.

My focus.

My ability.

"Your lack of explanation is concerning, Drew. What in the Sam Hill happened out there?"

I grit my teeth and stare at him.

I've overcome deficits, I've scrambled out of pockets, I've avoided blitzes . . . but this is one thing I can't run from. This is one thing a fucking Hail Mary can't fix.

My dad is going to die.

I stare at Roger and my stomach churns. The need to explain, to want to explain, is there and yet isn't he proving my mom right? One bad game and the press is already coming after me. Already assuming the worst.

Just. Like. Him.

I shove away the feeling of betrayal. The hurt.

Do not tell anyone, Drew. If the press finds out they'll say it's karma. They'll say it's justified. They'll vilify him all over again.

Mom, come on. Surely they won't say that. Surely they'll feel empathy for such a devastating diagnos—

No, Drew. Do not tell the press. You have no idea the things they will say. The mud they will drag our family through. We protected you from it as much as possible back then, but now . . . now that you're in the league that threw him to the wolves, I can't begin to imagine the unwanted attention it will bring to your career. Do not tell anyone.

"It all looks too goddamn suspicious. The Drew Hemmings out there today isn't the Drew Hemmings who has played for the past season. He never showed up. Instead I got a bush-league rookie who looked like he was doing everything he could to lose. Put that hand in hand with you being spotted with—"

"Fuck this."

"I need answers and I need them right now," Roger thunders, his voice reverberating off the walls of the empty room and forcing the point home.

He believes them.

Over me.

It's amazing how he's had my back when we were winning and now at the first challenge, the first bad outing, he gave up on me. I thought he believed in me—but now it seems he was only testing the waters.

I stare at him, blinking, trying to comprehend how my world is falling apart and all he can think about is the fucking score.

"Fuck this," I repeat as I kick one of the stools and it goes flying into the wall. "Fuck. This."

And when I walk out of the Tiger locker room, I leave behind the name Drew Hemmings with it.

Chapter
FORTY-ONE

Drew

I LOOK AT THE CLOCK ON THE SCOREBOARD AND GRIT MY TEETH.

Today has been a shitshow. Hobbs's head is somewhere fucking else and it shows in his concentration and passes.

I vibrate with anticipation that eats at me.

That owns me.

The crowd boos as Hobbs intentionally grounds yet another pass when he had two receivers wide open down the field.

"Fuckin' A," my teammate, Pete Umansky, yells to no one in particular. "Make the fucking play!" I glance his way and our eyes meet. "You need to be out there."

I nod, frustrated that I'm not.

"He's wet behind the ears," Umansky continues. "Playing scared. You can't play fucking scared or they'll eat you alive."

"Agreed," I murmur as Justin hands off the ball to a receiver and bobbles it in the process so that the receiver loses his footing and goes down.

"Hey Lonnie!" Pete shouts to our offensive coordinator.

Lonnie looks like a heart attack waiting to happen when he slips one ear from his headset and turns our way. His face is red, his vein is pulsing in his forehead, and his scowl hasn't changed once in the last half of the game. He throws his hands out to the side to ask what Pete wants.

"Get him out of there. The Pats are eating the fucking kid alive. His nerves are wearing on the rest of the guys out there. Quinton doesn't drop passes. Huxley doesn't miss routes. He's fucking up and it's making us look like shit."

"He needs to learn," Lonnie says as Hobbs jogs from the field when he fails to convert the down. But in true chickenshit fashion, he heads to the opposite end of the line so he's as far away from Lonnie as possible.

"And we need to fucking win," Pete snaps back. "Let him learn from the sidelines. Put Bowman in. He'll get the job done. It's who should be starting anyway."

I do a double take at Pete's words. At the unwavering conviction in them and the nods of the heads of the guys around him. I'm shocked as shit.

I know the guys respect me. I know they joke at practice that I should be the one on the field with them. But I thought it was because they were being cool. I thought it was them trying to placate me.

"Yeah, c'mon, Lon," Jergen pipes in. "We've told you we want Bowie in."

But now I know differently.

I meet Jergen's eyes and he nods. Something to tell me he means what he says and it's the push I need.

I storm over to our offensive coordinator as he starts to walk toward Hobbs. "Goddammit, Lonnie, put me in the fucking game," I demand.

He holds his hand up for me to calm down—or shut up—as he presses his hand to his earpiece so he can hear what's being said. He nods as if he's in agreement with the coordinators watching the game from above in the team press box, who are helping call the plays.

"C'mon, man. It's my job to step up. He's drowning out there and taking the rest of us with him." I throw my hand out in frustration.

"He needs to learn from his mistakes, Drew."

"He what?" I shout at him. "You're going to lose another damn game because he needs his hand held? Are you fucking kidding me?"

When I stalk off the field, it takes everything I have not to throw my helmet as hard as I can at the ground.

But I can't.

Team solidarity. And all that shit. Why can't this team get its head out of its ass and see that I should be playing? *I should be on that field. I should be the one leading them.*

But I can't see that changing any time soon.

Fuck.

Is it time I call my agent? Ask for what *I* want?

Chapter
FORTY-TWO

Drew

Brexton: That was a tough loss.

Me: Hobbs is in a slump. In his own head.

Brexton: You could come over. I could cheer you up.

I groan at the invitation. At the desire to get lost in her tonight after being so fucking frustrated during the game.

It pains me to type the response.

Me: I thought we said we were taking it slow. Three weeks? Isn't that what we agreed upon?

Brexton: I may have been intoxicated when I agreed to that. Three weeks is a long time.

Me: We can do it. This getting to know you stuff is fun.

I laugh out loud when I hit send, because I can already hear her groan when she reads it. It's the same sound she's emitted every time I've walked her to the door and turned away.

Brexton: Why three weeks? Why is that the time frame?

Me: Because three is your favorite number.

Brexton: You actually remember what my lucky number is?

Me: You used to count everything in threes when we were kids. How could I forget?

Brexton: Thank God it isn't twenty.

Me: No shit.
Brexton: Is that really why? The three?
Me: Yes.

I take a sip of my beer, sink back into my couch, and put my feet up on the table. There's a soft smile on my lips as I remember how bad we used to tease Bratty Brex about everything needing to be in threes. Skip over three cracks in the sidewalk. Three skips of a rock in the water were her only goal.

Brexton: Slow sucks.
Me: Depends on what we're being slow at.

Does she have any idea how bad I want her right now? How desperate I am to have my hands and mouth on her? My dick in her?

It's been two long weeks of grabbing coffee in that little café in Hoboken. Of phone calls where we talk so long the sun starts to lighten the sky. Of forcing myself to keep my hands off her to prove I want her for more than just sex.

But sex.

It's been on my mind twenty-four/seven. A goddamn stiff breeze would make me hard at this point.

Because that's what she does to me.

She turns me on with her words and her laughter and her intellect and opinions. She keeps me thinking and wanting. I can't wait until these three damn weeks are over so I can give in to the need that grows each and every time we talk.

Brexton: Is this slow enough for you?

And when the attached image opens on my screen, it's my groan that fills my entire house.

Garter belts. Stockings. A lacy bra. No panties. Heels.

All four are laid out on a bed with a card beside it that says: "Wish you were here."

Me: That's cruel.

So fucking cruel.

Brexton: Good thing there's only one week left out of the three.
Me: Good thing.
Brexton: Sweet dreams, Drew.

I laugh.

It's all I can do as my mind fills with images of Brexton and exactly what I want to do to her in the near future.

Too bad my immediate future entails a very cold shower.

Chapter
FORTY-THREE

Brexton

"OH MY GOD, CAN YOU PLEASE STOP TALKING AND JUST KISS ME already?" I ask as he grabs my wrist to try and prevent me from grazing over the denim seam of his crotch again.

His laughter rumbles through the night air as he wrestles me onto my back on the blanket we're on. The night is balmy and the car horns from stories below are loud, but this rooftop oasis in my apartment building is perfect.

"Stop touching my dick." He laughs.

I keep struggling though until he sits atop me, his legs straddling my thighs, and pins my hands to my side.

"Kiss. Me. Now." I pout.

"But I like getting to know you better," he says and grins.

"Drew. Seriously. Two weeks and six days of talking is enough."

"There's still one more day to make it a full three weeks."

"We've talked on the phone more than I've ever talked with anyone in my life. About politics and religion and favorite animals and bucket lists and, and, and. Take me downstairs and, pretty please, will you have your fucking way with me?"

His grin is taunting as it slides across his lips, his cock thick and heavy as it rests against me.

Talk about torture.

The man has done everything possible over the past few weeks to entice and seduce me. Like stopping by after a jog through the city to ask for a bottle of water since he ran out. So of course, he stood in my family

room, shirtless, sweaty, and looking hotter than hell as he downed the bottle I gave him in one fell swoop, only to grin at me, say thank you, and
then jog back down the fourteen flights of stairs and go back to his run.

Or asking me to come over for some takeout at his house only to
find him mowing the lawn—shirtless again—in a pair of gray sweatpants
that just might have outlined every hard line of his cock as he walked
around doing yardwork. The grin he wore told me he knew exactly what
he was doing. My stubbornness told me I wasn't going to let him catch me
looking.

But I looked. I definitely looked.

It's been one tease after another. A suggestive text. An oops, shirts
are overrated so I might as well take it off. A knowing look from him that
feels like he's undressing me with his eyes.

Sure we've gotten to know each other better than I ever thought possible, but in the interim, he's created the sweetest, most torturous form of
seduction. Knowing what he tastes like, feels like, and knowing that he
won't give in and let me have it.

I've been strong.

I've vowed to not beg or plead or open the door buck naked to prove
the point that I want him—although that has been tempting to do.

But when I opened the door tonight and found him standing there
with wine and dessert with rumpled hair and a shy smile, I knew I'd
reached my limit.

I knew I was going to beg, borrow, cajole, or bribe to feel him tonight.

"Only one more day though," he says. "I looked up topics online to
ask a girl you're interested in. The kind that allows you to get to know
them better, and so far, I've found that we've only covered about one of the
four pages of topics. Should I go get the list from downstairs so we can
make some headway on it?"

"You're kidding me, right?" I ask exasperated but giggling. The look
on his face says otherwise. "Oh my God, you're dead serious, aren't you?"

He nods. "The ones I picked to ask tonight are thought-provoking,"
he says in his most serious tone.

"You. This," I say bucking my hips up, "is not helping the situation
any."

"And what might that situation be?"

It's my turn to smile. "How wet I am. How much I want to feel you push into me. Fuck me. Lick me."

That definitely got his attention. His eyes widen and his breath hitches. "You're naughty."

"Take me downstairs and have your way with me, Drew, and I'll show you just how naughty I can be."

He tsks, and the sound elicits another groan from me. "Remember the rules? Extended periods of time indoors in places like residences where there are a lot of flat surfaces, are a no-go," he says, reiterating the stupid rules he invoked when our kisses grew hot and heavy, and I almost broke him of this promise. "They are too convenient to accidentally fall into bed."

"Who needs the bed?" I dart my tongue out to wet my lip.

"Or the couch," he says.

"There's always the table. Or the kitchen counter. Against the wall like in Miami. The shower works too. Then there is the possibility of bending me over the coffee table. Or—"

"Semantics," he murmurs but his eyes eat me alive as I taunt him. And when he leans down, when I think he's going to cave and finally give me what I want—his lips on mine—he presses a kiss to my cheek instead.

I think my groan of sexual frustration could be heard all the way to California.

"Let's talk about favorite places to—"

"No," I shout out in laughter. "I already know your favorites. Your foods. Your routines. How you like to have one leg out of the covers when you sleep. How you have an ungodly time for a quarterback sprinting the forty-yard dash but you hate to run. How you love cauliflower but think broccoli looks like brains—something that makes zero sense. We've done this, Drew—way into the wee hours of the night done this . . . and now, *kind sir*, what I'd really like you to do . . . *is me*."

"Demanding, are we?" he says and lines the tip of his tongue down my jawline where his teeth tug ever so slightly on my earlobe.

"Always."

He kisses his way down the line of my neck and murmurs against my skin, "I kind of like that about you." His fingertips trace ever so slightly down my arms. "That and how you bite your lip when you're frustrated with me." He presses a kiss to my bare shoulder. "Or the way you try not to watch me when I know you're watching me." His tongue lines the shell of my ear and shivers chase over my whole body. "Do you have any idea how hard it's been keeping my hands off you, Brexton? To see you, to want you, to tease you, but to not touch?"

Is it sad to say I'm thrilled to know this was as hard for him as it was for me? That I'm silently rejoicing in the fact?

"Drew." His name is a sigh on my lips. A thank-you, not for the frustration, but the reason behind it.

He leans back and our eyes meet. I feel like so many things pass between us. An acknowledgment that there is definitely more here than just sex. That this has been time well spent. Exasperating and sexually frustrating but well spent. That emotions are running deeper than we're willing to let our words express.

But even unspoken, the weight of the moment is still there despite the playfulness a moment before.

And then without saying another word, Drew suddenly rises off me and walks away.

"What the hell?" I say confused, but then quiet with a scrape of patio furniture and a sound of metal on metal. "What are you . . ." My words fade when I see Drew walking toward me, hands unbuttoning his pants, then one hand on his cock.

"Blocking the door. After waiting two weeks and six days, I definitely don't want to be interrupted."

My body hums with an anticipation I don't think I could ever put words to as he drops to his knees before me.

"There are things I've been dying to do to this body of yours, Brex. Things I want to touch." He grabs my legs behind the knees and spreads them apart.

Good thing for boho skirts and their easy access.

"Certain locations I want to lick." His fingertips trace their way up my inner thigh to their apex and run over the top of my panties.

I moan from his touch. It's almost unbearable having him so close yet feel so damn far away.

Much like it has the past twenty days.

"Places I want to fuck."

His eyes lock on mine as he dips his head down, hooks my panties to the side, and then licks his way between my seam.

I cry out. Buck my hips. Fist my hand in his hair. Lose all sense of everything but the warm, wet heat of his tongue dipping into me. Tasting me. Pleasuring me.

His groan is an aphrodisiac in and of itself.

But it's not like I need much to detonate. The back and forth of the past few weeks have been a slow simmer, a fireworks show without a grand finale, and this right here—Drew's tongue—is all I need to ignite and then explode.

It's in my soft sighs and fisted hands as he licks and sucks and pushes me easily into the oblivion I've been teetering on since Miami.

It feels like forever ago but when I crash hard over the edge, all time is erased.

The palpable frustration.

The searing foreplay.

The agonizing waiting.

Because it's just me and Drew and a deep-rooted connection I've never felt before with anyone else.

His eyes find mine as he rises from between my thighs. His grin is arrogant and his eyes are laden with lust.

And when he pushes into me ever so slowly, when my name falls from his lips in a sigh of desire, I know Drew Bowman owns more than just my body.

He owns my heart too.

Every damn piece of it.

And with that acknowledgment, I feel like I can finally breathe.

Chapter
FORTY-FOUR

Brexton

"I'm dying here, Kincade."

"Dying is hardly the term that comes to mind when I think of a starting NFL quarterback who is making more in one year than most people make in their lifetime," I say with a lift of my brows, as Chase sits across the conference room table from me and shakes her head. "But what do I know?"

"I don't find that amusing," Justin says.

"And the GM with the Los Angeles Chargers isn't exactly *amused* with your performances over the last two games, so maybe instead of dying here, you need to step it up out there on the gridiron."

Chase narrows her eyes and I write out "Hobbs" on my notepad and slide it across the table. She emits a laugh and rolls her eyes.

"You're supposed to have my back," he complains.

"No. Finn is supposed to have your back. I'm just the sidepiece who's trying to get you action without any commitment from you for the long-term."

"If we're talking in dating terms I should tell you ahead of time, I don't date. I prefer to fuck and move on."

"Lucky for her."

"That was low." He laughs.

"And you need to learn how to treat a woman properly," I deadpan. "I think you need to keep your focus on the field, Hobbs. Sell yourself there, because no one is going to want to take on your salary if you're not backing it up with your play."

"So you're still working on it then?"

I laugh. It's all I can do at his relentlessness. "Something like that."

And when he hangs up, Chase looks over at me and shrugs. "Please don't tell me that's the fucker who has put that extra bounce in your step because if he is, then you seriously need to have your head examined."

"I have higher standards than that," I tell my little sister.

"Not always."

"Screw you." I throw my pen at her and she dodges, so it falls with a thump on the floor as her laughter rings out. "Should we talk about you and your standards?"

"Honey, so long as they're hard and last long, that's all I need."

"Jesus." My father coughs the word out as he sticks his head in. "I think this is a conversation I don't need to be any part of."

"Wise move," I mutter as he backs away and closes the door to the conference room.

"You're just as crass as Hobbs is."

"I like to call it truthful. You need the fancy words and small gestures. I, on the other hand, need some back-bending sex, with a pat on his ass when I pass him face down in the bed as I leave, with no promises or words spoken. Simple."

"You're so full of shit."

"I wish I weren't, but it just makes things so much easier in the long run." She crosses her arms and leans back in her chair. "And since it isn't Hobbs who has your cheeks full of color, who, pray tell, is it?"

"Ah, so that's why you decided to come and sit in here with me."

"What do you mean?" She feigns innocence.

"You're the worst liar of the lot of them. Who asked you to try and get it out of me? Lennox or Dekk?"

"Me." She gives me a cheesy grin that confirms I've been the topic of discussion when I haven't been here.

"That's the biggest load of crap I've ever heard."

"Why all the secrecy?"

"It's not secrecy, it's just . . ." I sigh and shake my head. "This one matters, Chase."

Her head startles. "Haven't they all?" She chuckles.

"And that's why the secrecy. Thank you for proving my point."

"No. Wait," she says as I snap my laptop closed and gather my papers. "You're being serious."

I take a second before I meet her eyes. "I know my love life is a joke to you guys. I get you don't understand it. I'm more than aware that I date—*a lot*, that I fall in love, and then out of love—*a lot*. But there's something about this guy, Chase."

"Like what? He's a god in the sack?"

"There is that." I make no attempt to hide the grin that slides onto my face. "But it's more than that."

"Like what?"

"You wouldn't understand. You see men as an itch to scratch. As someone to use for some stress release when you've decided you want to take a minute to stop conquering the world. You're intimidated by anyone or anything because you have plans, and nothing is going to get in the way of that."

"Thank you, Dr. Kincade. I wasn't aware you'd gone back to school to get your degree in psychology," she teases with an annoyed edge to it.

"It's true. When was the last time you had a relationship? When you looked forward to talking to someone just because, and there was no ulterior motive to sleep together?"

My little sister stares blankly at me and then huffs out a breath. "Just because I'm different than you, doesn't mean it's a bad thing."

"Exactly," I say with a nod.

"So what if I have a list of things I want to accomplish before I fall down the rabbit hole of love? It's not that I don't believe in it, it's more that I don't want to be sidetracked by it."

"And I understand that and I love that about you . . . but that means you don't have a clue how I feel when it comes to this."

"Then explain it to me. I'm not emotionally stunted. I'm just busy—all the time—and feelings get in the way of my drive."

I stare at Chase, at the one who wants to conquer the world, and smile softly. "He scares me. The way he makes me *feel*. The way he makes me *want*. I'm terrified that letting outsiders know about us, will ruin what we have."

"But isn't that the test of any good relationship? Being able to withstand the outside influences and pressures?"

Always practical, she has a point there.

A point I'm not ready to feel out yet but know we'll have to tackle very soon.

Chapter
FORTY-FIVE

Brexton

"THIS IS JUST WHAT THE DOCTOR ORDERED," JULES SAYS, AS SHE LIFTS up the glass of wine and takes a healthy sip. Her auburn hair bobs as she does a little wiggle and a smile.

"A ridiculously long honeymoon to the Mediterranean was that rough, huh?"

"No. Not because of that." She rolls her eyes and swats at my arm. "More like I feel that the wedding consumed my every waking second for so damn long and now that it's over, I can breathe again."

"Well, everything went off without a hitch. It was gorgeous." I look around the outdoor farmer's market where we've taken up space at a table somewhere between a florist and an organic produce stand. People mill about from vendor to vendor on this warm evening. "And Mildred? She is incredible, and I'd like to thank you for seating me at her table."

Jules laughs. "She's one of a kind."

"She definitely is."

"Thank you for meeting me for a drink. I know you're crazy busy and time is sparse, but I'm glad to get to see you, even if it's only for a few minutes."

"I'm glad you called. It was—"

"Don't look now," Jules says, prompting me to look in the direction her eyes are focused.

"What?"

"Don't look yet. Two o'clock. A drop-dead gorgeous guy."

"You told me not to look and then gave me directions where to look." I laugh and wave my hand at her. "You're married now."

"Not for me! Jesus, seriously?" She laughs. "I'm talking about for you."

I level her with a glare. "Just because you are deliriously happy, doesn't mean you get to try and fix me up."

"Oh my. Is there nothing sexier than a super-hot guy who's a dad? And he's buying flowers. Probably for his wife. What a good man to show his daughter how she should be treated."

"Mm-hmm," I murmur, more than aware of how Jules takes one tiny thing and runs with it.

And running with it, she is.

"I mean look at his biceps flex when he picks up his little girl. Could you imagine arms like that framing you as he hovers over you and—"

"TMI and especially from a married woman."

"Honey, I'm picturing Archer over me, not him, but uh—you should picture it because *damn*. Those arms. That ass. That height." She lets out a long, low whistle.

"Whatever."

"I mean why does that make my uterus clench as if it's going to beg him to make it full?"

"Down, girl." I laugh but turn to look at the object of her attention more to stop her from going on than anything.

But my laugh fades into confusion when the man and little girl turn to face our way.

When I see his face.

When I realize—

"Isn't that Drew Bowman?" she asks.

So many thoughts cloud my head. All I can do is nod as I take in the little girl in his arms with the same eyes and coloring.

We're having a long practice tonight. I'll call you later.

His words from earlier run through my head as confusion grows. *And anger.*

"Drew!" She waves to him and his head snaps our way.

He freezes for a second—his eyes locking with mine as his expression falls.

Yes. You've been caught in a lie.

He recovers quickly but not fast enough. I catch his shock at seeing me there.

"If I were single I'd climb that man like a tree, Brexton," she murmurs as he makes his way over to us.

And for some reason, it's not Drew I stare at as they move, but it's the little girl. The blue of her eyes. The brown curls that bounce in her hair. The way her little fingers curl around his pointer finger.

My heart is in my throat as so many scenarios race through my mind. Is this why Drew has kept me at arm's length?

Because of her.

Drew has a daughter.

I don't even know how to put words to how I feel—confused, hurt, overwhelmed, surprised—and yet all of them ride a tidal wave through me as Drew steps up to our table.

"Ladies," he says and surprises me when he leans forward and presses a chaste kiss to my lips. "Hi."

My heart sighs through the confusion. How can he act like nothing is wrong, like this isn't a big deal, when it truly is?

He kept this from me.

He lied to me.

"Jules," he says turning to my gob-smacked friend as she looks at me then back to him with a knowing smile on her lips. "Good to see you again. I hope married life is treating you well."

"You two—do you—are you . . ." She points from him to me and back.

"Something like that," he says with an easy charm and a warm smile. One that I also have plastered on my face but is nowhere near being sincere.

"Who's this?" Jules asks the question that has been owning my mind despite Drew acting as if there is nothing odd here.

"This," he says with a dramatic flair and a roll down of his hand, "is my niece, Miss Charley."

Oh, fuck.

Not his daughter.

No.

His niece.

Maggie's daughter.

It takes a second for my brain to process this newfound information but when Charley giggles, there's no need to.

The sound is pure joy and the smile that it puts on Drew's face is even better.

"Hello, Miss Charley," Jules says as she reaches out to shake her hand. "It was a pleasure to meet you, but I must run."

"No. Jules—"

"Sit. Stay. Take my seat, Drew. Make sure Brexton here drinks another glass," she says with a wink and a smile and before I can utter another word, she's gone.

We both look after her and then back toward each other with astonished looks on our faces—before we laugh to fill the suddenly awkward silence.

When I turn, I find Charley studying me. She's a gorgeous little girl with curious eyes and a crooked smile just like her uncle. "What's your name?" she asks.

"I'm Brexton." I squat down so I'm at her level and hold my hand out. "Nice to meet you, Charley."

She looks at my hand but instead of shaking it, comes forward and gives me a huge hug that surprises the hell out of me.

"You're pretty," she murmurs as she plays with a strand of my hair.

"Thank you. You are too."

When I look at Drew, he has a strange look on his face as he watches our interaction.

"We got flowers for Nana," she says and points to the peonies that Drew set on the table.

"They're gorgeous. I bet they smell pretty too."

"They do." She nods and reaches out to touch their petals.

Drew clears his throat and I glance over to him. "Today is Charley and Drew day," he says as he holds his hand out for Charley to come to him. She moves to him and he hefts her up into his arms with an ease that says he's completely comfortable with her.

I stare at them, uncertain how I feel. My heart is warmed by his obvious ease and love for his niece. Who doesn't love a man who loves children?

At the same time though, if she is this big part of his life, why hasn't he mentioned her? How come he's felt the need to keep her a secret from me?

The thoughts erode at the feeling of security I've had when it comes to him and us.

"Brex?"

"What? Sorry." I shake my head and snap from my thoughts.

Drew studies me and concern glances through his eyes. "I said we were about to go feed the ducks at the park and then head back to my house."

"It's sleepover night," Charley says and throws a fist into the air.

"Sleepover night?" I exclaim.

"It's jammies and juice and Jenga." Her eyes are wide with excitement. "Can she come too?" She turns to Drew and asks.

He tugs on her hair and she giggles.

"Would you like to join us?" Drew asks.

"Thank you, but I don't want to interfere with your time."

"Uncle Drew says it's nice to include people. We never want to make someone feel sad. So let us include you." The innocence in her eyes and voice are everything that is good about kids.

"Yes," Drew says and reaches across the table to squeeze my hand until I meet his eyes. "Let us include you."

"I don't want to—"

"I want you to." His voice is soft, his smile is warm and inviting.

"I want you to, too," Charley pipes in. "Except for the sleepover part. Nana says boys and girls aren't supposed to sleep over at each other's houses."

I laugh, because it's something Brenda said many times when we were kids. "Your nana is very right." I wink.

"Then you'll come with us? For ducks and dinner at least?" Drew asks.

My smile says it all.

Chapter
FORTY-SIX

Brexton

"She really is a sweetheart," I say as I look at Charley. She's lying across the couch at his house, snuggled in unicorn-print footy pajamas, with her head on a pillow propped in Drew's lap.

Drew looks down at his hand where he absently plays with her curls and smiles softly. "She is. She can also be a stubborn devil but it seems she was on her best behavior for you tonight."

"Apparently I was known for being quite the devil at times too. Along with being quite the scaredy-cat." I shrug. "But I digress."

He chuckles and grabs his bottle of beer from the end table beside him, takes a long sip of it, and when he sets it down, stares at it for more than a beat before finally meeting my eyes.

"You're upset," he murmurs, his tone reticent. Concern etches the lines of his face. "I'm sorry."

"I'm trying not to be hurt that we've been dating each other this long, that we went through the three weeks of getting to know everything about you gathering, and yet I didn't know about this. About her when obviously, you guys are super close. About . . ." My voice fades as I look at her and a lump forms in my throat. "About your life before."

I wait to gain control of my emotions before I meet his gaze again. His nod of acknowledgment is so slight, so resigned, but it's there, and it kind of kills a little piece of me.

"There's a lot you don't know still, Brex."

"But why?" I ask, realizing this is going to be an interesting conversation with a sleeping child in between us. "Do you not trust me?"

"This has nothing to do with trust," he asserts.

"Do you not think that—"

"You simply wouldn't understand."

"Have you tried seeing if I do? Because we've talked about everything about me. My mom dying. How I felt after I had to withdraw from the Olympics. What it's like working for my family. We've talked about everything and yet here you are still keeping secrets from me. That's a hard one to swallow and not be hurt by."

His sigh is long and loud and feels as heavy weighing on him as it sounds.

"What is it you want to know, Brex? That our world fell apart? That since the day my dad walked away from the NFL my family has never been the same? That my dad no longer seems like my dad? That he became a shell of the man he was?" His voice is calm but there's devastation to it that I think only hints at the damage underneath. "That Maggs fell into a bad crowd and got hooked on drugs because she didn't have any guidance? That, for her, it was easier to be high than to deal with our house where we all walked around like nothing happened when our lives had been torn apart because everything did? Will it make any sense to you that I turned to football—to the very sport that ruined him—and he's never forgiven me for it? Almost like I betrayed him for being good at something that rejected him? Is that what you want to know?" Despite stroking his niece's hair, he is bristling with anger. It *looks* like it's directed at me, but that can't be the case.

What the hell did his dad do to his family?

And poor Maggs. Where is she now?

My heart hurts for him right now. For the teenager who went through it all alone and for the man now trying to live with all of it behind the scenes without anyone knowing.

I move toward him, needing to touch him, needing to comfort him. With Charley in his lap—her soft snores between us—I drop to my knees in front of him, take his hands in mine, and press a kiss to one of his palms.

"Drew . . . I'm sorry. I had no idea."

"No one knows. No one fucking knows, and it's been ingrained in our heads for the past fucking decade that no one *can* know. Our life is private and anyone who knows will use it against us." He shakes his head. "At first it was the notion that just one fucking story, one reminder of the past, would shatter the perfect world we all pretended to live in. And now it's if a story gets out, the stress of it all will make my dad's health decline rapidly as stress is a trigger with ALS." He pulls his hand from mine and runs a hand through his hair. "Is that the part of me that you need to know? The deep, dark secrets. Is that enough to make you happy?"

"That's unfair. I just want to know you, Drew. All of you."

Because I'm in love with you.

It's the first time I've allowed myself to think those words, to admit those words to myself. I stumble over the confession because there's so much unspoken between us—the blame he somehow lays at my family's feet—that has me fearing he'd never accept the words even if I did put a voice to them.

"Well, that's it. You happy? Every damn day I'm trying to keep all the plates spinning—my sister sober and alive, Charley feeling loved and oblivious to her mom's addiction, my dad proud of me when all he's ever done is shun me for playing a game that shut him out, and my mom in fucking la la land so that the nervous breakdown she's always teetered on stays at bay—so none fall off and shatter. It's exhausting, but if they all stay spinning, maybe, just fucking maybe, I'll get a chance to be me, to do what I need to do to be happy. To have my own fucking life."

His voice breaks on his last words and he slides out from beneath Charley's sleeping head and me sitting at his feet and moves about the room to abate his restlessness.

I watch him pace as I turn where I am and sit there. He's hurting and I don't know how to help. He's hurting and I'm afraid he doesn't want me to help.

"Drew," I say softly. A plea. An attempt at comfort.

"*Don't you know that's you?*" he whispers as he turns and faces me. "You're my chance, Brex. Taking the goddamn field in a game is my chance. And I'm fucking terrified that if I get an opportunity at either, that I'll screw them both up royally and never get a shot again."

There are tears in his eyes when they meet mine. There is a gravity, a somberness, to his expression that owns my heart in ways I never knew imaginable.

"I don't even know what to say."

"I've fallen for you, Brexton. Can't you see that? So you tell me what I'm supposed to do about it. I'm stuck in between a rock and a goddamn hard place when all I want to do is be with you."

I stare at him, eyes wide and heart soaring.

He loves me.

He's in love with me.

He drops to his knees in front of me. As I sit there stunned, he frames my face with his hands and whispers, "I'm in love with you, and fuck if it doesn't feel like maybe I have been my whole life."

And when his lips meet mine, it's the softest, most innocent of kisses, but it means more than any other kiss I've received in my lifetime.

He leans back to meet my eyes as if to make sure I'm okay with everything he's just said, and it's only then that I realize I haven't responded to him with words.

Right as I start to speak, Charley's little voice speaks up beside us. "Uncle Drew," she murmurs in a groggy voice. "Can you not kiss her? That's gross." We both chuckle. "And can I go to my bed now?"

"Of course," he says as he leans over and presses a kiss to her temple before carrying her up the stairs.

I startle and then smile when I hear them on a baby monitor I never even noticed on the kitchen counter. Her murmured *good nights*, his *sleep tights*.

What man has a baby monitor for when his niece decides to spend the night? Come to think of it, a room for her too? But now that I think back to how Charley talked about her Drew and Charley date, this seems like a pretty regular thing.

God, what a good man.

And in case everything Drew just said to me didn't make me love him, the way he is with Charley did.

I've almost drifted off on the couch when he comes down the stairs. He stands there and stares at me, his expression one of disbelief.

Is he regretting what he told me? Is he going to make excuses and take it back?

"I don't have much to give you, Brexton," he says as he makes his way across the room and sits down on the couch beside me. "I have a family who's fucked up. I have a career that is mediocre if not embarrassing at best. I have a shit ton of baggage that I can't unpack any more than I already have. And I have parents who might never accept the fact that I'm in love with you. I'm so . . . torn. To have worked my whole life to try and make him happy and finally the first time I feel happy, it's with you. *A Kincade.*" He laughs, but it's self-deprecating at best.

I cringe. There is so much in that last statement, how he thinks his career is mediocre, embarrassing. That's rough enough. But that bit about his parents? They used to think of me as one of their own kids. That was how our families were together. Would they really think of me like that? With disdain? That his choice of me is a poor one? *Do I deserve that?*

I crawl into his lap, rest my head against his chest, and simply hold him tight.

"I'd never ask you to pick between me and your family," I murmur knowing I never could either.

"I know. I just . . . I know how I feel and it's the scariest, most fucking real thing I've ever felt, and it's overwhelming. I thought if I held all of this back from you, it would let me keep my distance, it would keep this a little less *everything* . . . but I can't. This is me, Brexton. Warts and all."

I lift my face so he can see me, so he can hear me. "I've fallen for you too, Drew Bowman. I think I've been falling for you my whole life. It's only now I realize that I've compared everyone I've dated to the man I thought you'd grow up to be. Little did I know, that man was even more incredible than I'd imagined."

Chapter
FORTY-SEVEN

Drew

"I HAVE TO GO," BREXTON WHISPERS AS I HOLD HER TIGHTLY AGAINST me.

"No," I groan.

"Yes. Little Miss Charley is going to get up soon and wonder why Uncle Drew's friend Brexton is sleeping in his bed." She chuckles and fuck that sound makes me harder than I already am. "Remember, boys and girls aren't supposed to have sleepovers together."

But she has a point. One I'd like to ignore but a good one nonetheless.

I sigh. "Don't go yet. It's still dark out. Just five more minutes?"

She snuggles into me, her hand on my chest. "Okay, but no funny business."

"Promise," I murmur against the crown of her head as my finger traces letters on her hand.

It takes her a few seconds to catch on to what I'm doing. To try and figure the letters out.

"ILYB?" she says, looking up at me with her nose scrunched and her eyes narrowed in the most adorable of ways. But I see the minute she gets it. The four words. Her expression softens and a smile crawls onto those gorgeous lips of hers.

"I love you, Brexton," I say, surprised that I confessed my feelings to her last night but more so now that I'm just as comfortable saying it again to her.

"Take that, Ginnie Huber," she jokes. "I've got four letters to your two."

Chapter FORTY-EIGHT

Brexton

MY COFFEE IS STRONG AND THE MORNING AIR IS CRISP WITH THE first real traces of fall. The summer has had an extended stay in New York this year and as I sit with my knees drawn up to my chest on the rooftop of my building, I'm more than ready for the seasons to start changing.

This rooftop.

I smile with a shake of my head and think about how Drew and I made love here almost two weeks ago.

Yes, we made love.

That's what it was. Because words hadn't been exchanged yet, but our hearts had already decided.

It feels surreal.

It feels perfect.

And yet, why do I feel like I'm waiting for the other shoe to drop?

I take a sip and let the potent liquid scald my tongue as I debate the one thing that's been weighing on my mind: I'm hiding Drew from my family.

I'm in love with a man. A man who loves me, and the very notion I haven't told anyone or talked to anyone about it other than Jules, given she saw us at the farmer's market, is utterly fucking ridiculous.

But why aren't you, Brex? Why do you feel the need to keep things so private?

Is it because you're afraid Drew might be right? That Dad might have had a hand in whatever happened to Gary Bowman? If that's the case, it would shed a different light on the man you've put on a pedestal your whole life. *Make you look at him differently.*

The thought staggers me.

Then I immediately reject the notion, but it's already out there, the epiphany lingering.

Is that why I'm hesitant to say anything? Do I really think he knows more than he's letting on? Is it a possibility?

Drew certainly thinks so. He may not have said it outright but it's there, unspoken and hanging between us.

I snuggle back in my seat, my eyes taking in the city laid out before me but not really focusing on anything. I'm at a loss for words.

Because for the first time, I completely understand how Drew feels.

The rift is there, and we're both at fault for not confronting it.

The question is, how do we go about healing it? I'm not sure our past can stay in the past if it causes conflict, both now . . . and into the future.

Chapter
FORTY-NINE

Drew

3 years ago

I SHOULDN'T BE HERE.

I've had enough whiskey tonight, had too much time to think, and I fucking shouldn't be here.

And yet still I push open the door and walk into my parents' house. It's bright and airy and a goddamn farce to the weight I feel every time I step foot in this freaking tomb.

"Drew." My dad's head jolts when he sees me standing there.

"There's the man of the hour," I say. I don't give a shit that I sway as I walk into the family room where he sits with his reading glasses near the tip of his nose and his iPad in his lap.

"Drew?"

I chuckle as I shake my head and ask, "Do you know what I did today?"

He raises his eyebrows. "Apparently, drink."

"Bingo." I snap my fingers. "Do you know what else I did?"

"I don't have time for this—"

"I watched the team I was traded from, the team I was a starting QB on, win the fucking Super Bowl." The words feel like I'm chewing broken glass to get them out.

"It happens." His voice is measured.

"It should have been me."

He sets his iPad on the table beside him and sighs. "It could have been a lot of people."

"No, Dad. Me. Fucking me," I shout. "But it wasn't. You want to know why? Give you three guesses."

But he doesn't speak. He doesn't say a goddamn word other than look at me with that irritated look on his face. The one that says I should just *get over it*. I feel like I've been just *getting over it* for ten fucking years without an explanation why.

"All because of something that I had nothing to do with but that has affected me my whole goddamn adult life."

"We've talked about this before."

"No. Actually, we haven't. You stood there. You said you quit. You said it was never to be talked about again. Well guess what? I'm here to fucking talk about it, *Dad*." I walk from one side of the room to the other, my hands itching to grab him and shake the damn answer out of him. "Did you do it? Did you fucking slip off that perfect throne you sit on every damn day, judging all of us, and actually do it? Because you walking away without a fucking word says you did. You pretending like—"

"That's e-goddamn-nough," he thunders.

"It's never been enough. Not for Maggie, who's a fucking wreck. Not for mom, who stood by your side like a puppet on a string. Does she even know the truth? And sure as hell not for me, who you glare at every time I walk in this house. Why? Because you can't handle the fact that I'm trying to live out a dream you fucking walked away from."

"You could never be me," he shouts, knocking me back.

I stare at him, completely stunned by his words.

Hurt.

Crushed.

Sobered.

I blink as I process and the realization of what it is he's just said plays over the expression on his face. Anger. Disbelief. Awareness.

"That's not what I meant, Drew." He pushes up out of his seat but I'm already heading toward the door. "Drew. It came out wrong. It—"

"Don't you fucking touch me," I yell, as I yank my arm from his grasp and spin around with my fist cocked and no hesitation over willing to let it fly. A fury like I've never known before races through me. A debilitating feeling—one foreign to me—chases right behind the rage.

"Drew. Please." There are tears in his eyes, as if the ice man has thawed.

But only from regret.

Only out of fear.

"I hope to God you are never like me," he says, but it's too late. He's already said the words.

"No worries there."

When I walk out and slam the door behind me, he doesn't follow.

I run down the middle of the street as fast as I can until I can't breathe and double over on a sidewalk.

They're trading you out, Drew.

Even though they found nothing on me, even though I'm innocent, the Tigers no longer wanted a name on their roster like mine. One that has accusations tied to it everywhere he turns.

The Tigers win the Super Bowl. What an incredible game!

The announcers' declarations were like a taunt. Telling me what I missed. What I'll never have.

You should be happy Florida took you.

How could I be happy when I'm so far away from my family?

You could never be me.

Where I'm relegated to sitting on the goddamn bench week after week.

Alone.

All fucking alone.

Because of him.

Chapter
FIFTY

Drew

I ROLL MY HEAD BACK ON MY SHOULDERS AS FRUSTRATION EATS AT ME. Another fucking game stuck on the sidelines.

Another goddamn game where Hobbs's inexperience screams loudly.

And for what? For the Raptors to make sure they're not wasting their fucking money in that huge contract they're paying him.

He's a fucking flop. He has more talent in his pinky than most quarterbacks, so he needs to get past this block. His mental game is weak as shit. I know what that's like. But I kept fucking trying, even when knocked off my pedestal.

The Georgia crowd roars when his pass sails wide for the third time in as many downs. Thank fuck Georgia is playing just as poorly. The only reason we still have a chance is because they've made just as many mistakes as we have.

The stands explode in cheers when Hobbs fails to get the first down. Victory is so close they can taste it.

And it makes me sick to my stomach.

I turn my back to the game, unable to watch for one more second.

"Hey, Bowman?"

I turn at the sound of Lonnie's voice. "It's not your plays," I say, answering the question he's been giving me with every game as of late. "It's Hobbs. It's—"

"You're in next sequence."

I do a double take at his words. "Come again?"

Did I hear him right?

"We have five minutes left. You think you can pull this off? You think you can find a way to pull a touchdown out of your ass?"

My grin is my answer as I pull my helmet on and snap it into place.

The next minute goes by in a blur. Hobbs loses the ball in a turnover. He stares at me as he jogs off the field with a mixture of confusion and relief when he sees my helmet on talking to the coordinator.

Then I wait.

As our defense holds the line and prevents Georgia from advancing. As they force a punt into our hands.

It's showtime.

When I jog onto the field, the only thing I can hear is my pulse pounding in my ears. Not the fans cheering. Not the guys arguing in the huddle. Just my pulse and the confidence that I can do this. That all those nights putting extra time on a darkened field beside the stadium are going to pay off right now. *This is what I've worked for. This is my strength. I'm the goddamn QB1.*

Get the job done, Bowman.

"We've got two minutes left. Plenty of time to score," I say to the guys all looking at me in the huddle before reading off the play to them.

"Right out of the gate?" my tight end asks about my plan.

"Right out of the gate," I say with a nod and a grin.

The ball is set.

The cadence is shouted.

The ball is snapped into my hands.

I dance back into the pocket, hoping the line holds to buy enough time for Nix to get downfield.

C'mon. C'mon. C'mon.

I see the first break on the right side as a Falcon pushes through. I take a few steps to the right as he's yanked down by my lineman.

Get there. Get there. Get there.

Another breach on the right side.

But this time I don't move away.

This time I pull back and let it fly.

The ball sails in the air and a moment later I'm struck, thrown through the air, and hit the ground with a grunt. The lineman is on top of me but my head is angled to our sidelines so I see the entire bench celebrate.

Arms raised. Fists pumping. Fingers pointing at me as they jump up and down.

As my running back and my Hail Mary cross into the endzone.

Chapter
FIFTY-ONE

Brexton

I vibrate with anticipation as I wait for him to get here.

Pride all but bursts in my chest as I relive the moment over and over. Drew's unexpected substitution for Hobbs. My cheers of support in my empty apartment to a TV screen. The Hail Mary. Its gorgeous spiral forty yards downfield. The roar of the crowd when Nix caught it. The Raptors winning because of it.

I've been on a high ever since.

And not just for the Raptor's win. For Drew. For him to touch the field and make a difference has to be a huge boost to his ego. To his pride. To his status on the team. And all of the above hopefully do a number on that self-confidence of his.

Drew fucking Bowman just showed the world that he is the real deal, and I couldn't be more proud of him.

When he gets to my door, I fling it open before he can even finish knocking, and launch myself into his arms with a squeal of excitement.

My greeting comes in my kisses with my legs wrapped around his waist and "that was incredible" over and over.

It comes in laughter and praise and love.

So much love.

And I show him just how much of it when we stumble to the couch before I start stripping his clothes off.

Chapter
FIFTY-TWO

Brexton

"Do you really have to go?" I groan as he crawls over where I'm lying in my bed and plants another long, sweet kiss on my lips.

Then he winces followed by a curse and a chuckle as he sits up on his knees. "I forgot what it feels like to be hit like that in a game." He looks down to where a bruise has blossomed right beneath his rib cage.

"Poor baby. Let me kiss it and make it all better," I murmur and do just that. But then I let my mouth slide lower until he fists a hand in my hair and pulls my head back so my mouth can't reach where I was angling to reach.

"You don't play fair." His smile is devastating. Everything about him is really, as he sits in my bed in the bright morning light looking at me with eyes that reflect exactly how I feel about him back at me.

It's heady. It's wonderful. It's the best thing ever, and the grin that crawls on my lips says just that.

"Never." I press another kiss to right above the waistband of his jeans. "And that's a promise for later."

"Later?" He leans down and kisses me again. But what starts out as a peck ends up with my hands threading through the hair at the back of his neck and me deepening the kiss.

"I'm not ready for you to go yet," I say and then brush my lips to his again.

"Films," he says with a resolute nod as his fingers slide their way beneath the covers before he hisses out a groan and pulls it back. "I have to go watch films."

"Sounds boring."

He offers me a pained look that makes me smile. I'm glad it's as hard for him to leave my bed as it is for me to watch him walk away.

"It's especially boring when I know you're here." He scoots off the bed, grabs his T-shirt, and puts it on. "Warm and inviting—"

"And wet and willing." My smile is coy and his groan is one of regret.

"You're cruel." He laughs.

"And you're incredible." He stops mid-motion and stares at me as emotion pools in his eyes. "You are. You have to know that. Not just on the field, Drew, but in real life. Everything you balance, everything you try to do and try to be, you are simply incredible."

And I mean every word of what I say, because as I lay in bed this morning watching him sleep, I couldn't stop thinking about the weight of the world on his shoulders. Duty and integrity and his own career, and how he balances it all so that no one else knows the difficulties—because he hides them so well.

"Thank you," he says with the softest of smiles that tells me he hears me. That he knows I see the real man beneath his many layers, and I love him more because of them.

He watches me scoot out of bed, his eyes scraping over my bare skin as if he's remembering all of the glorious ways he pleasured it last night and before.

I hold his gaze and only break it momentarily as I slide an old V-neck T-shirt I commandeered the last time he left it behind.

"Tonight then?" I ask.

"Only if you promise to be waiting just like that. My shirt and nothing else."

"Oh, you didn't like the lingerie last night?"

His grin is lightning quick. "On second thought . . ."

We laugh as I follow him out into the living area of my place, our hands linked, and he places one more goodbye kiss on my lips.

"I'll see you lat—" But he never finishes his sentence because when he opens my door, my father is standing there just about to knock.

I can't see Drew's face, but I do see the jolt and the slow shock flicker through my dad's expression.

"Drew," my father says in greeting. My heart leaps into my throat with that sudden fear of being caught, causing my pulse to race.

Drew steps back and looks at me and then my dad. "Sir." It's all he says followed by a nod. But his eyes are wide and his skin is pale, and I can only imagine the million things running through his head right now.

"I didn't mean to interrupt anything," my dad says as he stands there, his cheeks suddenly heating when realization hits him that I'm in a man's T-shirt and nothing else. And Drew is the one here with me.

"You didn't—it wasn't—he was just going . . ." I shake my head and die a little of embarrassment, but it's Drew I'm worried about. When I glance at him, he looks horrified. I'm not exactly sure what it is he needs from me in this moment. There's nothing I can do to make this go away. His confusion, his discord, his discomfort.

"I saw the game last night." My dad steps into my apartment, as if he can't let this moment pass. "One of the best plays I've seen in a long time. It stands right up there with Rodgers against the Lions," he says referring to the Green Bay Packers quarterback and his famous Hail Mary in 2015 to win the game.

"Thank you, but I doubt it." Drew simply stands there and stares at my dad. It's like he's seeing a ghost.

"Nah, it was an incredible play. You should be proud of yourself."

"I need to uh—get going. Play review." He looks over to me and I smile trying to make this as normal as can be—when it's nothing of the sort.

"Okay. I'll call you later," I say.

"Sir," Drew says.

"Drew?" my dad says, causing Drew to pause. He doesn't speak but rather just meets my father's stare. He looks like a lost little boy, and I wish I could do something to take whatever is going through his head away from him. All I can do is stand by and watch him struggle. "It was really good seeing you again after all these years."

Drew lowers his head a beat before nodding and then shuts the door behind him without saying another word.

My father and I both stare at the closed door as I debate how to tip-toe around the incredible awkwardness. My lies, and my dad finding out, not to mention just the plain weirdness of being caught by my dad with a man in my place. I don't care how old you are, that's always embarrassing.

Anxious and needing something to do with my hands, I pull my hair up into a messy bun and start to make coffee.

"Do you want some?" I ask as if none of what just happened transpired.

"Sure. Yes." He blows out a sigh and takes a seat at my counter on a barstool. "*Christ.*"

"I'm hoping that last part isn't because I had a man in my apartment. I'm a grown woman who—"

"That last part was because you missed our morning meeting, you haven't been answering your phone, and I was worried enough about you to come and make sure you were okay since you've never done that before."

I drop my head and stare at the coffee percolating into the mug. Well, that's a first for me. I was so wrapped up in Drew that I lost track of time. "I'm sorry. I didn't mean to make you worry. I was—"

"Busy," he finishes for me. "So I saw."

I slide the first mug of coffee over to him without meeting his eyes and then wait for my cup to fill, as I try to figure out how to explain everything.

"Is this the reason you've been avoiding me?" he finally asks, breaking the silence.

"I haven't been avoiding you."

"No?"

I meet his eyes for the first time and hate the guilt that hits me immediately. "No."

"Because you've gone out of your way to make sure you're not alone in the office with me. We've had no talks over lunch in the conference room like we usually do. In fact, you've been scarce in person as of late."

"Like I said, I've been busy."

His chuckle is a low rumble that tells me he's not buying my excuse and honestly, I wouldn't either.

"Did you think I'd be mad at you?" he asks.

"No." The word comes out way too fast and I follow it up with a shrug, a long stare into my coffee, and then, "I don't know."

"It would be a shame and horribly unfair for someone else to hold all of the mistakes I've made in my life against one of my daughters." My eyes find his. They see compassion, lack of judgment, and hurt. "I'd hate that you'd think I'd do something of a similar nature."

I nod and hate that tears fill my eyes. "He thinks you were a part of it or at fault for whatever happened to his dad."

"He's told you that?"

"No, but it's been hinted at."

"And you've hidden your relationship with him because you're afraid if I was at fault, I'd be upset." The statement is made as if he's trying to figure out my train of thought.

"I know you didn't do anything. You never would."

"And yet you questioned it."

I don't respond but just meet his stare as my cheeks heat with shame.

"Gary Bowman was my closest friend. He was like my brother. All I can tell you, Brex, is that I know the character of the man I once knew. I know he loved his family with everything he had and loved his sport just as much. When the news came out that he was suspected of throwing a game, I was just as shocked as everyone else. Your mom and I couldn't believe it. Didn't believe it. But when he walked away without a word, I feared it was true. Whatever he did, he had to have a reason he felt that justified it."

I chew my bottom lip. "Then why does Drew think you were involved somehow?"

"Maybe it was easier for Gary to put blame on me. To salvage whatever relationship he could with his son, because that was more important than anything."

"Doesn't that infuriate you?" I ask.

"I'm simply speculating, honey, but if there's one thing I learned from being a parent, it's this: before you have kids, you swear up one side and down the other that you'd never do this or that . . . but when you're staring down an uncertain future and worried about the well-being of your children, worried you're going to lose them in some way or another—grief, anger, whatnot—sometimes you do or say things without thinking. In the moment, all you can think about is not losing that person too."

There's a sadness in his eyes that tells me he just might understand that feeling. Each of us went through stages of grief after our mom died. There was never a time when we were on the same page with the stage of grief we were in. As our father was trying to keep our family from imploding, he must have felt like a firefighter putting different fires out on a daily basis. Doing anything to help us while processing his own loss at the same time.

His words hit me hard. As a kid, I never thought twice about how we were taken care of, but now as an adult, I can only imagine that it must have been exhausting.

I stare at my father with so much love in my heart and wish Drew could see him for the incredible man I see him as.

"Can you talk to him, Dad? Can you explain that all to him? I mean—"

"No." He stops me with his soft smile and gentle voice. "It's not my place to step in between the relationship of a father and a son."

"But it's wrong. It's—"

"Who am I to Drew, honey? I'm no one but an old memory. If he's going to figure out the truth it has to be on his own accord, or he'll never really believe it."

I set my cup of coffee down and press my fingers to my eyes. Worry hits me again, that Drew and I can love each other all we want, but this rift will never be healed.

"He took me to Lake George. To see our handprints. *Mom's handprints.*" I'm not sure why I feel the need to tell him that, but I feel so much better sharing it with him. I've been desperate to share it with Dekker, Lennox, and Chase, but how could I possibly explain *how* I got the photos?

It's been eating at me.

All of this secrecy has.

His smile reaches his eyes as they grow misty. "She loved that place. Those memories we made as a family there."

And Drew gave them to me again.

My mind sticks on that one thought and I can't let go of it.

"I love him, Dad."

"I know."

"How?"

"He's important enough to make you lose track of time, that's how I know."

It's my turn to smile. It's my turn to realize how wrong I was keeping this from my dad. "What now though? This *thing* will always be between us somehow."

"You'll figure it out."

"That doesn't help." I laugh.

"If love were easy everyone would be in it. But it isn't and everyone's not."

"That didn't help either."

His smile deepens as he rises from his seat, walks over to where I stand, and presses a kiss to my temple. "If Drew's anything like the kid I once knew—intelligent, contemplative, curious—he'll figure it out."

"But what if he doesn't pick me?" My voice breaks and his expression falls at the sound of it.

"You never want someone to have to pick between you and their family. It would never work. There would always be resentment and bitterness that lingers." He pulls me in for one of those bear hugs that makes you feel like a little girl again and that he has all the answers. "He has to *choose* you. To want to be with you. To know things will get sticky sometimes but that is how life is."

"And if he doesn't?"

"You and Drew have had a connection since you were kids. You finished each other's sentences, you annoyed each other, you stared at each other when the other wasn't looking, hoping to be noticed. Stay the course. Have patience when you feel like there's nothing left to hold on to, honey."

He knocks on the doorjamb with his knuckles, almost as if he's completing the one he never got to land when Drew opened the door. I'm not sure why that strikes me, but it does.

He could have come here in anger, scowling and in no way kind to Drew when he first saw him. He could have scolded me for making him worry.

But he didn't.

Rather, he evaluated the situation in the present instead of harboring anger from the past. He treated Drew with respect, praised his game even, when I'm sure every part of the protective father he is wanted to ask questions and demand answers.

He treated me like a daughter in love, not like a best friend who had been scorned.

And now, finally, all that guilt for keeping this from my family has eased. It's like a weight has lifted off my shoulders.

You and Drew have had a connection since you were kids.

He's right. We did. I see it and realize it now. With that being said, will we get past *this* challenge?

Chapter
FIFTY-THREE

Drew

FILM REVIEW HAS BEEN POSTPONED FOR SOME REASON AND THANK FUCK
for that, because I was going to be late anyway.

There's no way I could sit there and concentrate after what just happened.

Instead, I'm sitting in my truck across the street from my parents' house
trying to figure out what in the hell I'm doing here.

I just came face to face with a man I've believed to be the monster who
undid the Bowman family. The villain in our story. Kenyon Kincade.

And yet, he was nothing like the man I'd led myself to believe and like
everything I'd seemed to have forgotten. The kind man who loved his girls
more than his next breath, and with a laugh that you couldn't help but join
in with.

Seeing him . . . Christ, seeing him has brought about a tidal wave of
memories and the emotions that came with them. More so than when I saw
Brexton for the first time, because Kenyon was . . . Kenyon was the stable
one. The adult of the four parents who everyone listened to and went to
for advice.

Is that why it was so easy to believe he could be the monster? The one
at fault?

My hands grip the steering wheel as I stare at the house.

Details.

I squeeze my eyes and try to recall what it was my dad had said that
Kenyon did. The intricate details of it all. My mind draws a blank. Because
isn't that like everything about this whole situation? Fuzzy. Unexplained.
A goddamn fucking mess.

Is Kenyon innocent? Is the man with the kind eyes and the warm smile I just met in my girlfriend's house blameless?

"You did it didn't you?" Fury and disbelief twist and turn and claw at me as I stare at my dad's oldest friend. His eyes are wide and his mouth is open.

He's shocked.

Fucking shocked that I'm here calling him on his bullshit.

"Drew?" My dad's oldest friend moves through the lobby of Kincade Sports Management. "Son? Can I help you? What are you talking—"

"Don't you dare call me son," I shout, hands fisted and teeth clenched.

"Let's go to the conference room so we can talk in private."

"Why? So all of these people don't hear how you ruined my family? How you did it and pretended to be my—"

"Goddamn it, Drew," he shouts and pushes me through the open conference room door before slamming it behind me. I jerk my arm from his grasp, and it takes everything I have not to let my fist fly. Not to do something—anything—to abate all of this fucking rage.

"Why don't you want me to talk out there, huh, Kincade? Why don't you—"

"So you don't make an ass out of yourself, that's why."

"Me?" I laugh the word out and glare at the man I'm supposed to be able to trust. For the life of me, I'm finding it fucking difficult to meet his eyes. "Me? You're the one who did this to us. You're the one—"

"Drew, I understand you're upset. I know your world just turned upside down, but I'm not going to stand here and take your abuse."

"But it was you. You're the one who should be ashamed. You're the one who ruined my dad. You ruined us all."

I shake the thought off because if he's not at fault, that only leaves one explanation.

That means my father is.

The man who stood before us time and time again and told us it wasn't true.

There's no way.

He couldn't have.

He wouldn't have done this to our family. To Maggs. To my mom. *To me.*

I reject the idea. Not because I believe it, but solely because it's the only explanation that I can handle right now.

Talk about the highest of highs to the lowest of lows. From last night to today.

Pick.

Choose.

Decide.

C'mon, Drew.

But I don't want to do any of them.

I can't.

Instead, I grab my cell, scroll through my contacts, and hit send.

"What's up, man?"

"Can you rack the tees up, Steve? I need to get some work in."

"Today's not a practice day. It's a rest day. Film review later. Didn't you get the email?"

"I know. I did. I just need to . . ." *I just need it.*

The one solace I've had my whole life. The sound of my feet on the turf. The whistle of my hand and ball as it whips past my ear. The feeling of being in control of something in my life.

Football.

While I'm suddenly afraid the game was the sin of my father.

It's been my savior.

Chapter
FIFTY-FOUR

Brexton

THE STADIUM SEEMS SO MASSIVE WHEN IT'S EMPTY.

Empty save for me and the man currently running up and down its steps. The man who owns my heart.

He climbs one after another from the field level to the lower loge to the top loge. One step after another without slowing, as if he's hellbent on solving the world's problems in this one workout session.

But I know he won't be able to solve a thing by doing it. Maybe quiet his head. Abate some anger and confusion. I can only imagine what he's trying to work through. Seeing my dad again after all this time. Figuring out how we can be together when his family might just disown him for dating a Kincade. Worrying about the Raptors and if he'll get more playing time. Or perhaps figuring out how we can be together when his family would hate that he's dating a Kincade?

I'm not sure how long I watch him but in the time I do, I can tell the weight of the world is on his shoulders. I only wish I could help alleviate it somehow.

But my dad was right—this is something Drew needs to figure out on his own.

And that scares the hell out of me. I can only hope that when the dust settles from the impending explosion I predict is on the horizon, I'm still standing here.

I know the minute Drew sees me. He trips over the next step going up but catches himself and keeps going as if he didn't.

So I take a seat and wait for him to finish the zig-zag of rows until he can't avoid me anymore and I'm right in his path.

"You're not answering my texts," I say when he slows to a stop in front of me. I'm standing with my ass against the gate that he needs to get onto the field to go into the tunnel to the locker rooms.

His eyes meet mine, a torrent of emotion raging through them. "I was busy."

"Running till you collapse isn't going to solve anything."

"Like you have a fucking clue what would, huh?" Instead of going through the gate at my back he just hops over the railings at my right and onto the field.

"Excuse me?" I say scrambling after him, kind of surprised by the comment.

"You heard me."

"Running and hiding isn't going to fix a thing, Drew."

"Why don't you go back to your fucking family and give me some space."

"Seriously?" I yell at his back. "You're going to turn this on me? Blame me? All because you saw my dad? Did you think we'd just keep on dating and that would never happen?"

"Will you keep quiet?" he barks and turns around, looking over my shoulders.

"There's no one else here. I sweet-talked old Barry," I say of the groundskeeper, "to let me in before he locked the doors on his way out."

"What do you want, Brexton?" he asks in a resigned sigh, shoulders slumping, head rolling back for a second as he takes in a deep breath.

"You tell me."

"What the fuck is that supposed to mean?" he shouts and takes a few steps toward me, shoulders squared, tendons tense in his neck.

"Pretty self-explanatory considering how things were left between us this morning. Add to the fact that you're not answering my texts, I'd think there's lots to say."

"I don't want to do this right now."

"Why not, Drew? Let's get it all out. Scream at me. Yell at me. Tell me what the fuck is on your mind because I'm so goddamn sick of guessing and worrying and wondering. It would be nice to finally hear it from your lips." I bait him, because I'm primed and ready for a fight. I feel like this has been bottling up for some time. As great as we are, there's this constant underlying tension between us—the past we can't control, a third party to all the good between us.

And if that's how I feel, I can't imagine how he feels being the one left to decide what to believe.

"What's on my mind? No one gives a fuck what's on my mind. All they care about is that I believe them when I'm not sure what the fuck to believe anymore."

"I think you do."

"Don't!" he shouts like a little boy not wanting to hear something. "Don't you dare tell me what to believe when you stand there beside your perfect family and pass judgment on me."

"That's what you think? That I'm passing judgment on you?" I brace my hands on top of my head and walk away from him before turning back. He looks at me, lost but determined. "I'm not passing shit on you, Drew, but I'm lost here. All I want is to know what you're thinking. How you feel. I want to stop feeling like I'm in love with a man, yet waiting for the other shoe to drop. Surely it's going to come down to me or what I feel like are a set of lies and you sure as shit aren't going to pick me." My voice breaks and the first tear slides down my cheek when I don't want it to.

"Brex." My name is a resigned syllable with so many emotions woven into the four connected letters. "What do you want to know? That it fucked me up seeing your dad today? I feel stupid because it did. When I left, I was more confused than ever before, because for over ten years it's been insinuated that he's to blame. And fucking hell, Brexton, in that moment when he looked me in the eyes, I knew he had nothing to do with it." He paces from one end of the tunnel and then back, and I swear if he could punch something right now he would. "Do you know what it feels like to realize you've been lied to by the person you idolize? It's not exactly the easiest thing to swallow or even face."

"I'm so sorry."

"Don't," he shouts when I step forward and try to touch his arm. He squeezes his eyes shut as a tear slips out. Its slow descent as he tries to rein in his emotion breaks my heart.

"Don't push me away," I plead. "Don't—"

"Just shut up, would you? Just ..."

And then he crashes into me with a fervor I feel but don't understand.

His hands are on my face and his tongue demands to meet mine. He picks me up so I can wrap my legs around his waist, while he carries me into the trainers' room. He sets me down—long enough for our hands to shove down our bottoms so we're bared and ready to connect the minute he lifts me onto the trainers' table.

Anger turns to passion. The defensiveness to lust.

There are no words when he enters me. No soft murmurs. No sweet nothings. There's just our guttural groans as I give and he takes.

There is nothing gentle about our joining. It's aggressive and dominant. It's completely selfish, and I don't care. He's hurting and if this is what he needs right now, then I'm here for it.

Especially when I didn't have words to fix it for him.

So I give him my body to get lost in. I give him my moans to smother with his lips. I give him scratch marks down his back and a nip of teeth on his shoulder so he can feel the sharp contrast against the pleasure and know that this moment is real.

That I am real.

And with his head buried into the crook of my neck and his hands holding my ass in place, Drew Bowman comes hard, fast, and without warning.

His hands tighten, his body tenses, and his strangled cry is muffled where his lips meet my neck. But even when the last ounce of pleasure drains from him and his breath is still ragged, he doesn't move.

He needs a moment.

Hell, we both do.

So I run my hands up and down the length of his back. I allow him to regain some of his pride I know admitting all of that to me took from him. I *urge him* with my actions to feel surrounded by my love for him.

I can't be angry at him. Sure he said shit that was hurtful, but if I were in his shoes ... if my father had lied to me for this long over something so life-altering, I would be devastated. I would be hurt. I'd lash out at anyone and everything trying to tell me otherwise. I can't imagine how hard this is hitting him.

I want to be his safe space. The place he can turn to when he needs solace from it all. The arms that will hold him when uncertainty owns him. The heart that will love him above all else.

"Sometimes, I just want to go back to before," he murmurs. "To when you were Bratty Brex and I was Dreadful Drew and everything was normal."

I press a kiss to the side of his head. "But then it would have been a single kiss from a spin-the-bottle dare instead of what we've found between us."

He leans back and looks at me with a clarity that makes me feel like we can figure this out. And when he moves forward and kisses me, it's so haunting and slow that it steals my breath.

When it ends, I keep my eyes closed as he rests his forehead against mine, his thumbs brushing back and forth over the line of my jaw.

"I'll figure this out. I promise."

I nod to reinforce his words with a soft smile. "Mildred was right."

"What?" His head startles.

"Hate fucks are the best."

He throws his head back and laughs. "I wouldn't exactly call that a hate fuck. No one said anything about hate."

"Well, let's make sure that's the closest we get to the hate part, okay?"

He presses a kiss to the tip of my nose. "It's a deal."

Chapter
FIFTY-FIVE

Brexton

"Dekker, I think you got flowers again from that sickeningly sweet man of yours," Chase calls through the office with a dramatic roll of her eyes, as she carries in a gorgeous arrangement of anemones from the reception desk.

"Really?" Dekker asks as she jumps up like a giddy teenager and takes them from Chase. But it's after she sets them down and looks at the envelope buried in the arrangement that she laughs out loud.

"I don't want to hear about what Hunter wrote that he wants to do to you. Or"—Chase holds up her finger to stop Dekker—"what it is you did to him to earn those."

"If they were mine, I'd make sure to tell you so you could be madly jealous, but they're not for me." Chase and I look at each other as Dekker continues. "You'll have to ask Brex what she did and to whom, because this card is addressed to her."

It feels like all eyes in the office of my sisters and our staff shift to look at me. "For me?" I ask.

"For you." Dekker dangles the card by her two fingers as I walk over to the bouquet on the table.

I hold my hand out. "May I have the card, please?"

"Only if you tell us who they're from." She quirks her brow as Chase steps up beside her to form a unified front.

"I can't exactly tell you if I don't get to open the card, now can I?" I snatch it from her fingers and take a few steps away so I can open it without their prying eyes.

And when I open it, I can't help the giddy feeling and the grin that forms on my lips.

You're the only one I want to spin the bottle with.
ILYB.
-DD

Dreadful Drew knows the perfect way to end an awesome week.

ILYB. Four letters that say and mean so damn much.

As if waking up snuggled in bed beside him every morning for all five days wasn't enough. Now this.

"We're waiting," Dekker says in a sing-song voice when I walk back, bury my face in the flowers, and draw in a huge breath.

"Who are they from?" Chase adds, looking over my shoulder at the card. "ILYB?"

"ILYB?" Dekker says looking at me and then Chase again. "Oh. *Oh.*" She looks back at me. "*I love you, Brexton?*"

"Yep. They're from my boyfriend," I say as I pick up the vase and head toward my desk, noting that their mouths have just dropped open. "Drew Bowman."

And when I turn on my heel to their shocked gasps, I meet the eyes of my dad across the room and smile when he winks at me.

I know I have only seconds before the barrage of questions start so I get a good head start into my office before they do.

But no such luck. They look like Cinderella's evil stepsisters as they fight each other to get through my door and talk to me first.

"Drew? Drew? That Drew?" Dekker asks with an incredulous look on her face.

"It's the only Dreadful Drew there is," Chase answers for me.

"How did this happen? How is it possible? I mean—"

"What Dekker means is holy shit, you're dating Drew?" Chase continues.

"That's exactly what I mean," Dekker says with a nod, "except for my comment would have had a lot more curse words in it."

"True. She does cuss a lot more than we do," Chase says.

"Are you two done?" I ask, "because I'm curious why you barged your way in here when it's clear I don't even need to be part of this conversation."

"Lennox," Chase says. "We need to tell Lennox. Does she know?" she asks, turning to look at me.

"Of course she doesn't know," Dekker says. "If she knows and we don't, then we'd have to kick her ass for not telling us."

They both laugh and then it slowly fades when they realize they are so caught up in the excitement of finding out who I'm dating that they aren't letting me talk.

"This is serious, isn't it?" Dekker asks me.

"I love him." Saying those words out loud has chills chasing over my skin.

"Oh. My. God," Chase says dramatically as she plops into the seat in front of me. "I've never seen you this sure of being in love before. Are you sure, sure?" she asks as if I'd just told her I was abducted by aliens.

"She's definitely sure," Dekker says.

"And how would you know?" Chase asks her.

Dekker turns to me with tears welling in her eyes and awe in her voice.

"Because when you know, you know . . . and Brexton here, knows."

Chapter
FIFTY-SIX

Drew

I scramble.

It's all I can do as the offensive line crumbles for the third time in as many plays. The 49ers have our goddamn number today and it shows.

I'm able to throw the ball and see that it isn't going to be caught—by either team—milliseconds before I'm tackled to the ground. I hit with a thud and a grunt and then a wince as another guy adds to the pile.

I've been given five more minutes. Five precious minutes to show off what else I can do after Hobbs took hit after fucking hit.

But I'm not going to be able to do shit.

Not with our offense folding with every single goddamn play.

And when the clock runs out and the game is over, I've accomplished little to fucking nothing other than putting zero points on the board to counter the seven our defense and their shitty coverage all but handed to them.

I glance toward the stands as we walk off the field, the kid in me still looking, still hoping for my dad to be sitting there, proud of me.

I'm an idiot for thinking it. For hoping for it. For even thinking it after the events of the past week.

And yet just once, I want him to be proud of me. Just once I want him to not put himself and what people think of him first, and think about what it would mean for me to see him there—whether I'm sitting the bench or the off chance of me taking the field.

"It was a fucking slaughterhouse out there wasn't it, man? Goddamn team sucked ass today."

I glance over to Hobbs and nod. He's right. Fucking dead-on right, but that's not shit you say to a team that just got their asses handed to them and are sore and pissed off. That's not how you lead them.

"It happens. Now we're going to go into the locker room and after Coach speaks, you're going to take the floor. You're going to tell them they fought hard and we came up short, but that's okay because we have six days to fix our mistakes before the next game."

"But they didn't fight hard. They—"

"You're their leader. Go lead them with positivity."

Hobbs falters in step momentarily as our eyes meet long enough for me to catch that he understands what I'm saying.

The question is, will he step up to the plate, or is he going to strike out?

"Hey, Bowman."

I stop at the sound of my name as we enter the tunnel and look up to a couple of guys dressed in Raptors gear with beers in their hands, hanging over the railing.

"You had five fucking minutes and you couldn't perform. No wonder you've been second string your whole career."

"If he can call it a career," the other sneers.

"Yeah, loser. Walk away like I read your old man did."

"Walk the fuck away."

I keep walking into the tunnel without giving them the time of day.

But their words stick.

They eat at me.

Through our team meeting and the press junket afterward.

When I text Brex and tell her I'm not going to be able to make it to her place tonight.

The entire drive home.

Even when I pull into my driveway to find Brexton's car parked in the driveway and her sitting on my porch with her legs stretched out and ankles crossed over the other.

I get out of my truck, not sure if I'm pissed or happy to see her. "What are you doing here?" I ask as I cross the short distance from the driveway to the porch.

She holds up a six-pack of beer and a bag of takeout food. "You need to eat, right?" Her smile is soft as she pushes herself up and angles her head to the side to stare at me.

"I'm afraid I'm not much company tonight. I've got a lot on my mind."

"Hey," she says. "We celebrate losses as much as we celebrate wins."

"Are you crazy?" I laugh.

"For you, yes." She gives me another smile before stepping onto her tiptoes and kissing me.

"This is ridiculous."

"Maybe." She shrugs. "And maybe it's just what the doctor ordered."

I stare at her standing under the porchlight and smile, despite feeling sorry for myself.

How did I ever deserve this? Deserve her?

"Are you going to let me in?" she asks and bats her lashes.

I chuckle and shake my head as I take the pizza box and bag of other items from her and unlock the front door.

"You really are something," I say, walking toward the kitchen as she shuts the door behind us.

"Hey Drew, will this help take your mind off the game?" she asks, prompting me to turn around.

And when I do, the game and thoughts of it disappear completely. Brexton is standing in my foyer with her dress pooled around her ankles and nothing on but a black negligée.

I drop the pizza without seeing where it lands and cross the room to her. "I think that might be a very good start."

꩜

"If that's what I get when we lose . . ." I blow out a whistle as her finger traces absent lines on my chest.

"Funny." She presses a kiss to the underside of my jaw, and I close my eyes and let it soak in.

Her being here.

Me wanting her here.

Because as much as I wanted to be left alone tonight, as much as I wanted to wallow in my thoughts over what those assholes said, Brexton showing up only served to show me I was wrong.

Her lips pressed to mine is what I wanted. Knowing she is here for me, win or lose, is what I needed. That she knew what I needed . . . knew how to love me . . . blows my mind.

She validates me.

Believes in me.

As it seems she always has.

The lingerie and incredible sex were just the cherry on the top of it.

"You want to tell me why you were so upset about a game that you had no hand in losing?" she asks. "The 49ers are a good team and they had your numbers tonight. Fair and square. Sometimes that just happens."

I don't respond.

"You're not telling me something."

"There were just some assholes after the game. Same shit, different day."

"What do you mean same shit, different day?" she asks, propping herself up on her elbow so she can look at me. I'd much rather look at her gloriously naked body instead of have this discussion.

"What I said. There's always one asshole in the crowd, always a comment linking me to my dad somehow or some shit like that."

"Fuck them," she states so matter-of-factly.

"I wish it were that easy."

"Why is it not? You can handle all the other criticism with a grain of salt, treat it the same."

"I used to be able to, but this time around with everything that's going on, I think it hit a little closer to home."

Is that why it did? Because I've spent years thinking my dad was wronged by the NFL and for once I think he is the one who did the wrong?

"At some point you're going to have to put this to bed with your father for your own well-being. You have a right to know the truth because it affects you daily. And when you do, then you can figure out the next step after that."

She's right.

I know she is.

But it's so much easier to put my hand on the back of her neck and pull her closer so I can taste her lips again.

So I can lose myself in her.

Chapter
FIFTY-SEVEN

Brexton

"Congratulations." I shake Mark Whittier's hand. "You are now a Los Angeles Charger."

"No shit?" His grin spreads from ear to ear.

"No shit." I pat him on the back.

"Coach told me I had to come up to the small meeting rooms and I was freaking out a little. I thought they were going to cut me like that after everything . . ." He blows out a breath and shakes his head. "Los Angeles? Really?"

"The contract was sent over about twenty minutes ago. I figured I'd swing by and tell you in person."

He scrubs a hand over his face. "Shonda is going to freak," he says about his wife, who has been trying to get back to her home state for years.

"Then let's make sure you finish the season healthy and strong, that way there'll be nothing that stops you when you start there come spring."

He nods, his expression priceless as he takes it all in. "Thank you. Truly. Thank you, Brexton."

I smile, feeling more than content knowing I just made him and his family very happy. And days like these, appreciative athletes, make this job so worthwhile.

"I'll review everything just to make sure it's what they said it was going to be and then get it over to you to sign electronically."

"Sounds good." He takes a few steps toward the door before turning back to face me. "Thank you, again."

I smile and watch him walk away before I turn back to my laptop to send a few things.

"So you could get him a deal with the Chargers but not me?"

Of course.

Hobbs.

It's Justin's voice at my back. I should have assumed that Mark would tell everyone, but not this fast.

"I overheard," he says as he enters the small closet-like space.

My sigh is heavy as I lean my ass against the desk and turn to face him. "We've been through this, Justin. I told you I couldn't promise anything, especially when I have absolutely no authority to negotiate for you."

"So then you were just bullshitting me?"

"Not at all. I included you in my discussions with them. I made suggestions on how to make their offense stronger. I told them they needed you."

"My guess is that you weren't convincing enough." He squares his shoulders as he takes another step closer.

"And my guess is that you haven't exactly been shining on the field lately to help your own case."

"Oh, so that's what this is? Bash me so you and your boyfriend can ride off into the New York sunset together?"

"My boyfriend?" I laugh.

"You think I don't know Bowman has a thing for you?" he sneers, and I hope I don't look as taken aback as I feel.

But I recover quickly. The last thing I want is Drew coming into this conversation when he has no place there.

"If that were the case, Hobbs—if I were screwing you over as you're implying for Drew's sake—then I'd want you the hell out of here so he could be starting QB." I take a step toward him, using my finger to point at him. "I'd have done everything in my power to get you there, but I don't play like that."

"Sure you do," he says, his voice lowering as he steps into my personal space. He emanates such unexpected anger. "And since you didn't play like that for me, I think you owe me."

"Owe you?" I scoff, but when he takes another step closer, I don't like the position he's put us in—he towers over me. Especially noticeable when he's this close.

Alarm bells sound off in my head when I can usually keep them at bay.

Crap.

"I don't owe you shit, but I'll tell you the same thing I told you back then. Talk to Finn. Tell him you want California. Make him work for you, because I'm beginning to think this was all an exercise in futility. Even if I made it work, you had no intention of signing with KSM. You just need that big ego of yours fed. You need to feel like everybody is running around like chickens with their heads cut off trying to please you."

"I know a way you could please me," he murmurs, and I swear to God, if he reaches that hand out to touch me, my knee is going straight into his crotch.

No hesitation.

"Watch your step, Hobbs," I warn.

"What's little ol' you going to do about it? Huh? Because I can think of about ten things right now that would make things so much fucking better."

"Like you taking about ten steps the fuck away from Brexton."

My head whips over to the voice in the doorway. I'm shocked as hell to see Finn standing there, arms crossed, and fury in his expression.

I let out a breath I didn't realize I was holding, when Finn glares at Justin until he does as Finn asks.

"Finn." I gulp in a breath of air.

"Go get changed," Finn orders Justin. "And don't you dare fucking leave. You and I are going to have words."

Justin stands there and looks from Finn to me and then back to his agent. "It's not what it looked like."

"I heard enough to know exactly what it was." Finn raises his eyebrows and motions toward the door.

With an annoyed sigh, Justin strides out of the room without another word.

And when he's gone, both Finn and I take a second to consider what happened.

"I never thought I'd be happy to say this, but it's good to see you, Finn."

He throws his head back and laughs. "You couldn't give me more than that?"

"Nope," I tease, but then my expression falls as realization hits me. I've dealt with men my whole career, and I'm proud to say that's the first time anything like that has ever happened. I'd like to keep it that way. "Well, I always thought he was a harmless prick but now I know he's an entitled asshole too."

"That he is." He purses his lips and nods. "You want to tell me what that was all about?"

"Your client was trying to pit us against each other to get a trade to LA."

"And you took the bait?" he asks.

"Of course I did. If there's a chance that I can steal someone from you and add one more pea between that stack of mattresses you sleep on in your tower, of course I'll take it."

"Fucking unbelievable." But he chuckles.

I shrug unapologetically. "But I told him from the get-go that it was a long shot. That he needed to talk to his agent, because there was really nothing I could do."

"And what exactly did you do?"

"I dropped some hints to the Chargers GM. I let them know Hobbs was interested in playing there, but there wasn't much else I could do. Do you see that?" I ask as I hold my hand out to him.

"What's that?"

"I'm passing the baton to you. He's your client. After that little show, his allure has faded for me."

"No shit."

"I lied," I say with a sigh.

"Uh-oh."

"I do feel a little bad trying to steal him from you. I mean you did just kind of save me."

"Nah. You Kincades don't ever need saving. I saw that your knee was primed, ready to connect with his dick. You would have done just fine."

I chuckle and look over at him. "Thanks, Finn."

He nods. "If it's any consolation, I was coming to tell him that the Las Vegas Raiders are interested in him. It's not California, but it's the next state over."

I lift my eyebrows in surprise, upset the self-righteous prick will be getting what he wanted—a trade toward the West Coast—but I'm glad it's not California.

I'll take the victory no matter how small it is.

"The Raiders? That's a good fit for him."

"It is."

I stare at Finn for a beat and shake my head. He's not supposed to be the good guy. He's the one I want to hate. My little sister's ex-boyfriend who hurt her and a rival agent I like to think of as our enemy.

He's not supposed to be a guy I'm smiling at right now and thankful that he's here.

"Hey? When you negotiate Hobbs' terms with the Raiders, do you think you could give him a pay *cut* in the process? I'm thinking he doesn't deserve to be rewarded for being an asshole and trying to screw you over by going to a rival agent."

Finn gives me a half-cocked grin. "*You mean you?*"

"You win some. You lose some. And this time I'm glad I'm losing to you. He's all your problem."

He laughs with me. "I'll do my best on the pay cut part. No guarantees though. If it's any consolation, I'll draw negotiations out as long as possible to make him sweat."

With my bag on my shoulder, I stop in front of him. "You know what? You're not so bad, after all."

"Shh." He winks. "Don't let the secret get out."

Chapter
FIFTY-EIGHT

Brexton

Drew: Where are you?

Me: In Philly. Why?

Drew: I'm starting today.

Me: Are you serious? OMG!

Drew: Lonnie just told me

Me: How? When? Why? I'm so excited for you. What happened to Hobbs?

Drew: Karma

I shake my head, my smile widening at the comment that I can all but hear him say in that sarcastic tone of his. I can still picture the look on his face when I told him the stunt that Justin pulled and that Finn helped me out of. To say he was pissed is an understatement, but I made him promise me that he wouldn't act on it. That he wouldn't jeopardize all of the hard work he'd put in with a bullshit act—like getting into a fistfight with a teammate—when he's finally making headway and getting playing time.

He'd relented.

Eventually.

Only after I told him it didn't make him any less of a man for not sticking up for me, but more of a man because he trusted that I could handle myself.

And now, look what happened.

Thank God, he listened and didn't jeopardize this opportunity.

I stare at the text and then look up at the stadium I'm about to walk into. The one where I have six clients about to play and know without a second thought that I won't be seeing them take the field.

Not even for a single down of the game. My heart leaps at the sight of his words. At yet another chance for him to prove himself to the Raptors—and the world—who he is and what he's capable of.

I bite my bottom lip. I know it seems unprofessional to bail on a few clients to go watch my boyfriend play, but then again, this was an unannounced visit. My clients are no worse for wear, and I have no meetings scheduled.

Some things are more important than work, and that something is starting a game for the first time in what I'm sure seems like forever.

Sure the traffic will be brutal, but I'm pretty certain I can get there by half-time.

I know where I need to be.

I know where my heart already is.

Me: I'm on my way.

I'll move heaven and earth to get there.

To be there.

To cheer him on.

Chapter
FIFTY-NINE

Drew

I'M EXHAUSTED.

I'm amped.

I glance up to the big screen on the opposite end of the stadium from where I stand in the huddle and know we've got this.

The win.

And a berth to the playoffs.

The Panthers have been battling toe to toe with us all goddamn day. We get points, they get points. We turn it over, they turn it over.

Like a damn see-saw.

It seems this game will be won by whoever is the last to score.

And time is running out.

I glance over to Lonnie on the sidelines and get a nod, his words from minutes ago back in my head.

"What are you thinking?" I ask Lonnie, who's standing beside me with his arms crossed, that heart attack waiting to happen kept at bay for a little while longer.

"I'm thinking they are wearing us down. They know our plays. They've got Donnell's number," he says of one of my offensive linemen. Pretty soon he's not going to be able to stop them. "If that happens, you better hold tight to that fucking ball, because he's a goddamn tank when he hits you."

"He won't hit me."

"Funny," he murmurs as the crowd erupts when Grandy sacks the Panther's quarterback in the backfield. "But that just helped some."

"So? What's the game plan?" I ask.

"I trust you to figure it out."

"What?" I ask, head whipping his way and away from our special teams running on the field to receive the punt.

"I'm going to leave it up to you. You know the plays. You're reading their field position well. They've recognized what we're going to do a few times and it's too late to change, so I'm leaving it up to you."

If that's not the ultimate show of confidence in my abilities, I don't know what is. I stare at him, at the man who has denied me time and again but who is now telling me he trusts me, and it takes me a second to fully grasp it.

"Showtime, Bowman," Lonnie says and smacks my ass as special teams come off the field.

"We've got a minute left. A lot can happen in that minute," I say, meeting each one of my guys' eyes.

"We need to score, man. They're killing us in the backfield," Muncy says, looking frustrated.

"I know. I see it." I find Fulton's eyes and say, "Texas Fifteen."

His eyes light up. "No shit?" he asks as the guys start smiling. They know the Panthers are expecting a run. It's been our pattern all damn night and now that I'm in charge, and not the guys up in the booth making the call, I'm going to play to what I know. To what I trust. *My instincts and my arm.*

"No shit," I say.

His smile spreads. "Copy that."

"Let's do this, boys!" I shout and then say, "Break."

We clap to break the huddle with a glance at the clock and a quick prayer to the football gods.

This is my chance.

My proof that I can start and finish a game strong. That I'm worthy of a starting position.

"Texas Fifteen. Texas Fifteen. Hut. Hut. Hut."

I shuffle back in the pocket. Fulton runs in front of me where I hand the ball off to him. He runs to the right and sells the run as the whole field shifts and follows him. The offensive line holds just as Fulton dodges a tackle and lateral passes it to me. I have a millisecond to glance down-field where Muncy is wide open.

The offensive line breaks. Number fifty-five is barreling down on me as I pull back and let the ball fly the fifteen yards to Muncy.

He catches it, cradling it in his arms as the stadium erupts around us.

But he's not done.

He turns and runs into a full sprint down the almost wide-open field and crosses into the end zone.

My arms go up to match the referees calling the touchdown, and the roar in the stadium is deafening.

There are hugs and pats on the ass, and I look over to Lonnie and catch his wide grin and the shake of his head over the Pop Warner-like play.

But it worked.

It fucking worked.

And that's all I keep thinking as we take our time wearing down the play clock. There are thirty-five seconds left and the game clock says twenty.

A simple knee will do it.

We don't need the extra point after. We just need to take a knee and let the rest of the game clock tick to zero.

And we do.

When Stussy hikes the ball into my hands and I take a knee, the stadium erupts into a frenzy of deafening noise.

We won.

We fucking won, and it was with me at the helm from start to finish.

With me leading this team.

Tears threaten. The mental exhaustion and toll the last seven years have taken on me hits like a ton of bricks. Even when the clock runs out, I sit with the football in one hand, and my elbow on my knee with my head in my hand—and soak it all in.

When my teammates keep slapping me on the back in congrat-ulations, I finally look up at them and then toward the stands. Toward where my dad would sit when I was a kid and watch. I know he's not going to be there, because he'll never set foot inside a stadium again, and yet I look out of an old, irrational habit.

And I startle when I see Brexton standing there, unbeknownst to her, right where he would have been. Her grin is huge, and she bounces on her toes in excitement when our eyes meet.

In that moment, there is nothing else on my mind other than hugging her. Not the Raptor's PR person waiting to guide me, not the media standing by waiting to talk on-air live, not my teammates waiting to relive a play.

It's just her.

Just the girl I fell in love with all those years ago who's waiting for me on the sidelines as if she knew just where to be.

I push through the people with, "I'll be right back," "one second," and "I have to do this first," until I reach Brexton. She squeals as I climb up the rungs of the railing, and all but launches herself into my arms when I'm at the right height.

I give no thought to the cameras or the media or the fans. All I can think about when I press my lips to hers is that she's here.

That she believes in me.

And that I'm one lucky son of a bitch.

Chapter
SIXTY

Drew

"You're going to be sore in the morning." Brexton glances at me over her shoulder where she's putting food in bowls on the kitchen counter. "You took some hits today."

My body aches and my throwing shoulder needs to be iced again. "Nothing some beer and some of this won't numb," I say as I press my lips to hers in a slow, sweet kiss.

I slide my hands down to her ass as my lips find hers again. She smells of soap from my shower and, just when I sink into the kiss with thoughts of a quickie on the counter before everyone gets here, she bats my hands away.

"Uh-uh-uh. You're the one who invited the guys over to celebrate, therefore none of that until later." But in complete contradiction to her words, she fists her hand in the front of my shirt and pulls me toward her for another kiss. "You know how madly proud I am of you, right?" Her eyes light up with the smile I barely see because I'm too busy focusing on the emotion swimming there. "If there was ever someone who deserved today, who deserves this, it's you, Dreadful Drew."

Her tongue flicks against my lips and it's a no-brainer to let her take control for a beat. To let everything feel like it's fucking perfect in my world for the first time in what feels like so fucking long, it's ridiculous.

"You keep teasing me like that," I murmur against her lips, "and the only thing I'm going to be setting out on this counter behind me is you."

She chuckles against my lips and wiggles her body against mine. "Promise?"

"Christ, woman," I swear as I break from the kiss and step back from her and her glorious distractions. She just stares at me with the cutest pout before erupting into a fit of laughter.

"Greet the guests with that," she says motioning to my dick straining against my jeans, "and they're going to think this is a whole different kind of party."

"Funny."

"I know." She winks and then motions to the counter behind me. "Can you grab that bowl over there for me—"

The doorbell rings and we both look at each other and laugh.

"Would you look at that," she says. "Good thing we held off. You said seven, right?"

The clock reads six. "No doubt one of the assholes was hit too hard in the head today and can't tell time. I'll get it."

"You going to take care of that situation before you get there?" she asks, motioning to my crotch.

"Always the comedian," I say. She gives me a cheesy grin and wipes her hand on the dish towel as I head toward the door. No need to take care of anything, seeing as one thought of one of my teammates being behind the door has me back to normal.

What an incredible fucking day.

My grin is still wide and my sarcasm loud and clear when I swing open the door and say, "I said six o'clock, you asshole." But my double take follows right behind it when I catch sight of who is standing there.

"Mom? Dad? What are you doing here?"

Have they come to congratulate me? They drove all the way over here to let me know they saw the game and they're proud of me?

But the thought is short-lived when my dad simply glares at me, his jaw clenched, and disbelief raging in his eyes.

"Who was the woman?" he asks as my mom clings to his arm.

"*The woman?*" And then it dawns on me. The press. The cameras. My kissing Brexton.

"Charley pointed to the TV and said it was Brexton." He looks at me with a fear I've never seen before. A fear that has me wondering what it is he's so petrified of? Is he worried that maybe I've asked questions of the daughter, and maybe even the man, who he's blamed all of this on? Is he worried this world he painted my family into might be coming undone?

"Why?" I shrug, studying his every feature, not sure if I'm hoping he lets me down so I know I'm right or not.

"A *Kincade*. Are you crazy?"

"I'm sure her father would say, 'A *Bowman*. Are you crazy?' *But he didn't*," I all but taunt to get a reaction from them.

"Don't mention *that man* to us," my mother says, voice cold, eyes full of fury as she stares at me with astonishment.

All I can do is put my hands in my pockets and chuckle as I stare at the two of them in utter disbelief. If I doubted my father's story before, the two of them just solidified it for me now.

I don't know why the thought crosses my mind but it's there and it won't go away. They didn't drive across town to congratulate me on something I've busted my ass for. They came to make sure their lies stay intact and honestly, I'm not sure which one I should be more upset about.

"Are we done here?" I ask with a raise of my eyebrows.

"Drew." My name is a warning from my father's lips as his body starts to tremble, and by my mom's quick intake of air, she noticed just as I did. "After *everything* that family has done to us? *How could you?*"

Hasn't this been my dilemma? How do I confront him without damaging his health? How do I look at my idol and tell him I no longer believe him? Hasn't this been what I'd been stressing over?

And now the moment is here. The rubber is about to hit the road. When I look at him, I feel all the love in the world but at the same time so much betrayal.

So much loss.

A decade of misplaced blame that makes no sense and yet happened.

"Answer me, son," he demands as I take a step back.

"I think you're the one who owes me answers," I say quietly.

"*Drew?* Who is it?" Brexton asks at my back. The widening of my father's eyes shows me he has seen her over my shoulder. The tendons in his neck strain and his whole expression freezes.

He stares at her long and hard. Studies her. Recognizes her.

And then he looks back at me with narrowed eyes and lines etched on his face like I'm the one who's betrayed him. Like I'm the one who has hurt him. His mouth is in a tight line as his hands tremor. My mom clings to him with determination like if she squeezes his arm tight enough, this will go away.

"What have you done?" my mom asks, her voice barely audible but the accusation is there.

"Nothing, Mom. Absolutely fucking nothing, but try to live my life out from under the web of lies Dad spun around us."

My dad's chin trembles, and his eyes swim with so much emotion that I don't know if he's going to run or stay and fight.

Let's hope he loves me more than the game of football. Let's hope he fights for me.

"I did it for you." My dad's voice is all but a whisper, and I'm not sure if it's because he doesn't want Brexton to hear or because he's overcome with emotion.

"*For me?* You haven't cared a day in your life about anything other than yourself, so don't you dare turn this on me. Don't you dare stand there and act so fucking pious. You turned our lives around because you were too goddamn weak to either fight for what you stood for or to admit you were at fault."

Chapter
SIXTY-ONE

Brexton

MY HEART LURCHES INTO MY THROAT AT THE SIGHT OF A FATHER AND a son who look so much alike but who are at complete odds.

I can't tear my eyes off Gary. The man I used to joke with, play catch on the beach with, and consider an uncle. He's older now. The years haven't been kind to him, but I'm uncertain if that's the illness or the stress of everything.

The expression on his face is what holds my attention. I can't figure out if he's relieved and is masking it with fury or if he's really as angry as he seems.

Either one is heartbreaking when it comes to its consequences for the man I love.

Then there's Brenda.

She's clinging to Gary's arm as if they're one and the same person and it's part pathetic, part what I could picture my parents being like if my mom were alive.

Drew glances back at me for a moment and I note the intensity in his eyes that reflects everything about him in this moment. Defiance. Anger. Confusion.

I feel completely out of place and uncomfortable and struggle with whether to go or stay. So instead, I just stand right where I am with feet that feel like they're weighed down by lead.

"She needs to leave," Gary says to Drew, as if I'm a child he can't stand to address.

"She stays," he deadpans without looking at me or asking if I want to be here.

I don't.

Not in the least.

While Gary may have somehow put the blame on my father, me being here is only going to complicate matters.

"This is a private matter, son. It's to be discussed among our family."

I see Drew tense from his words and hear his stifled laugh of disbelief. "This is my house. Are you fucking kidding me? You don't get to stride in here and give me orders. I've lived by your rules my whole goddamn life and I'm done. Fucking sick of them. You don't get to tell me what to do anymore."

"Don't do this," his mother murmurs.

"Do what, Mom?" He throws his hands up. "Do what we should have done years ago but we were so goddamn afraid to upset the precious fucking peace?"

"Don't you dare bring disgrace to this family," Gary warns.

"Yes, right. I forgot. I disgraced you by playing football when you told me I shouldn't. I disgraced you by not being good enough for the Bowman name. And I fucking disgraced you by falling in love with the enemy. That's right," Drew's voice thunders. "I love her, goddammit, and the two of you can go to hell if you don't choose to accept it."

There is stunned silence in the house. One that's suffocating and smothering. It makes me feel like I'm watching two cars in slow motion about to hit head-on and there is no amount of screaming I can do to stop it.

I shouldn't be here. This is between them and my presence is only going to make matters so much worse.

I walk to the counter for my purse and grab it, needing away from this and wanting Drew to be free to say whatever it is he needs to say without fear of hurting me when it comes to my family.

"Brex?" Drew asks after he hears the jingle of my keys when I walk back into the room.

"I just . . . you guys need to sort this out. He's right," I say and Drew winces. "I shouldn't be here right now."

He opens and closes his mouth. The tears that well in his eyes break my heart. But he doesn't speak or try to stop me when I get the courage to walk out the front door and right past Brenda and Gary. I meet their eyes but don't say a word. It's so damn silent you can hear a pin drop.

The calm before the storm.

Too bad I have a feeling the minute I leave, the thunder that roars will be deafening.

But as I pass by, no one says a word. No one stops me. And a small piece of me breathes a sigh of relief that even Drew doesn't. I run from the house with the click of my shoes the only sound made.

My hands are trembling as I open my car door and start the engine. I'm not sure why tears threaten as I drive down the street, but they do.

A part of me fears what Drew's about to go through. Fighting with your parents is never fun. The other part of me fears that this might be the last time I see Drew.

Yes, I heard what he said to his parents, but the pull of family is much stronger than the pull of a new love.

And then I feel selfish for feeling that way.

For thinking of me and us when more than anything, Drew needs this for himself. Answers. Closure. A new start.

I drive. Here. There. Everywhere through the suburbia adjacent to his neighborhood, hoping, willing, wanting, a text or phone call from him.

Anything to know that he is okay.

Anything to know that we're okay.

Surely their discussion is over by now. But by the time I've wasted hours driving and have arrived home, I decide to take the plunge and call him myself.

He doesn't answer.

I text him.

He doesn't reply.

And that selfish feeling starts to return. The one that wants to know what happened. The one that fears he believes the ugly lies once again.

The one that warns me that a heartbreak just might be on the horizon.

Chapter
SIXTY-TWO

Drew

THE BOTTLE OF WHISKEY IS EMPTY.

My phone buzzing alerts is face down on the couch beside me.

My house is pitch-black.

But my thoughts don't stop.

They walked away. Fucking walked out the door minutes after Brexton left when I demanded answers.

"She's a Kincade." My father's voice is low, his expression unmoving, as Brexton's taillights are still a glimmer down the street.

"Why don't we address why the thought of me being with her has you in an absolute panic, Dad? Why don't we talk about how scared you are right now that the goddamn ruse is up?"

"Her father ruined our family," my dad says with a quiet steel to his voice.

"So you've said, but you know something?" I ask and make a show of scratching my temple. "It doesn't make any sense. Why would he burn a big-time client who he was making a shit ton of money off of in commission? Why would he hurt the friends who were like a family to us? Only a coward would do that and from what I remember, Kenyon Kincade wasn't a coward."

But I'm beginning to see that you were.

I plant the seed. The bait. I wait for the reaction. I need to see if he's going to stand and fight or turn away like a coward.

Two completely different reactions. Two completely different truths.

He lied about what happened. I know deep in my bones he did. Maybe I always have but was too much of a coward myself to admit it to myself. Maybe

I needed to hold on to the hope that my father was the man I'd always wanted him to be.

"You've made your choice then," my father says.

"No. You're making the choice. Not me."

My father's eyes meet mine and I swear there is something in them akin to devastation, but it's fleeting and wiped away by a harsh bout of tremors. My mom's face falls, and I want to reach out and help support him but fear the reaction I'd be met with.

Emotion is thick in my throat as my mom murmurs to him to calm down and guides him down the walk away from me.

"Fuck," I mutter into the darkness, into the loneliness, as the events replay over and over in my head.

I should have gone after Brexton.

I should have left my parents and their non-answers behind and run after the only person in as long as I can remember who is true and real and honest.

Goddamn Brexton.

My savior. My sounding board. My best friend.

But I didn't chase after her. Now I'm left feeling like the asshole who didn't do enough to stand up for her *and* the son who just walked away from his sick father.

Last time we fought, we didn't talk for over a year.

Over a goddamn year.

What if the same happens now? Because I won't bend this time. I won't unless I have answers. I deserve that much.

But what if he won't give them?

Will the disease have ravaged him by then? Will I lose out on time my father has left before it's too late?

But he didn't give answers . . . just ultimatums.

He didn't say a fucking word other than to point fingers at Brexton and the Kincades.

I guess, perpetuating the lie is more important than mending fences.

And how the fuck is that supposed to make me feel? That whatever the fuck he did was more important to him than me?

So I drank whiskey. So much whiskey, I lost count but the bottle is empty on its side on the floor by my foot.

And there was rage. A swipe of the kitchen counter and all the preparations for the celebration went flying to the floor. Dishes breaking, food flying.

Then there was knock after knock on the front door as my teammates came and then left probably wondering what the fuck was going on. Still texting to make sure everything is okay.

And now? Now I'm trying to understand the measure of me as a man. How gullible I was to be held under my father's spell. How easily I've tried to please a man so fucking selfish that he chose a game over his family.

He did this. To us. To our family. To him.

It wasn't Kenyon, and it sure as fuck wasn't anyone else.

It was him and whatever weakness he caved to.

And even worse? I'm sitting here, drunk as fuck in the dark, wondering how I can feel sorry for him. I worry that tonight affected his health. I still want to know if he's proud of me for the game I played today. I wonder if I've just lost my family.

What kind of man does that make me?

A pussy? Lacking character? Spineless?

I scrub a hand through my hair and rest my head on the back of the couch.

There's shit I need to figure out, need to find answers to, before I can be worthy of a love like Brexton's.

She deserves better than this. Than me. So much fucking better.

She deserves the white knight when I'm nothing but a Montague destined to be at odds with her and her family forever.

Figure your shit out, Bowman.

Sleep on it. Get your head straight. Then figure your shit out.

The answer is a simple one.

At least it should be.

I don't know how long I sit and stare at the ceiling or how many times I replay tonight in my head, but when my phone buzzes yet again, I finally pick it up.

Text after text fills my screen. From my teammates wondering what the fuck happened tonight with the party.

From Brexton.

She's worried.

So am I.

But I open her text and respond.

Me: I just need some time to sort through the shit in my head.

Brexton: Okay. I'm here if you need me.

I should type something else. A *thank you.* A *come over.* An *I need you.*

An *I love you.*

But I don't. Instead, I toss my phone back where it was and close my eyes.

I just hope she can still love me after I didn't stand up for her more, tonight. Didn't chase after her.

I didn't fight hard enough for the one thing I love.

Doesn't that make me just like him?

Chapter SIXTY-THREE

Brexton

THREE DAYS.

It's been three goddamn days since I walked out of that house, since I got that text that felt like a death sentence to our relationship, and not one word since.

I know he's been at practice but nothing else.

Did they fight it all out and Drew's mourning whatever the outcome was? Did Gary reassert his truth that my family is to blame, and Drew fell back down that rabbit hole and is afraid to tell me that we're over?

"Quit overthinking it," Lennox says in my ear.

"I'm not."

"That's total bullshit and you know it. He didn't have to answer your text but he did. In fact, he was specific that he needed time to figure his shit out. I'd say that's progress. I'd say that's a man letting you know what is happening instead of shutting down when it comes to communication like most do. I know it's hard, but you need to hold tight to that."

"Perhaps."

"No perhaps about it. It's a fact." She chuckles. "If he was going to end things he wouldn't have responded. He would have blown you off and that would be that. Instead he asked for time, for grace, and you're giving it to him. Sounds like the perfect give and take if you ask me."

"Except that I'm sitting here in the dark."

"True, but you're also being the person he needs you to be right now. And that is one of the most important things in any relationship. You both had to bend and bow at different times. You might not always like it, but it's true."

"Of course, because you're a relationship expert now that you've found Rush."

"Far from it, but I'm learning as I go. Oh, and don't think for a second that I don't know why you call me for this shit. Because you don't have to see me face to face so when I'm right, you can still save face."

"Whatever," I say but know there's an iota of truth in what she said. With her living in the UK now, she's my go-to advice person because it's easier. "Things with Rush still good?" I ask.

"Gloriously so," she says. "And speaking of the devil, he's calling for me from the other room. You good?"

"Yes. Thank you."

"You can thank me when I'm proven right."

"Funny."

"Love you."

"Love you more."

And when the call ends, I feel a little better but still worry about him. Still miss him.

I have a million contracts to review—because life goes on even when my heart wants to stop and wait for the man I love—but I'm mentally exhausted. So even though it's early, I snap my laptop closed and crawl into bed.

But sleep doesn't come.

Just staring out the window at the stars trying to shine through the bright lights of the city and my thoughts running wild in the darkness.

"Go away, Bratty Brex. I don't want company. Don't feel like talking," Drew says.

I can't tell you how many times I've heard that this trip. Dreadful Drew has become Moody Drew, always wanting to be alone, and while I've tried not to feel hurt by it, I'm still hurt.

He's never minded my company before. In fact, he's been fine with just sitting in silence if he didn't feel like talking.

But not this trip.

And it stings more than ever.

I bet if Ginnie Huber were here he wouldn't say go away to her.

"What's wrong?" I ask.

"Nothing."

"Nothing? Then why are you so grumpy?"

"I'm not grumpy, it's just . . . stuff."

"Like what kind of stuff?" I ask, imagining him heartbroken. How I could swoop in and save him from it.

"This is why I want you to go away. You keep asking questions."

"Yeah, well, you keep being grumpy."

"I said it's just stuff, okay? Stuff you don't understand."

"Humph." I cross my arms and stare at him. "Maybe I don't want to talk to you either, Dreadful Drew. Maybe I'm just here to look at the stars and you're the one who should go away."

"I was here first."

"So?"

He looks over at me and rolls his eyes, but he doesn't object when I take a seat beside him. "My mom likes to look at the stars." I point to the star-filled sky above. "She says there's nothing better when you need to think than to look at the stars."

"Why?" he asks and glances over at me. I lie on my back beside him and put my arms behind my head.

"Because the sky and its stars remind you that your one problem is so very little in this great big world. It makes you feel like you're not all alone."

"Is that so?"

"It's a fact."

"A Mom fact," he says with a snort but copies how I'm lying.

"And now you need to make a wish."

"A wish? For what? It's not my birthday."

"It doesn't have to be your birthday." I sigh. "You're looking at this great big sky. How do you not know that someone else who is looking at the same sky—somewhere—doesn't have the answer to your problem? So make a wish. Maybe they'll hear it and help you."

"Another Mom fact?" He nudges me.

"Nope. A Brexton fact."

He laughs out loud, but he stays there beside me for well over an hour until our parents call us in.

"Hey Brex?" he asks when he stands, offering me a lopsided grin as he pulls me up.

My heart flutters in my chest. "Yeah?"

"Thanks. Maybe looking at the stars with someone is better than being alone."

An idea hits. One I'm not certain is smart, but I can't stay away from him any longer. I grab my phone and text him.

Me: Remember that time we stared at the stars and made silent wishes? I'm looking at the stars right now, Drew. I'm making my wishes. If you want to join me, you can call me. We don't have to talk, but it's nicer looking at the stars with someone than being alone.

I hit send and then feel like an idiot the minute I do. He probably doesn't even remember that night. He probably doesn't—

I startle when my phone rings and his name is on the screen.

"I'm here," I say when I answer the call. "I'm here."

"I know."

It's all he says as we stare at the stars together, feeling less alone tonight.

Chapter
SIXTY-FOUR

Drew

"MAY I COME IN?"

I stare at my mom standing in my doorway and hate that I actually want to say no. The last thing I need is more bullshit when my head is finally clearing.

"We have a team meeting I have to get to," I lie.

"No, you don't. You forget you're talking to an NFL wife. Meetings are for mornings. Practices after that. Film review on Mondays. I understand that you don't want to talk to me, son, but there's something I think you need to see," she says motioning to the box at her feet.

"Mom." The word is a plea. "I can't do this again. If he's not going to give me answers then I can't do this. Don't you think I deserve that much? Don't you and Maggs and Charley deserve it?"

"Please?" she asks with tears in her eyes.

I open the door and hold her gaze until she walks inside. We move in silence as I carry the box and set it on the coffee table, which is situated between the two couches.

"What's this?" I ask.

"The other night there were a lot of things said."

"More like a lot of things left *unsaid*," I argue, not wanting to let her off the hook this time. She was an enabler in this whole thing so my resentment toward her is strong too.

She levels me with a look that says to give her a chance. I sigh and sit back, already frustrated.

"You told your father he never cared about anyone else a day in his life."

"It's true."

"You are his pride and joy, Drew. How can you say that?"

"How?" I scoff. "Because when he walked away from the sport, he left me behind with it. He never showed up to a single one of my games. He never said anything positive. Most dads would be thrilled to have their son follow in their footsteps. Mine resented me for it and let me know I'd never live up to his legacy."

"On the contrary, son. Dad was staying away so you could have your time to shine. If he was there, it would only draw attention to him. He was staying away so he wouldn't be selfish and take the light away from you."

"Those are just words, Mom. They mean shit because even when he wasn't there, the whispers and comments still were. Every goddamn game. Don't you think it would have been easier if I'd had him in my corner? Wasn't it selfish to leave me to face all of that alone? Was it too hard for him to come to a game or simply say he was proud of me? Or did he resent me so much because I played a game he was too chickenshit to fight for?" I shake my head.

She pushes the box across the table. "Open it."

"Why? Whatever is in that box isn't going to solve our fucked-up family."

"Open the damn box, Drew, and stop being difficult."

When I lift the lid off the box, I uncover a bunch of binders or maybe scrapbooks. I glance at my mom as I pick one at random and pull it out.

"Open it," she urges.

And when I do, I'm met with an image of me during a game. The black and white photo of the newspaper cutting is one I remember vividly. It was a conference championship in college that we lost in a nail-biter.

But just as clearly as I remember that first article, when I flip the pages, there are dozens behind it that I don't. Little scraps with a mention of me. Squares of game stats glued to a page. A faded picture in action. A college team brochure.

I look at page after page, each one chronicling my history. Each page documenting a moment in time I never would have remembered.

"He did care, Drew. He followed every single step of your career. The highs. The lows. The in-betweens. These are his proof. And what you find in that binder, there are dozens more just like it."

I don't bother hiding my tears. This is a little boy's wish answered and in the way I've always wanted.

I've looked for him. In every game I've taken the field, I've looked for him, so why didn't he tell me he'd been following me? Why couldn't he have sent text messages, emails, picked up the fucking phone, anything that said he was proud of me?

Is proud of me.

The visible proof is here in front of me that he cared, but what am I supposed to do with it now? It's like a belated birthday card—nice to get, but a reminder someone forgot the big day.

"Wouldn't saying it have been easier?" I ask as I stare until the words in the article become blurred.

"Would you have believed them if he had said the words? Or would you have thought he was justifying his absence?"

"I don't know, but I still needed to hear from my dad that he thought I could be starting quarterback. I stayed on the sidelines, not believing I had the talent."

"I know you think he only cared about himself—and I can understand why you think that, but I also thought you should know there are two sides to every story, Drew. When it comes to you, this is his side. His proof. You're who kept him going most days." She rises from her seat and walks around the table to press a kiss to the top of my head. "I'm sorry you never knew about these until now."

"Mom?" I ask, struggling to accept all of this.

"As a parent, all you want to do is protect your children from everything. And sometimes, you don't see until it's too late that protecting them is what ends up hurting them."

"Okay. Fine. But why won't he give me answers? *Us answers?* Don't I deserve an explanation about why our life spiraled into such chaos?"

Her somber eyes meet mine and a bittersweet smile ghosts over her lips. "I did just explain," she says softly before turning and walking out of my house, leaving the box behind.

As a parent, all you want to do is protect your children from everything. And sometimes, you don't see until it's too late that protecting them is what ends up hurting them.

What the hell does that mean?

And a man who thought he had it all figured out, is now conflicted once again.

Chapter
SIXTY-FIVE

Brexton

"HEY, IT'S ME," I SAY TO DREW'S VOICEMAIL. "I KNOW YOU NEED SPACE but I wanted you to know I'd never ask you to choose between me and your family. I don't want you to feel like that's a choice you have to make. I do love you, Drew. *Madly*. And I'd walk away from us if that's what it takes for you to be happy." I almost choke on the words but know I'd do that for him. "And I hate that you're hurting. I only wish there was something I could do to help you, but I understand this is something you need to figure out or confront on your own. I'll be here whenever you're ready to talk or . . . whatever."

I stare at my cell phone for a beat as I vacillate between whether I should have said all of that or not, but it's too late now as it's been said. I can't take it back so I end the call.

But this not talking to him thing is killing me. It's making me doubt myself and how strong I thought we were together.

The one thing I keep thinking is that I know silence speaks when words can't, but I'm struggling to hear what Drew's silence is saying.

Restless and preoccupied, I walk to my office door and then turn back, already forgetting whatever it was I was needing to do.

Get a life.

Hear from Drew.

See Drew.

Any of the three will suffice.

"Hey? You okay?"

I startle at the sound of my Dad's voice and when I look up, find him standing across the office studying me.

How long has he been there?

Did he hear me on the phone?

I've been trying desperately to put on a brave face so that no one knows what's going on. At least until I know what's going on, that is.

"Brex?"

"I'm good. Sorry, I was lost in thought." I nod and give a smile that I'm more than certain he realizes doesn't reach my eyes.

"Is it Flatley?" he asks about my NBA player, who is currently causing problems with his teammates on the Chicago Bulls, and the management is demanding I try to control him. "If it's too much on your plate, I could have Dekker or Chase go for you. I could even go. I know you have a lot going on and—"

"No need. I'm fine. I already have my flight booked for tomorrow morning. I'm heading there and then have a few meetings set up the day after next with some clients I've been neglecting in the same vicinity. Just a quick trip. I'll be back on Sunday afternoon."

"You sure? I can take your place." He gives me the once-over, and I try to be more convincing with my smile this time around.

"One hundred percent. You know me, I like to keep busy." I lean against the doorjamb of my office and then take a deep breath. *This is your dad, Brex. You know you don't really have to put up a front of indifference.* "I've just been running ragged, I guess. I feel like shit for not landing Hobbs, but even if I had landed him that spot with the Chargers, I still wouldn't have signed him with the shit he pulled."

"I agree. There's no need to feel bad, honey."

"But I do, and so I'm just tired, trying to pull in some other new clients to make up for it is all. Then this crap with Flatley, and I'm just frustrated. That's it. Frustrated and tired."

Quit talking. Quit overexplaining. He'll definitely know something is wrong.

"We'll survive without an asshole like Hobbs. I already told you that. And Drew? He's good too?" he asks and purses his lips.

"Yes. Of course." I offer a tight smile that wins me a narrowing of his eyes followed by a nod.

"I have a good lunch." He holds up his lunch bag. "I overpacked per usual. Do you want to share it with me? We can have lunch together in the conference room like old times?" His smile is soft, his eyes knowing. He can see I'm upset about something.

But he doesn't ask.

I swallow over the lump in my throat and nod. "I'd like that. Thank you."

And before I follow him, I toss my cell on my desk. I'm uncertain if I'm leaving it behind because I'm afraid Drew won't respond to my voicemail or if he does, his response might be something I'm not ready to accept.

But I leave it.

Because right now it's okay to be uncertain. It's okay to feel a little lost.

At least I'm in the best place possible while having those feelings.

Next to my dad.

My rock.

And it doesn't hurt that he packs really good lunches.

Chapter
SIXTY-SIX

Drew

"You're distracted this week," Lonnie says as I walk past him on the field. "You're not the same Bowman I've seen week after week during practice. You break up with your girl? Need to get laid? What's the deal?"

Stopping with my helmet in my hand, I turn to face him, unaware that all the shit in my head was affecting my on-the-field play. I thought I was hiding it well enough.

"I'm good. Everything's good," I say.

"You sure?" He tucks his clipboard under his arm and takes a few steps toward me.

I nod. "I'm sure."

"Good, because I need clarity on the field tomorrow, Drew. I need to know you can focus and secure us the home-field advantage for the playoffs."

I stare at him. There's no way I just heard that right. "I thought you told me it was a one-time thing last game? That Hobbs's shoulder was sore and—"

"Yeah, well. Maybe I didn't want you to get in your own head too much if I told you otherwise." He winks and laughs. "But I spoke to Neil and Coach, and we think you're the best-suited QB to lead us against the Steelers. You're starting, so do whatever it is that you have to do to get your head straight and your mental game strong."

"Yes, sir." I stand there and stare at him.

"Did you need something else?" he asks.

"No." I blow out a relieved breath. "Just taking it all in, is all."

Lonnie pats me on the shoulder and squeezes. "There's something to be said about fighting your way to the top. I've always found it's those guys who appreciate the top much more."

He walks away and leaves me standing in the stadium, one hand on my hip, one hand holding my helmet, and a sense of belonging for the first time with the Raptors.

Pride swallows me whole.

I did it.

It took me way too fucking long, but I climbed back here. I proved myself and my talent even with the Bowman last name.

"Brexton," I whisper.

I need to call her. To tell her. To see her. She's definitely one of the reasons I'm standing here right now.

. . . do whatever it is that you have to do to get your head straight and your mental game strong.

There's something else I have to do first.

Chapter
SIXTY-SEVEN

Drew

"DREW?" MAGGIE'S FACE LIGHTS UP WHEN SHE OPENS THE DOOR TO see me standing on her doorstep.

"Hi." My smile is timid but genuine. "You look good."

And she does. There's color in her face and the hollow of her cheeks are now filled in with the weight she's gained.

"I'm taking it day by day." She steps back and motions to the inside of her apartment. "Would you like to come in? It's a mess but—"

"Just for a sec."

"If you're coming to check if I'm using, I'm not."

"That's not why I'm here," I say and take a look around her place. It's bright and sunny with the curtains pulled back, whereas the last time I was here it felt more like a tomb. There's a plastic kid's table in the corner where coloring pages are half done and some building blocks are stacked.

"She's with Wayne. I mean, if you're looking for Charley. I don't get to have her just yet. Just visits for now," she explains.

I don't have the heart to tell her that I spent a few hours with her yesterday, needing a bit of her innocence to ground me.

I'm not quite sure that I found it, but Charley's sweet smile and belly giggles definitely helped.

"I'm not here for her either." I walk to the kitchen and open the refrigerator out of habit to make sure there is food in there. No tin foil. No bent spoons. No lighters.

I hate that I look, but I do.

"What do you need?"

I turn to stare at my sister and shrug. "I'm not exactly sure."

Her laugh is anxious as her eyes narrow. "Drew?"

"Why?" It's a single word but it's asking so much.

"Why what?"

"Why did this happen to you? I mean, was it Dad? If his scandal had never happened, do you think you would have gone down this path?"

"I'm not following you." She takes a step closer, concern filling her eyes.

"I'm in love, Maggs. I'm in love with Brexton Kincade." Her lips form an O in shock and her eyebrows lift. "And—"

"Do Mom and Dad know?"

"Yes," I say and explain what happened the other night. She has her hand over her open mouth as she listens. Our parents going to my house. The fight. The ultimatum. Letting Brexton walk away without chasing after her.

"So what are you asking me?" she whispers, and I immediately feel stupid for coming here and involving her when she's in such a fragile state.

"It's stupid. Never mind."

"You know, in recovery, you have to ask yourself a lot of hard questions. You have to make amends for all the lies you've told others and the ones you've told yourself before you can move on with a genuine clean slate."

"What if the people you apologize to don't accept them?" I ask.

"It's not about them accepting, it's about you acknowledging the hurt you've caused and the damage you've done. It's about you owning up to it. They can do with it what they will."

I twist my lips as I stand with my hips against her kitchen counter and my hands shoved in the pockets of my jeans. "I think Dad did it."

"Okay." She stretches the word out.

"And I'm mad at myself for believing him all these years, because if I had really listened to what he wasn't saying, then maybe I could have stopped this years ago. Our family's pain. Your battles with addiction. The lull in my career—"

"No one is to blame for my addiction other than me, Drew." She moves forward so she's standing right in front of me. "Sure, I was lost and needed something when our world went to shit, but that's one hundred percent on me. Not Mom. Not Dad. Not you. *Me.* It took me a while to comprehend, but one of the rehab mantras is this: *Grant me the serenity to accept the things I cannot change, the courage to change the things I can, and the wisdom to know the difference.*" She pauses, closing her eyes and taking a deep breath. When she opens her eyes, she says, "*I* took that first hit when Bobby Bufford offered it to me. If I blame Dad, then I also have to give him credit for *my* recovery and I refuse to do that. I'm doing this on my own and I deserve all of the credit."

"You do." My smile is wide. I couldn't be prouder of her than right now. "You deserve all of the credit."

"So go do it, Drew."

"What?"

"Confront Dad, once and for all."

"How do you know that's what I'm going to do?"

Her smile is soft as her hands come up to frame my face. I'm forced to look into my sister's bright and cloudless eyes, which is so damn welcome. "Because you've always looked out for me. And right now, you're here because you're afraid that I might not be stable enough to handle whatever fallout ensues from you demanding answers—our family pulling together or possibly falling apart. You don't want me to relapse."

I nod. It's all I can add as an answer, because isn't that why I came here? To make sure she's okay? To know she's on board with the decision I've already made?

"We've been both, Drew. Together and apart. You have a life you deserve to live. Get your answers. You need them. And then go and live that life. Go and love Brexton. Go and step out from under this shadow."

When I wrap my arms around her and hold tight, I know I was right to come here first. Whatever she said wasn't going to alter my decision to confront Dad, but I sure as hell didn't expect it to make me more confident in my decision like it just did.

"I love you, Maggs."

"Drew," my mom says when she opens the door, her eyes wide and the pitch of her voice high. "I didn't expect to see you. I—thank you for coming by."

"Don't thank me yet. I need to talk to Dad. *Alone.*"

"Yes. Okay. You sure?" Nerves dance through her as she probably fears what I'm here to say.

"Yes. This is something I should have done years ago."

My mom stares at me with tears misting and gives me the slightest of nods. She understands.

"He's in the study."

I hold her stare for a few more seconds before I set off toward the back of the house. When I reach my dad's office, I'm struck how everything that lines the walls is about a sport we've been forbidden to talk about. Pictures, memorabilia, and game balls in glass cases line the bookcases and walls and my dad sits at his desk in the middle of it all.

"Dad?"

He startles and starts to stand immediately, his defenses already up as surprise reflects in his expression.

"Drew."

"Stay seated," I say as I walk into the room and close the door at my back. There are a million questions in his eyes but he doesn't say a word. Instead he simply stares at me with a wary expression. I inhale a measured breath and then say what I came to say. "Did you do it?" My voice is calm and unrelenting.

"We've already gone over this."

"No. You told us to shut our mouths and we have, but can't you see that your silence is tearing us apart, Dad? So I'm going to ask you one more time for the truth. And if I walk out of this door because you refuse to give it, then don't ever plan on seeing me come back."

The words stick in my throat. A horrible threat given to a man with a terminal illness. But I can't do this anymore. I can't keep living for him and pretending that I'm not. I've reflected on my mom's words the other day, and I don't understand how he was protecting us. It makes no sense.

But I need to know.

I need to get my head straight.

"Son, I—"

"I've got the start tomorrow. Not because Hobbs is injured, like last time, but because I've earned it. It's been seven years since the last time I started. Now, I need to know the truth. You owe that to me." I clench my fists out of frustration and from years and years of not knowing. "I need to be able to go out there and play for me instead of playing to clear our last name."

"I never asked you to do that." His voice is so cold, so stoic, that all I want to do is shake him to get some emotion out of him.

But then again, is that something he's actually capable of?

"You didn't have to. You're my dad. You *were* my idol. And no matter what I've done in my life, everything about what you did overshadows it. I have a chance here—at my dream on and off the field—and the only way I can walk into both so that I can succeed is if I know the truth . . . so I'm going to ask you again, *did you do it?*" Anger floods my voice as I jab my finger with each and every word.

"It started out small. A few bets here and there on baseball or college football."

Fuck.

"The funny thing is, the more you make, the more you bet. What's a huge dollar amount to someone else is chump change to you." He sighs and leans back in his chair, his hands trembling as they try to clasp in front of him. I can't take my eyes off them.

"I started betting more and more, began loving the high I'd get waiting to see the outcome of a game and whether or not I was right or wrong. I'd reached every pinnacle that could be reached playing football and placing huge bets was the next closest feeling I could find to say winning the Super Bowl."

"You were addicted."

"I didn't see it then, but yes, I was addicted."

"Did Mom know?"

"I hid it from her. Or at least I thought I did. But you can only hide something like that for so long before the lies run out."

"So you threw the game." My voice breaks when I say the words.

I wish I were wrong. I wish I'd come here and received any other response—anything—because it would be so much easier to accept. So much easier to process. So much easier to save face.

"Let me finish. Please?" When I don't say anything, he continues. "I got into trouble with bookies. It started around the time we were in the Keys. I spent that whole trip stressing how I could keep pretending I was living the high life when all my money and then some was going to bets. I had loans to pay. Big amounts, and it wasn't like I could make any more money than I was making."

"Bookies? Are we talking about loan sharks and mafia—"

"Yes. Drew. I owed money—*a lot of it*—to some very bad people."

Jesus Christ.

I stare at the man before me and wonder how someone so strong could fall into that trap, how he could have been so weak, but it's not like he's the only one who ever has.

"I was so in the hole, and I was convinced that I could make one more significant bet and win, and that would turn things around. But it never happened. The payout never came and they wanted their money back." He falls quiet for a beat before continuing. "They came to the house one night. You were in the street playing catch with the Merriman kid, and they pulled in the driveway and let me know that they were done waiting. That I either pay up or they'd take my pride and joy away from me." His breath hitches and he averts his eyes to stare at his hands. A tear drops onto where they are clasped as he takes in a shaky breath. "I'll never forget that feeling when they threatened your life."

The words are deafening to hear.

The memories faint. My dad in the driveway. Three guys talking to him. Me squinting from down the street trying to figure out who they were. The SUV driving away and my dad telling me to get inside. I asked what was wrong but he said nothing.

"They made sure to let me know they knew everything about your schedule. When your practice was over. The name of the girl you'd been kissing at the party you'd gone to the night before. The route you jogged when you went for a run. Fucking everything, Drew," he says when he finally lifts his eyes to meet mine. "And it terrified me because I knew they weren't joking."

I move for the first time since I've come into his office, and perch my-self on the edge of the chair across from him. I'm looking at a truly de-feated man. One I barely even recognize. *Have I ever seen that in this man?*

"They let their threat sink in for a few days before I heard from them again. That's when they told me how I could clear my debt."

"Throw a game."

"Not just any game, but a game against the Colts. We were, by and large, a huge favorite, and a win against them would have put us in the AFC Championship." His sigh sounds like the weight of the world is on his shoulders. "They were going to bet on the long shot, the Colts, and when they won the point spread, they'd make back what I owed them plus interest."

"Why didn't you go to the cops? The league—"

"Because they told me you were the consequence. If I told the cops, if I didn't throw the game . . . you were the consequence, Drew."

Chills snake down my spine. This conversation went in a direction I never expected it to go. I'm at a loss, trying to comprehend it all.

"So I did it. I missed passes. I dropped handoffs. I threw the game even when every bone in my body revolted against doing it."

"You threw up on the sidelines during the game." The memory comes out of my mouth without realizing it. I remember it though. The com-mentators wondering if he was ill and trying to play through it. The spec-ulation afterward that he was using—his excuse.

"I did. I was so sick to my stomach but I had no choice. It was you—my everything—or a game I loved. There was no question who to choose." He shakes his head. "But I was naïve. I thought I could throw the game and no one would know. I thought I'd be able to pull it off. But weeks later, someone tipped off that a large bet had been made on the game. The gamblers were long gone with their winnings but their threats were still present while I took center stage."

I remember those first days after the accusations came. The yelling behind my parents' bedroom door when they thought we'd fallen asleep. The press camped out on our lawn. Their sudden clinginess to Maggs and me and our every move.

"I thought I could ride it out. I thought it would blow over. Kenyon was trying to tell me what to do, but I shut him out. I knew if he looked closely he'd know the truth. He knew me too well, and I couldn't stomach letting him down either. So I went to meet with my team without telling him. They told me the NFL was launching a full investigation into the game and my actions. They told me that the NFL was possibly going to strip the club of our Super Bowl win the year before. They were questioning if I let the Colts get closer in points because I was betting the split."

"Did you?"

"No. I don't expect you to believe me, but no. I didn't. I told them it was a load of crap. They responded with their own offer. If I walked away from the game and never spoke of the situation again, they'd pay out the rest of my contract. They said they believed me that I didn't do it, but they couldn't risk the NFL taking the championship away or investigating all of our other games. They said it was a one-time offer and I had to accept right then and there or I could face the investigation." Tears pool in his eyes again. "I took the deal, son. I was broke, I'd ruined my career, and if I took the deal I had a way to provide for my family."

I lean back in my chair and close my eyes as I replay his words over and over in my head. As I try to poke holes through things I have no knowledge of. But why would he lie? Why all these years later would he lie?

But then I remember he had.

"You blamed this on Kenyon. You even stood in my house last week and told me to kick Brexton out because she's his daughter. You gave me the ultimatum—her or you. Why? Are you that weak a man you had to blame somebody else?"

"Yes." He nods and then shakes his head. "Do you remember that day I told you? You were so angry and I was more than devastated over what I'd done to my family and walking away from all I'd ever known. You yelled at me. You questioned and demanded and, for the first time in your life, you looked at me like you were ashamed. I deserved it. Fuck did I. But I will never forget that look in your eye and so when you asked if Kenyon was at fault, I took the chickenshit way out and ran with it. And I've sold the lie, protected it, fostered it, ever since because I needed you to believe that I was a good guy, son. I needed to know that even after I did all of this, you didn't hate me."

I shove up out of the chair, brace my hands on the back of my neck, and walk to the windows, looking out at the pitch-black beyond the panes.

"But you blamed somebody else," I say, my voice rising in pitch. "Couldn't you just once, own up to something? Couldn't you just—fuck!"

Frustration eats at me. I understand why he did one thing but not the other. I understand making a reckless, split-second decision in the moment, but I can't comprehend carrying it on for ten years.

"Son—"

"Please, don't *son*, me right now. Please don't . . ." I scrub my hands over my face and blow out a breath. *Fuck.* I lost the Kincades due to my father's selfishness. I lost two good men in my life, and look how that has screwed with every aspect of it. I lost respect for a man who still deserves it. And Kenyon then lost Claire. And Brex . . . *My mom should have been there for Brex and her sisters when they lost their mom. But because of this man in front of me, she lost my mom too.* Fuck. So fucking selfish. That's what I can't reconcile. He could have made this play out differently. "So even if this is all true—"

"It is true."

"Even if this is all true," I repeat, "it doesn't make any sense why you kept me at arm's length. If I was threatened, if you did all of this to save me, why did it feel like you didn't love me anymore? Why did it feel like you wanted nothing to fucking do with me?"

And isn't that the goddamn question of the year? Because even if I believe all of what he said, I can't bring myself to understand why he acted like he did.

"They picked you because you were my world. Yes, I love your mother and Maggs in their own ways, but you were a carbon copy of me. Right or wrong, Drew, the sun rose and set with you. I thought, I figured, if I stepped back and didn't outwardly show that it did—that you'd be safe. That they'd know nothing mattered to me and therefore there was nothing more they could threaten."

My chest aches beneath my breastbone and my head swims with all of *this*.

"But your debt was paid. Life moved on. At some point that no longer became a valid excuse."

"At first, they left notes letting me know they were still watching, that they would know if I told anyone the truth . . . but you're right. Everything moved on except the fear I lived with every day that someone wanted to hurt you because of me."

"I don't buy that. I can't. I spent every goddamn game looking in the stands at all the other fathers cheering their sons on praying there'd come a day when I'd see you there. Even if it were in the shadows with a hat hiding who you were, I wanted you there. I still do." It kills me to admit it but it's true. "I spent week after week trying to make you proud, trying to make you feel anything when it came to me other than indifference. Maggie could overdose and have a kid and fuck up time and again and it was okay, but I played a game you walked away from and you hated me for it."

"I never hated you for it, Drew." He shakes his head frantically. "Never. I was so proud of you but I was terrified you'd fall into the trap I fell into. I was worried that you were so like me in every other aspect that—"

"That what? I'd be weak like you and fuck up my whole life?" my voice thunders. "Well, guess what, you still fucked it up."

He nods. His shoulders sag and his posture is defeated. "Until the one thing you love the most has been threatened, until you are in my shoes, you have no clue the lengths you'd go to, to save your kids. Even if that means being hated when all is said and done."

"I think it would make you hold on tighter to the things you love."

"Perhaps." He nods and meets my eyes with a clarity I haven't seen in some time. "I only hope in time you'll be able to forgive me."

I stare at the man I used to idolize and wonder if I'll ever be able to forgive him, or if the years of hurt and what felt like neglect are too powerful to overcome.

I think of the endless unknown we lived with, the lies we were covered in, and wonder how different things could have been without them. For Maggie and Charley. For my mom. For me.

"I don't know." It's the most honest thing I've said in the moment and when he meets my eyes, I can't stand the sadness I see. The hope is erased. The realization that even though he told his truth, it might not be enough.

My mom has been in hiding, rather than the socialite she loved to be. Maggie lost a present father all those years ago, and all it took was some asshole showing her attention, and we lost her too. *Did his addiction foster hers somehow? Or would we have eventually lost her anyway?* And my story is just as disappointing.

Until now.

But I refuse to let it be.

I need to turn this around.

I will turn this around.

And without another word, I walk out of the house. Emotions and realizations spin and whirl and own every part of me.

At the end of the day, I'd been right.

My father's selfishness destroyed our family. Our lives . . . to a point.

Hell yes, I'm doing well, but it has nothing to do with him and everything to do with me. I think of Brexton and smile.

I cannot right the wrongs of my past, but I can make better decisions going forward.

I can be the man I want to be.

I can be the man she deserves after all.

Chapter
SIXTY-EIGHT

Drew

I DRIVE.

With no destination in mind.

With no direction predetermined.

I just drive.

To consider the consequences that now I know the truth to.

To clear my head.

To quiet my restlessness.

His story makes sense but it infuriates me at the same time.

Hours pass. They feel like minutes one moment and infinite in others.

I end up at the beach where I stare at the stars above and listen to the waves crash against the sand.

Finally, I find the courage to pick up my cell and dial.

"Drew?"

Every part of me sighs at the sound of her voice. I fucking miss her. I miss everything about her. Her contagious laugh and her no-nonsense attitude. Her quiet advice and astute observations. Christ, I could name a million things about her but what it comes down to is that I just miss her. All of her. Completely. *And it's time to fix that.*

Chapter
SIXTY-NINE

Brexton

My heart pounds in my chest as I sit up in bed in my Chicago hotel room and wait to see what Drew called for.

"Hi," he finally says.

"Are you okay?"

"I'm going to be."

"I'm so very glad to hear that." I close my eyes and breathe for what feels like the first time in a week.

"I'm at the beach." He pauses. "Want to stare at the stars with me?"

My smile is slow but steady at that simple question. "I'm in a hotel in Chicago," I say, repeating his phrasing. "I'd love to stare at the stars with you."

And we sit in silence on the phone with the steady rhythm of each other's breathing to keep us company.

I think of the utter loneliness I've felt over the past week with his absence and marvel how a simple phone call, the sound of his voice—his breaths—has erased it and then some. I can imagine he's hurting, but I'm more than thrilled he turned to me when he wanted to process whatever happened.

When he wanted to wish on the stars.

When he didn't want to be alone anymore.

The silence feels a little less lonely with him to share it with.

"Do you want to talk about it?" I ask softly after some time has passed.

"I finally got answers, Brex. I'm not sure how they make me feel, but I finally have answers."

With a pillow hugged to my chest, a tear slides down my cheek. "It took you ten years to get answers, so it might take ten years to understand them," I whisper.

"I need to tell you about it, but later. Right now I just want this. I just need this."

"I'm here, Drew."

"I miss you."

That one tear turns into more at those three words. "I miss you too."

I love you, but then again, I always have.

Chapter SEVENTY

Brexton

Dekker: Where are you?
Me: On my flight back home. Why?
Dekker: Buy the Wi-Fi.
Me: WTF?
Dekker: Trust me. Buy the damn Wi-Fi. Turn on the Raptors game.

My pulse begins to race when I read my sister's text. I scramble to grab my laptop and power it on.

Me: Okay. Why?
Dekker: You'll know the minute you see it.

It feels like it takes forever for my computer to turn on and to navigate the slower-than-shit process to get Internet on the plane.

But when I do, when I pay the extra fee for faster Wi-Fi and finally get the game to stream, I'm vibrating in my seat in anticipation.

The score is seven to nothing in the Raptors' favor as their defense tries to stop a fourth down-push from the Steelers. They succeed, and I stare at the screen expecting Hobbs to be running on the field and am surprised when I see Drew.

He's starting. *Again.* Oh my God. *This is huge.* Two starts in two games.

Two starts in two games leading into postseason.

My eyes are glued to the screen as Drew runs onto the field with the rest of his offense. They huddle together for a moment and just before they break, the camera swings around to Drew's back.

It's then that I see it.

Dekker wasn't telling me Drew was starting.

She was telling me I needed to see this.

She was remembering a conversation way back when just like I do right now.

"Like I'd ever put that shit on my helmet." He snorts and crosses his arms over his chest in annoyance.

"Not even if you were madly in love?" she asks.

"Nope," he says and emits an exasperated sigh.

"You're telling me if it was the only way to profess your undying love for someone that you wouldn't do it?"

"Dekker." Her name is a frustrated warning.

"Well?" she asks.

"Sure. Yes. Of course. That's exactly how I'd profess my undying love for someone. A public statement for everyone to see, because I especially enjoy the guys razzing the shit out of me over it just like I am to the dude on the TV right now."

"I'm serious," Dekker adds.

"So am I. Better yet, I think that's the way I'll propose to the woman I plan to marry. Nothing like ridiculous fucking gestures to make the whole moment that much sweeter."

"But you've always said you're never going to get married."

"Exactly," he says with a definitive nod and a chuckle as he drops the remote control in mic-drop fashion before striding out.

I gasp out in surprise and then cover my mouth when my seatmate glances my way.

But I can't help it.

How can I?

Not when I see the ILYBK in big black letters on the back of Drew's helmet.

Letters he swore he'd never put on a helmet unless it was a woman he wants to marry.

"Oh. My. God." It's Dekker's voice in my ear, but it's my heart that I'm listening to.

The one that is so full of love for the man I'm madly head over heels for.

The man I'm going to marry.

Wishes do come true after all.

Chapter
SEVENTY-ONE

Brexton

I can't get to my door fast enough when the knock sounds. I fling it open to see Drew standing there, his grin wide, but his demeanor nonchalant as can be.

"Hi." I breathe the word out as it takes everything I have not to launch myself at him. "Great game. Congrats on the win."

"You saw it?"

"Bits and pieces on the airplane." I tilt my head to the side, completely consumed by the man in front of me and all that he makes me feel.

"Just bits and pieces?"

"Enough."

"Huh." He purses his lips.

"How did you know I was home?"

He shrugs. "Because this is our thing. I come here after a game or you sit on my porch in lingerie, and since you weren't there . . . here I am."

"Our thing?"

"Yeah. We have lots of things like that," he says.

"We do?"

He nods. "Staring at the stars, spinning the bottle, initials on hands."

"Oh," I murmur. "I was kind of liking the initials on the helmet thing personally, but only saps do that."

His grin grows from ear to ear as he steps into me, hands to my cheeks, and presses his lips to mine in a toe-tingling kiss that owns every part of me. "Then call me a sap, baby, because I'm all yours."

"Is that so?" I ask and press a kiss to his lips in between every word.

"Completely." He runs the backs of his fingers down my cheek while his eyes hold mine. "There's nowhere else I'd rather be. There's no one else's initials I'd wear on my helmet."

"Sorry, Ginnie Huber." I'm still smiling when he kisses me again.

"She didn't stand a chance against you."

"No one ever did. It's always been you for me, Dreadful Drew. There's no one else I'd rather stare at the stars with."

"I love you, Brexton Kincade. I know it took a long time to find you, to fight for this, but there is no other way I'd want it to be."

And this time when he kisses me, he kicks the door shut behind him, and I know he's home.

I know we've found our home—in each other.

I want to scream from the rooftop and tell every teenage girl waiting awkwardly in the corner for the hot guy to notice her that sometimes it happens.

And I want to shout out loud to every grown woman who has had her heart broken over and over that they need to just believe in love.

Because it happens.

Look at Drew and me.

It really happens.

Epilogue

Drew

FORGIVENESS IS A FUNNY THING.

It's something you say you'd give easily but when the time comes, it feels like a glob of peanut butter stuck on your tongue that you have a hard time swallowing down. But you try and try again and then eventually you're able to get it down entirely.

That's how it's been with my father and me.

I try to forgive, the sentiment gets stuck for a while until I realize that he's reaching out time and again and so then, I try again.

I think of the man who spun our lives into chaos. The one who lied about the reason and then blamed it on someone else, and I wonder how I can look at him and still love him. I wonder how I can be in the same room when so many were hurt by his actions.

But then I realize time is precious.

I know that when he goes, it would be me who suffers with the guilt of not saying more, of not loving more . . . and so I'm glad we've worked on it. There are days the resentment burns bright. Days when I watch Maggs still struggle with her sobriety and I see the fallout . . . but then there are days when I get a text after an away game telling me I did a great job, or when I can look in the stands and see him there and know he's there only for me.

And I know he's trying just as hard as I am.

Then there are days like today when I blow out a deep breath, knock, and hope the man who answers the door will be just as willing to forgive.

Kenyon and I have a stronger bond now that I've confessed the truth, but I still feel pain. The more time I've spent with him of late, the more

I've resented all the years spending time with him that were taken from me. And now, I need to ask this man to look beyond what he shouldn't be asked to look beyond. *A betrayal that my father has not yet broached or healed with him.*

When the door swings open and Kenyon Kincade stands before me, my pulse begins to race.

"Drew? What a surprise. Come in, come in," he says and steps back from his front door.

"I won't stay long."

"Stay as long as you like." He goes through the niceties of offering me a drink and making small talk before we take a seat. "So, what can I do for you, son?"

"I know there's history here and I don't want you to think in any way, shape, or form that I'm ignoring it with the question I came to ask you."

"History is called history for a reason. It's something we live, we learn from, and then we move on from. Besides, the history you're referring to had absolutely nothing to do with you."

"I know." I swallow nervously. "But I also know that Brexton loves her family dearly and I'm slowly working on repairing mine."

"And?" he prompts and then takes a sip of his beer.

"And I love her. Everything about her. Even the things she dislikes about herself—I love." I run my sweaty palms down the thighs of my jeans. "And I want to ask you for her hand."

"Is that right?" he asks, eyebrows raised.

"Yes. And I can't ask that question without telling you there might be times when we have to be together with my family—like say, a wedding." I chuckle nervously. "But they've said they'll take a step back to not make you uncomfortable. They said that they know she's it for me and so whatever you want—"

"Drew." He smiles. "Son. You love her, right?"

"I think I always have."

"Then the rest will sort itself out."

"Does that mean . . ."

"I've never seen her happier. You helped make her that way. I give you my blessing."

Epilogue 2

Brexton

"CAN WE SPEND EVERY SUMMER HERE?" I ASK WITH A LAUGH AS THE cool breeze coming off the lake has my hair tickling my cheek. While Lake George is laid out before us in all its splendor, the dock beneath us is still slightly warm from the sun beating down on it all day, but the sky has darkened.

It's been a year since we were here last. A year full of ups and downs and absolute utter perfection. I'm here right now with the one I want to be with.

The man who puts up with my bad days just as positively as he puts up with my good days. The one who loves madly and sports my initials on his helmet despite his teammates calling him a sap. Fitting and funny but awesome nonetheless. The lover who is the other half of my broken whole. Where he zigs, I zag.

"Every summer? You're not going to hear me argue about that request," Drew says as he shifts and pulls me back into him so my back is against his chest. His legs shadow mine and his arms wrap around me. "In fact, I already looked into reserving dates for next summer."

"Great minds, Drew Bowman. Great minds." I squeeze his arms and lean my head back on his shoulder. "Maybe next summer we could bring Charley with us. She'll be old enough then that she'll be able to do everything. Paddleboat, kayak, ice block sledding down the hill."

"Eating ice cream until her stomach hurts," he adds and then presses a kiss against my cheek that heats up more places than the dock does. "She'd like that." Another kiss to the side of my neck. "I'd like that."

We sit in silence as I think about our last seven days here. Hours spent relaxing in the sun and sailing on the lake. Barbeques and watching fireworks. Late-night passion and early-morning lovemaking.

Teammates have come out for a night, adding to the laughter that has filled this gray clapboard house on the lake's edge.

"How did we get here, Bratty Brex?" Drew asks softly. I can hear the smile in his voice. "How did one game of spin the bottle end up here, eleven years later?"

"A lot of persistence. A lot of patience. And a lot of one fifteen-year-old girl making promises to give up this or that to the powers that be that *Dreamy Drew* might notice her."

"You made promises to give things up?" he asks.

"I sure did."

We fall silent for a beat. I still feel like I should pinch myself to make sure this is real. That this life is real.

"You were right you know."

"About?"

"Brexton facts."

"What do you mean?" I chuckle, trying to follow him.

"All those years ago, you told me that looking up at the stars made you not feel so alone."

"I thought we said those were Mom facts," I say and then smile softly at the thought of my mom.

"You're right. You didn't let me finish though," he teases. "Remember what else you said that night?"

"The make a wish part?"

"Mm-hmm. The make a wish part. The *Brexton facts*."

"I remember vaguely."

"You told me that I should make a wish, because maybe someone else staring at the same sky would hear it and help me."

"Sounds like something I'd say when I was trying to impress my crush."

He presses a chaste kiss to my bare shoulder. "You were right, Brex," he whispers against my skin.

"As a teenager, I wished for a girl to fall madly in love with me. As an adult last year, I wished for that girl to be you. And now I'm going to throw up one more wish and see how it will be answered."

"Drew..."

"Marry me, Brex." I gasp as I turn to face him as best as I can with our positioning. I meet his eyes through the moonlight and see everything I want in them—love, devotion, friendship, and respect. "I know we've had tough times and I'm sure there are more to come, but no one has ever made me happier. No one has ever made me want to be a better man. No one has been my last thought before I go to sleep and my first thought when I wake up. Do me the honor of being my wife. Make my wish come true once and for all."

My lips are on Drew's in a heartbeat.

Tears stream down my cheeks as I lean back to look at the man I love. There is no person I'd rather be with. "Yes." I hiccup over the word as he slips a ridiculously gorgeous ring on my finger. "Yes." My lips meet his again. "Yes." And another. "Yes." And another.

"I love you, Bratty Brexton."

"I love you, Dreadful Drew. And that's *Brexton facts.*"

And when our lips meet again, when we sink into the kiss, when our souls sigh at a beginning completely fitting for the two of us, all I can think about is how perfectly *us* this is.

Kissing on a dock.

At Lake George.

Under the stars.

Together.

Coming Soon

Did you enjoy Drew and Brexton's story in *Hard to Score*? Fall in love with the rest of the Kincade sisters and their love interests in the other Play Hard books:

Hard to Handle—Out Now

Hard to Hold—Out Now

Hard to Lose—Out March 17, 2021

ACKNOWLEDGMENTS

I must take a moment to acknowledge the crew that helps keep me afloat most days:

Chrisstine—for always questioning my creativity and pushing me to dig for more

Alison, Stephanie, Marjorie, Michele, Ninfa, Janice, Kara, and Chrisstine—for always being my first set of eyes who help me catch the things I miss.

Christy—for being the master of all things including late night texts for tech help.

VP Pit Crew Admins—for helping to keep our reader group going.

Stacey—for making my words look pretty on the page.

Marion—for polishing my words because they're a mess when she first gets them.

Helen—for designing pretty covers so you want to read my words.

Valentine PR—for helping to keep me visible.

And YOU!! My readers because without you, there would be no one to write for but myself . . . and that might get a little boring.

—Kristy

ABOUT THE AUTHOR

New York Times Bestselling author K. Bromberg writes contemporary romance novels that contain a mixture of sweet, emotional, a whole lot of sexy, and a little bit of real. She likes to write strong heroines and damaged heroes who we love to hate but can't help to love.

A mom of three, she plots her novels in between school runs and soccer practices, more often than not with her laptop in tow and her mind scattered in too many different directions.

Since publishing her first book on a whim in 2013, Kristy has sold over one and a half million copies of her books across twenty different countries and has landed on the *New York Times*, *USA Today*, and *Wall Street Journal* Bestsellers lists over thirty times. Her Driven trilogy (*Driven*, *Fueled*, and *Crashed*) is currently being adapted for film by the streaming platform, Passionflix.

With her imagination always in overdrive, she is currently scheming, plotting, and swooning over her latest hero. You can find out more about him or chat with Kristy on any of her social media accounts. The easiest way to stay up to date on new releases and upcoming novels is to sign up for her newsletter or follow her on Bookbub.